The Life

of

Captain Reilly

The right of J.T. O'Neil to be identified as the author of this work has
been asserted in accordance with the
Copyright Designs and Patents Act 1988.

The Life of Captain Reilly
Copyright © J.T. O'Neil 2011
daisyPress print edition published 2013
978 0 9569150 7 8

First published by daisyPress as digital books in two volumes
The Life of Captain Reilly Part 1
ISBN 978 0 9569150 0 9
The Life of Captain Reilly Part 2 - Descent
ISBN 978 0 9569150 1 6

Typeset in Minion Pro 12/15

With thanks to my editor – the girl with the flaxen hair
and the red pen, Fiona Cox PhD.

The Life
of
Captain Reilly

J.T. O'Neil

daisyPress

The Life of Captain Reilly is a work of fiction – the kind of fiction that plays out everyday in the airline world.

Prologue

Many a true story …

Captain John Reilly is the pseudonym of a full time (and boy, does he know it) commercial airline captain. His identity, and those of his colleagues, must remain hidden to protect the guilty, the innocent, the foolish and the embarrassed. He also wishes to prolong his career making dreams come true for thousands of Spanish bar owners who salivate at the sight of drunken Brits waddling towards their otherwise deserted bars. With this in mind, and a stiff tongue in his cheek, Captain John Reilly wishes to remain incognito.

Fortunately for those wishing to discover what really goes on behind the locked door of the modern flight deck, Captain Reilly has regaled his friend, confidante, and fellow aviator, Captain J.T. O'Neil, with his aviation exploits so that his life may be recorded for all eternity.

In no way is it suggested that captains John Reilly and J.T. O'Neil work for the same company, or heaven forbid, that they are one and the same person.

The implausible, preposterous and outrageous story told here is based on true accounts. Mostly. This is what happens when you mix highly trained professionals with expensive machinery and add a sprinkling of attractive young ladies. It's the grown-up (and I use that description with caution) equivalent of pulling wheelies on your BMX bike outside the shopping mall on a Saturday afternoon: you could easily end up looking like a twat, but still not get to play with one.

All the events recounted in *The Life of Captain Reilly* most definitely happened (to someone, somewhere, sometime). And on this, you have the word of a professional, responsible, conscientious, respected, impeccably presented, perennially sober, highly educated pillar of the community: your commercial airline captain.

J.T. O'Neil (maybe)

Volume One

Glamour doesn't fly anymore

Chapter 1

Long Haul Husband

It all starts the night before. If I agreed with the aviation authorities, I would have gulped down the quarter filled tumbler of whiskey a few minutes ago. If I agreed with my employer, I would have finished drinking two hours earlier.

I was quite sure I'd be sober by morning, even after draining the alluring glass that sat next to me on the bedside table. I'm quite used to it. My employer thinks ten hours of joyless abstinence is essential if they are to protect my passengers and crew from the effects that the sour fruits of libation might have on me. I'm afraid I can no longer live with that. And I'm not the only one.

I twisted my arm round to peer at the watch strapped to my wrist. It had been a gift from my wife when I got my command, a Breitling – the pilot's watch – and my only extravagance. She had told me it was the perfect present, explaining that whenever I looked at my watch I would think of her. She had been right.

With a sigh of resignation, and with eight hours before reporting for duty, I raised my other arm to drain the glass that had been waiting since I'd filled it half an hour earlier. I didn't agree with the aviation authority's abstinence laws, but sometimes my conscience was irritatingly pious.

I scooped up the last few Hula Hoops from the far-too-shallow depths of the crinkly packet lying on the bed, and shovelled them all into my mouth at once. It was an inelegant display, but there was no one there to see it.

Perhaps you think that, as an airline captain, I should have been enjoying a selection of cheeses with some water biscuits, or maybe some duck liver pâté on crisp french toast, to complement my single malt. Well I'm afraid I missed those days; they were long before my time. We are now in the age of the lo-cost airline (even too mean to fork out for the 'w'), and cheese boards belong to a bygone era of aviation and a bygone type of pilot. These days it's cheap snacks and cheap uniforms.

There was no point going to bed early to ensure what our operations manual calls, 'sufficient rest' since my body has never really understood the company's roster-ing protocol, and it certainly isn't wired up to follow it. I'd been on late shifts the week before and my body was wide-awake long after midnight, every night. Only after a few days of forced early wake-ups and mid-flight naps would it understand that it now needed to sleep by 9.00 pm. But, to show willing, I undressed, pulled back the floral duvet and settled into bed. It was 10.10 pm.

I didn't even think about sleeping, though; it was far too early for my confused body clock. With nothing on the television, and no Internet access, I opened the un-creased pages of a new novel and read until my eyes stung with the effort.

But I even my book – one a passenger had left behind a few days earlier – couldn't send me to sleep. Perhaps another glass would help me on my way, I thought. The whiskey bottle, which I'd positioned out of easy reach on the old walnut sideboard, was only a glass shy of full. There was no way I would be unfit to fly in the morning if I made it two glasses shy. But lack of sleep, well, that's a big killer. Besides, I had another packet of Hula Hoops in my bag. *Sod it!*

I slipped out of bed, already feeling chilly in the vaguely heated room, and grabbed the bottle from its resting place. A small measure should be enough. I poured the bronze liquid until it rose level with the top finger of the two I'd wrapped around the base of the glass.

It was 10.45 pm, and I'd settled back into bed with the novel before I realised the Hula Hoops were still in my bag. After a few moments of indecision and mild cursing I decided I could live without the little snack.

I was pleased that I didn't yet need glasses for reading (though I'd been warned the day fast approached), but I certainly needed more light than the eco-bulb beside my bed offered. By about 11.00 pm I gave up with the book and, blinking hard, settled down for a typically restless night.

The first day of early duties is always a shock to the

body. The only compensation comes when, predictably, I wake about 1.00 am and I can enjoy the luxury of lying in bed delirious in the knowledge that I have the time to doze off again. Bliss.

But that night, like every other, I couldn't doze off again. I lay turning and fidgeting, glancing at my travel clock every few minutes, and worrying that I couldn't sleep. I stared at the two blinking dots between the hours and minutes, hoping they would blur, but my vision was still crisp. The beeps would sound in four hours and I was still fully awake.

The next day's duty was a 6.00 am report for an easy two-sector day taking holidaymakers to Spain and back. The Malaga flight is a breeze: two and half hours down to the bottom of Europe, a little jostling with the charters for some air space, and a spot of breakfast somewhere over the Bay of Biscay. Not a bad way to begin the week.

I say 'begin the week', but it wasn't actually Monday morning, it was Saturday. My week doesn't begin on any particular day; it varies with my roster pattern. Whilst a regular guy is out revelling on a Friday night, celebrating the end of his week, I'm settling down for an early night without the cocoa. Equally, though, my week could end on a Sunday and I could be smiling into my pillow come Monday morning. The days of the week hold little relevance to airline folk (except the management, but let's not get into that just yet).

It's a worrying feeling to consider a Malaga trip as 'a breeze', since it's actually a seven hour working day. When you consider there are no breaks from duty during this time, it becomes equivalent to a standard nine to five office day. And we consider this a short day. What's more, there's no respite: it was the first of six consecutive days of work before my days off, and they weren't all short like this one.

It seems I did doze off again because the next thing I knew, some chirpy bastard on the radio was telling me it was 5.00 am. Why couldn't it be 1.00 am again so I could wrap myself tightly in my duvet and luxuriate in being awake without having to get up?

I lay in bed listening to the news for a few moments before remembering I never allow even a minute for such luxury when I agree a wake-up time with myself. I had to get moving.

I'd shaved the night before, just prior to opening the whiskey; it's a time saving task that I can get away with since my fair hair spares me any dark stubble. All I needed in the morning was a quick shower. I hoped the water would be warm.

My landlady is used to airline crew; her B&B is a popular choice for displaced pilots and she usually fires up the boiler in time for our early starts. But when I arrived the night before I'd heard a couple of pilots discussing their 4.00 am report time so I wasn't sure if there'd be any hot water left by the time I got up.

I stepped out of the shower after just thirty seconds. Shivering pathetically, I reached for my towel and scrubbed away the tepid water. Our body temperature falls to its lowest point at around 3.00 am and since it was only

5.05 am, I resigned myself to freezing my follicles off for a short while.

Damn! My shirt was still stuffed inside my suitcase. Lovingly ironed by my wife; carelessly creased by me. I pulled it out of the bulging trolley case and held it up as though its own weight might stretch out the creases. It didn't. But my jacket would hide it for most of the day, so I dressed quickly, grabbed my flight case, and dragged my languid body down the stairs to the front door.

I never allow time for breakfast when I'm on earlies, but there's always a carton of juice in the car to help kick start my metabolism. It was 5.15 am – time to leave.

The journey to the airport is about twenty minutes at that time of day, but it always takes longer to travel from the staff car park to the crew room whatever time of day it is. I needed to leave plenty of time if I hoped to report for duty by 6.00 am.

Passengers are generally advised to arrive at the airport up to a couple of hours before their flight, but I think this is largely a ruse to trap them in the terminal for as long as possible.

Airports make much of their revenue from the money travellers spend in the terminals, and so the concept of 'lounge' is largely missing from the creative brief given to airport interior designers.

Airport owners now view their terminals as shopping malls, which is why modern examples have considerably fewer seats for passengers to lounge about in than the good old days of air travel.

Their philosophy appears to be as follows: if you want to sit down then go to one of our 'food outlets' and spend your money. If you don't want to sit down, then browse our 'retail outlets' and spend your money.

It's also why the gate for each flight is announced only minutes before boarding begins; they don't want everyone waiting at the gate where there's nothing to spend any money on.

Airline crews, on the other hand, are expected to arrive just one hour prior to departure; the airline doesn't want us to buy anything in the terminal, and there's no financial value in paying us to be there any earlier than the legal minimum. Rostering an earlier report time would simply reduce the length of flight duty that could be legally squeezed from our pip-like bodies, so it's never going to happen. However, to get all our flight preparations done in a diligent and conscientious manner, an earlier report time is often essential. Airlines do occasionally apply some moral pressure to persuade crews to arrive earlier than their rostered report time, but with 12-hour days becoming increasingly usual, pilots and cabin crew stick two proverbial flying digits up to such tactics. An hour is rostered, so an hour it is.

The unfortunate ones, like me, who work out of London Gatwick Airport, are allocated staff parking as far away from the airport as possible. Truthfully, the car park may well be in central London given the time it takes to travel between our cars and the airline crew room.

If you're lucky enough to be in the regions then even

the most remote point on the airport is likely to be within walking distance of the crew room. I could once count my lucky stars for being based at a sleepy provincial airport, but that was before my airline bosses realised they could make an extra few quid if they moved a couple of aircraft elsewhere. Before long someone will identify a new airport where even more money can be made and the same relocated aircraft will be moved again, as will the crew who fly them.

It's the same story everywhere these days: itinerate directors, goaded on by faceless investors, pursuing bonuses and enhancing City reputations before scurrying along to their next high profile appointment. It's the modern way, and it's the reason I've just woken up alone in a B&B two hundred miles away from my family. But at least I still have a job.

I arrived at car park X and drove around for several minutes, cursing the airport owners for not providing more parking spaces or even another car park. To be fair, though, I doubted they owned any land far enough away from the crew room to turn into a staff car park.

The minutes marched on as I continued driving round and round – then, I spotted it: a space, halfway along the next row.

I pushed my toes forward and accelerated with blinkered determination. My eyes fixed on that simple little gap like a small child playing musical chairs at a party – though without the jelly and ice cream, or prizes for that matter.

As my sportless Škoda screeched around the corner at

the end of the row, another car came from the opposite end. *NO!* It was a white VW Beetle and it was close to the only chair left in the game.

My toes squeezed the accelerator again. The Beetle was almost there. We raced towards the space at selfish speeds. As I came close, I saw one of those oversized plastic flowers that commonly sprout from the dashboard of the new Beetle. What's going on there? Is it an optional extra? I allowed myself a few moments of cynicism:

> *'Would you like climate control, Madam'?*
> *'Oh I don't think so, thanks.'*
> *'Alloy wheels?'*
> *'Not really.'*
> *'How about a plastic flower sticking out of the dash board?'*
> *'Ooh yes, that would be lovely, could I have a pink one, please?'*

Her mobile allotment was just metres from the space – *my* space. The driver avoided eye contact. She dragged her arms violently to the left and somehow defied Newton's Laws of Motion as she turned the car skilfully into the envied little spot. It was almost a hand brake turn. Fair play to her, I thought, though it wasn't my first thought.

The damned flower had distracted me. *Foul play!* I was still sitting, motionless, halfway along the lane when the winning driver climbed out to take her applause. She was a lady of *un certain âge* with tightly coiffured blonde hair – not her natural colour, I suspected – and a face that looked as though it had been rendered. She wore a dark blue uniform with a brilliant white blouse. No way had that blouse been stuffed in a suitcase all night. She held a small leather bag in her right hand and a clipboard in the other. As she approached my car she smiled widely but briefly at me. By the time she passed the window I expected she'd already discarded my existence. Undoubtedly some kind of customer services representative, I thought, but not with my airline – we didn't have any.

Finally (I'm afraid that word is going to crop up an awful lot during the course of these pages since the life of an airline pilot involves a good deal of sitting around waiting for things to happen), I found a rhomboid shaped space between two badly parked cars at the back of the car park. Both vehicles were large, expensive tank-like monstrosities; probably owned by pilots in a hurry, like me.

I expected there was enough space for all the staff members allocated this unpopular plot of land, but staff also park here when they go on holiday. Others, as I know too well, simply don't leave enough time to park carefully within a single bay.

I contorted myself to fit through the narrow gap between my Škoda and the neighbouring tank and climbed out of the car. My legs aren't particularly long – I was 5 feet 10 inches at my last aviation medical examination (and since there are no ejector seats in commercial aircraft, I suspected I remained the same height) – but it was still a struggle to avoid dirtying my dark trousers on the sills.

I wasn't particularly fussed if the tight squeeze resulted in a dent or scratch to my car; the clichéd Porsche was abandoned long ago for that very reason. I don't really care if the old Octavia gets scuffed; it's one less thing to be stressed about.

As I locked the boot I turned my head round and noticed the shuttle bus just leaving the stop. If I ran quickly I could meet it at the next one along since I was parked equidistant between the two. Surely the driver would see my athletic commitment and wait for me. *Yeah, in Dream World!* I rolled my eyes at my own naivety.

The sight of a uniformed airline captain racing across the car park might goad the driver on as though someone had pulled alongside him at the traffic lights, grinning moronically and revving the engine. I could almost hear him shouting to his passengers, 'Hey, look at that this guy! Watch this, I'll wait till he gets within ten feet and then pull off!' Such is the attitude these days. Selfishly I deprived him of his fun, and chose to wait for the next bus instead.

I'd misjudged the weather again that morning, and I stood shivering in the bus shelter wishing I'd brought my overcoat. In my defence, though, it had been overcast when I'd looked through the window in my bedroom, and a blanket of cloud usually keeps things a little warmer. I smiled glibly at my meteorological incompetence.

The bus stop was already re-filling with more zombie-like crew and airport staff. There are dozens of airlines operating out of Gatwick, and most have early morning departures.

I've always wondered why passengers accept an airline's twenty-four hour timetable. Why would you want to get up at 4.00 am on your day off to go on holiday? Just say 'No!' then we can all have a lie in.

A cabin attendant, who had been part of my crew the week before, stood inside the shelter. I tried for a few moments to catch her eye and say hello, but she blanked me. That would never have happened at my old base. Everyone knew everyone else, and if we saw an unfamiliar face, we introduced ourselves. But things were different at the company's largest base.

A captain arrived and plonked his flight case down on the damp floor. I recognised him as someone I'd flown with when I first arrived in Gatwick twelve months earlier. I hadn't seen him since, but I was pleased to see he'd gained his promotion. We chatted while waiting for the bus. I asked him how things were going now he'd been promoted, but his reply was drowned out by a Boeing 777 coming in to land – probably an overnight flight from the US; it was about that time.

The bus arrived. There was no mad scramble to get on-board as there was still plenty of space available. By the time the bus reached the last few stops, it would be crammed to its limits. I guessed this was why it was always so difficult to find spaces in this section of the staff car park.

There was surprisingly little chit-chat among the passengers on the bus. Airline crew are recruited, in part, for their gregarious nature, but perhaps the thought of being friendly and outgoing all day depressed some of them into being tacit commuters. My colleague and I were the exception.

'So, Stefan,' I asked, as the bus pulled into the next stop. 'How long have you had your command?'.

'Just three weeks, but it's going well.' Stefan smiled like a kid who'd inherited a sweet shop.

'You're enjoying yourself then.' It didn't need to be a question; I could see how happy he was. But he drew breath sharply in the way Swedish people do when they're agreeing with you.

'Jo, it's fantastic, man.' Stefan was part of a large community of non-British pilots who joined the airline when its rapid expansion outpaced the Brits who wanted to apply. These days, even Chesley Sullenberger, the Hudson River-ditching captain, wouldn't be allowed to fly our planes unless he stumped up his life savings to join as a self-funded cadet. It's all about cost now.

The bus jerked to a halt outside the building that housed our crew room. All those standing, like me, fell forward, outstretched arms clinging on to the chrome poles like exotic dancers. I looked into the driver's rear view mirror expecting to see his face grinning, but he appeared to be ogling some red-suited girls crossing the road ahead.

Many of the airlines and service companies based in Gatwick used this building, and the entrance courtyard was milling with staff. People were beginning to wake up and find their personalities. Greetings and gossip filled the small space – some staff showing reluctance to enter the building, others running through the doors in panic. Lateness is next to theft in the eyes of management, particularly cabin crew management.

I exchanged a few smiles and nods with one or two fellow flyers before showing my pass to the security officer and entering the building – and the world of airlines. Stefan headed off to the bike shed for a quick last smoke.

The Airline
Flight Operations
Department

Let me be honest with you: the days when a pilot would turn up to work and begin planning his flight (and pilots would have been almost exclusively male, in those days), plotting his route, calculating the fuel burn, choosing flight levels, filling out and filing a flight plan, are well and truly over (I feel fatigued just writing it, and don't mention fatigue to an airline pilot). Perhaps, in the crazy world of corporate aviation, a biz-jet jockey may well have to work like a one-person airline, but for the rest of us, life is far cosier.

Your standard airline pilot arrives around one hour before departure – up to two hours for long haul flights – and attempts to persuade a cumbersome, cheap computer system to recognise his or her (for things have moved on) presence in the crew room. It's a brain blowing task that only the spiritually content could cope with long-term without nose-diving towards an early grave. Sadly, pilots aren't generally spiritually content, so accessing the company's IT system on a daily basis often results in clenched fists, barely concealed curses, and indeed a few early graves.

Half a dozen angry clicks of the mouse later, he or she gives up and tries to bring the next computer to life. This could go on for several minutes, eating into the minimum report time rostered for our weary pilot. But occasionally, with one deity or another smiling on its wayward child, this simple process can take as little as just a few minutes.

Sooner or later, pilot and computer do become one, and 'The System' allows the plucky pilot to check in. Now, a clever system would indicate whether or not the other pilot has already checked in, and whether they have printed the rainforest worth of paperwork associated with the intention of transporting passengers around the skies. A cheaper system wouldn't.

And so, in a large crew room bustling with bewildered aviators, it is highly likely that when both pilots eventually meet, they will each be clutching an identical set of paperwork. Of course, this assumes that the captain is of the modern type.

Not that long ago many captains would refuse to collate the paperwork for their flight, believing that it was the co-pilot's responsibility to do so. You can imagine that such an attitude has been shown to save a whole rainforest over the lifetime of an individual captain, and so shouldn't necessarily be frowned upon like some other habits from the bad old days. After all, there's only so far you can take this touchy-feely modern approach, and I for one have always preferred to do my touchy-feely stuff on the nightstop. Before Mrs Reilly was around, that is.

Before I was married I regularly nightstopped in various exotic – and unexotic – destinations. Once, some years ago, I was in a bar with a great bunch of people including a young French crew member who was making it clear just how good she was in bed. Not solely for my benefit, but for anyone who cared to be listening (though I was the only bloke there). The little minx was 'a giver', she appealed; 'unselfish', she lured; 'wild as a devil', she enticed. After a whole evening of these clear-as-a-see-through-negligee clues from the little French fire lighter, I obviously wasn't seeing the wide open door in front of my face (though wide open legs would have been clearer). So, back to the bar – actually, we'd moved on to the beach, but no matter – where little Mademoiselle Feu was unconsciously drawing lewd images in the sand with her finger, whilst lamenting that she hadn't had a good man *pour longtemps*. I was the only man, good or bad, within combustible distance of Mme Feu, so I started to wonder if she really was pointing her flamethrower at me.

Not used to dealing with thickos, the poor girl was forced to become a little more direct.

Now, a lesson in the language of love that may serve you well one day. Un baiser is a masculine French noun meaning 'a kiss'. Baiser – without the article – is a verb meaning to fornicate like a rabbit on Viagra. But it's easy to get the two mixed up when your French is a bit dodgy.

Fortunately for me the English version followed swiftly, and when a French girl says, "I want a fuck" – I'm sorry but I'm quoting here – then you can safely assume she doesn't want a peck on the cheek. But it's always polite to start with one.

It's worth clarifying, before we go any further, the use of the terms 'co-pilot' and 'first officer'. They are one and the same, of course. Co-pilots were always called co-pilots until someone decided that first officer sounded grander, and could be differentiated from second officer which sounded less grand, but grander than junior co-pilot. It is a rank that also suits the modern function of the second pilot.

You see, in the bad old days of 'The Right Stuff' (when most pilots were Second World War veterans) the captain would fly the plane and the co-pilot would merely assist. But in these modern times both pilots take turns to have a go at taking off, flying around and landing the plane. But there are some people, notably the cabin crew at the back of the plane, who would undoubtedly welcome a return to those halcyon days of aviation since aircraft geometry ensures that hard landings are most keenly felt by those seated rearwards of the wheels.

The modern approach, however, is best. It provides for some variety, helps to stave off monotony, develops the skills of the first officer, and allows the captain to fall asleep shortly after take-off.

Hopefully, the daily routine of reporting for duty usually

results in two pilots – one of each (though some are both) – arriving at the briefing table with all the paperwork, pens, coffee and doughnuts appropriate for the duty ahead. And if they could achieve that within 5 minutes or so, it would be considered an outstanding success.

Note I didn't include newspapers in that little list. This is because we rely on passenger donation for much of our in-flight reading material; it would be jolly decent if passengers were to leave a selection of newspapers and magazines behind for our enjoyment when they eventually bid *au revoir* to our dedicated cabin crew.

Where were we? Oh yes, pooling our resources at the briefing table. To assist us in our time-critical task, airlines employ armies of operations staff to plan flights and file flight plans on our behalf. It saves time, money, time that is money, time that money can't buy, and money that we haven't got time to make. So all in all, it's a better system than forcing pilots to do it themselves; which we couldn't anyway, given we all forgot the basics of flight planning just seconds after handing the exam paper to the CAA invigilator all those years ago.

So what do we get from our operations department? A flight plan for starters. This official document normally contains the following essential information:

The aircraft type
This is in case you don't know what type of aircraft you're qualified to fly).

The five letter aircraft registration
So you don't take the wrong plane, it happens.

The commercial flight number and ATC call sign
This is sometimes different (but not to confuse the cabin crew).

The date and time
So you know it's not a day off.

The city pair
In other words, the departure and arrival points and and how you're going to get from one to the other (this hasn't always stopped pilots landing at the wrong airport).

Fuel calculations
A breakdown of how an office oik with a degree in computers has attempted to work out your fuel requirements.

With some airlines the fuel usage information is a concoction of statistics, forecasted weather conditions, flight levels proposed, and payload predicted (you and your bags, but don't try getting on with plural bags – that's forbidden).

Fuel calculations can be reassuringly accurate, but they can also be woefully wrong. How do we deal with that? Well, we're not completely slaves to the system so we just take the fuel we think we need despite the stunning work done by a nerd with a calculator back at HQ.

The filed route (the one which operations has told air traffic control we're going to fly) is worked out based on cost. Yes, we pay to use the motorway in the sky; it's a bit like a toll road.

Some motorways (okay, they're called airways) cost more than others, and it all depends on popularity and which bit of the earth it happens to sit over.

The busiest airways in Europe are over and between London and Paris. But it could still be cheaper to fly through this popular airspace despite the higher charges levied. Weather, longer routings, and slot delays all have an impact on the overall cost of the flight.

Generally speaking, it's a complex process working out exactly which route to fly on any particular day, and one that is far beyond the interest levels of your average pilot. Suffice to say, we just tell the flight management systems on board the aircraft which route someone else has told us to fly, and then let the aircraft follow its own sat nav.

The operations staff also, very kindly, compile the appropriate weather information for our flight. These include some familiar weather pictures (though without the little white cloud, sun and rain symbols you may have seen on television) but the report itself is in coded format. Fortunately, since we all went to pilot school and studied meteorology, we can read this special language – even if some of us can't tell if it's going to be cold outside by looking through the window.

J.T. O'Neil

An aerodrome weather report is called a METAR or METeorological Actual Report and a typical example might look like this:

```
EGKK 020950Z 27008KT 4500 BR OVC002 9/9
Q998
```

This string of letters and numbers decodes as follows:

EGKK

The four letter International Civil Aviation Organisation code for the airport. One eventually learns all these ICAO codes, but until then the novice pilot must hope the captain recognises the appropriate airports from among these codes and gleans the correct weather conditions for his (or her) day out. EGKK represents London Gatwick; I know because I've looked it up.

020950Z

This figure is the date-time group stating at which time the weather conditions were observed.
In this example it's the 2nd of the month (it's assumed you at least know what month it is) at 9.50 am. The Z represents ZULU which is a military way of expressing GMT.

The RAF uses letters of the alphabet to label each time zone, and the Greenwich Meridian is located in the zone represented by Z. Obviously we're not the RAF but we use Zulu because we're not supposed to say GMT anymore but can't bring ourselves to say UTC.

So what is UTC? Well, despite GMT being chosen in 1884 (almost unanimously – the French abstained) by an international conference to be the basis of calculating world time, and regardless of the revolutionary clock making skills of Yorkshireman John Harrison that allowed accurate time keeping, not to mention the pioneering work on international maritime navigation by the scientists at the Royal Observatory – IN GREENWICH – the official term for GMT is now UTC. It stands for Universel Temps Coordonné, and yes, it's French! I'm not sure what their contribution has been in this field, but someone has decreed that we have to use a French abbreviation for expressing Greenwich Mean Time. *Que faire?*

27008KT

The wind speed in knots (nautical miles per hour). The wind in this case is blowing from the direction of 270°, in other words from the west towards the east, at a speed of 8 knots. The Knot comes from a method of calculating the speed of a ship through water by dangling a knotted rope overboard. Obviously we can't do that at 39000 feet so I'm unsure why we continue to use a unit of speed that has no relevance to modern jet airlines. But what can you do?

9/9

The temperature is 9 degrees Celsius and the dew point is also 9 degrees. The dew point is an indication of humidity, and can be used to calculate the height at which clouds will form. Alternatively we can just read the cloud base information from the METAR.

Q998

The atmospheric pressure at the airfield. This is used as a reference for the altimeters on board the aircraft, which then measure atmospheric pressure differences from this reference level and convert the reading into an altitude. We generally work on height above sea level (which is called altitude) rather than height above the ground (which is called height!). Since we obviously only ever land on, well, land, this makes perfect sense. Obviously.

Other codes used include:

CAVOK

Ceiling And Visibility OK. Basically, it's a nice day. We don't see that very often in the UK.

FG

Fog (the 'o' must feel a little discriminated against)

BR

Mist (from those 'great pioneers' of aviation, the French, BRume = mist).

All right, I accept I'm being unfair on the French. They gave us the Montgolfier ballooning brothers, and Louis

Bleriot – the first person to fly across La Manche – but that was only because the Brits preferred the ferry with its cheap booze.

RA
Rain (we see this a lot)

+RA
Heavy rain (we see this a lot, too)

DZ
Drizzle (ditto, but mostly in Bristol and Manchester)

TS
Thunderstorm

GR
Hail (again, from the French grêle – hail)

CB
Cumulonimbus – the vindaloo of clouds

In addition to these actual weather conditions we also get weather forecasts. The TAF, Terminal Aerodrome Forecast, codes look similar to the METAR, but, by their nature, introduce an element of uncertainty.

We are also presented with snow reports, runway state information (if affected by snow or ice) and lots of pretty pictures. These pictures feature weather patterns, turbulence, icing conditions, and volcanic activity – sometimes.

Finally, our diligent colleagues in 'ops' list all the notices that may affect our day out. We call these NOTAMs – NOTice to AirMen (so not for women, it seems) and they include information such as airport closures or restrictions, fuel availability, industrial action (we see this a lot for French destinations), navigation issues, or construction work at airports (we see this lot for Spanish destinations). Basically, it's the job of the flight operations department to provide us with any information deemed relevant to our task of conveying unwary passenger to faraway places.

Chapter 2

First date

My airline's crew room is on the top floor, but there's no view, and a penthouse it certainly isn't. It is, however, cheaper than the lower floors, and these days that's all that matters.

The lift held about three people, so with a gaggle of cabin crew already crowding the door, I elected to take the stairs, as usual. It saves on gym membership.

I reached the top step of far too many and felt a little dampness against the shirt on my back. I was in good condition but my body resented this level of exertion at 5.55 am. There was also a little stiffness in my calf that I rubbed away with my free hand before following a first officer into the crew room.

'Where are you going to today?' I asked, for want of something better to say.

'Marrakech.'

'Oh, then we're not together,' I concluded. It had been

a long shot since there are dozens of departures every morning about this time. But you've got to say something.

The official starter's pistol for my working day fires when I attempt to persuade a cheap, overburdened computer system that logging me in is not an optional part of its day – or when I imagine pointing a real pistol at the Chief Pilot's head. That day, though, neither of these two contrasting outcomes applied: the computer logged me on like an old friend, and the Chief Pilot survived another pilot's mid-career crisis.

The next challenge involves identifying one's flying partner for the day. In a room bursting with garishly coloured uniforms it's often difficult for the eye to zone in on individual people. I thought about reaching for my sunglasses to tackle the glare, but even for a pilot, at six in the morning – indoors – that would be uncool.

Despite the twelve months I'd been in Gatwick I still didn't know anyone. There are several hundred pilots, and almost as many different pilot contracts, so finding someone who shares your roster pattern is unlikely. You would, perhaps, think it simpler to keep all pilots on the same contract. But that might encourage us to band together and seek some kind of collective representation Who knows, we could even cling to the right to a family life.

I scanned the busy room for anyone with fewer stripes on their sleeve than my four. Hopefully there would be someone, usually younger, searching round like a bloke on a blind date. I just hoped he wasn't carrying a bunch of flowers. I felt a hand on my shoulder.

'Are you going to Malaga?' asked the voice.

I turned and met my first officer, relieved by the absence of flowers in his hand or on his lapel. We shook hands and exchanged names (though not phone numbers at this stage). Chatting amiably, we shuffled and stapled the lumbering computer's output of fallen trees, otherwise known as the flight-briefing package. I hadn't flown with this guy before but he seemed to know what he was doing, so I asked him on which sector he would like to think he was flying the plane. He told me that he'd been on leave and would prefer a gentle easing back into things. He chose the return sector.

We were getting to know one another, chatting away with all the conviviality of old friends, whilst pretending to analyse the fight plans and associated bumf. Eventually I mumbled a few figures out loud, waved my pen aimlessly around the fuel breakdown column, and then opted for a fuel figure slightly higher than the one computed by the flight planning system – the one, in an indirect way, chosen by the geek who had written the flight planning software. My first officer agreed with my fuel figure with barely more interest than I'd shown but, to be fair, none of this was rocket science – oh wait, some of it was – kind of.

The first officer, Dan – a decent name for a pilot – went over to the phone to join the growing queue of first officers waiting to speak to the handling agent.

The handling agent is a dedicated organisation that provides passenger and baggage services to an airline operator. Sometimes the airline and its handler are one and the same, but more usually they are contractors (or business partners, in modern lingo). In this case, the handling company is the organisation that actually loses your bag, not the airline. As contractors they are beaten down on price so much that many of their ground workers earn close to minimum wage, and this is unfortunate when it comes to relying on their services.

Whilst Dan queued for the phone, I tried to identify our cabin crew from among the forest of uniformed bodies in the room. There were wall-to-wall standing tables, each with at least one yawning crew member slumped against it. I looked down at my crew sheet. There was only one female among the crew so I looked for a group of three guys and a girl.

My head swivelled around the room, briefly checking each table in turn, before I remembered that this combination of cabin crew was not that rare – in Gatwick, at least.

My eyes were about to pass from one uni-girl table to another when I noticed someone staring straight at me. A young man appeared happy that he'd caught my attention. He waved and mouthed Malaga at me with bright glossy lips perched on a lightly freckled face. Rather theatrically, he raised a pair of ever-so-slightly ginger eyebrows to form a visual question mark. I nodded and smiled a remote greeting, then raised my index finger and mouthed back 'One minute.'

Dan came back to the table muttering something about another first officer who he'd handed the phone to.

'She's so full of herself, that one,' he said

'Who, the blonde?' I asked, looking beyond him.

'Yeah, Claire Pippings, have you flown with her?'

'I don't think so.'

'Oh, you'd remember, John, never shuts up about how she should be a captain already, but claims she's been overlooked because she won't sleep with the Base Captain.'

'And how's she upset you today, mate?' I asked.

'I was trying to talk on the phone but all I could hear was her gobbing-off loudly about a captain she had reported for sexual harassment.' Dan was shaking his head.

'From the sound of it,' I ventured, 'if she'd been as open with her legs as she is with her mouth, perhaps she'd be Chief Pilot by now!'

We shared a schoolboy snigger before Dan read out the gate number for our plane, together with the good news that, so far, there was no air traffic control delay on our flight. With nothing left to do, we wandered over to the cabin crew and introduced ourselves.

'You look like your photo,' explained Sebastian, the freckled young man who'd waved at me moments earlier. 'That's how I recognised you.'

There should have been a reproduction of each crew member's security pass photo next to the name on the crew sheet, but most people have somehow avoided this incriminating feature. I instinctively looked down at my sheet and the small grainy picture beside my name. It was an old photo, taken when I joined the company ten years earlier and, inevitably, not a faithful likeness. These days there is rather more grey on top, and a growing collection of lines below. But I supposed Sebastian had an eye for these things.

I noted that the only other crew member with a photo beside her name was Kelly, the token girl. Glancing over at Kelly's sheet I could see that she had done a bit of doodling. *Must have been a riveting crew briefing, Sebastian!* She had drawn little devil's horns on our respective heads, which struck me as an interesting start to the day. She was probably half my age, but she looked at me with a tempting grin – or at least I thought she did. Perhaps it was a look of encouragement. I needed to be careful: happily married with no record of ill discipline. I wasn't about to start now.

I glanced down at the name badge on her purple blouse – an unnecessary act, but instinctive – and spotted the little Portuguese flag beside her name. So, she spoke Portuguese. That was unusual – unless one of her parents was Portuguese, I supposed. But with the surname of Wellington I guessed it wasn't her father. *Kelly Welly, bet she's heard that a few times.* Thinking about it, she was probably a few years younger than my first guess, probably more like twenty. Not that any of this mattered.

Several seconds had now passed in silence, and I became aware of my crew staring at me.

'Right, yes, hello everyone,' I said. 'How are you all?' I felt my cheeks tingle, so I dipped my head and pretended to study my crew sheet once more.

There was general mumbling before Sebastian asked for the flight times. Awkward.

I read out the relevant information and vaguely suggested that the weather would be warm and sunny in Malaga, but crap back here. I could see they were impressed with my thoroughness, but Sebastian interrupted my meteorological masterclass by asking what I'd like to drink during the flight.

The words 'pint of Stella' formed on my lips but I doubted Kelly would find such an obvious joke even remotely funny. Quickly, I stifled the words before they could do any damage. *I'm not interested in what Kelly thinks!* Playing it safe, I simply asked for coffee-white-none, and chose to have breakfast on the first sector. I noticed that Kelly wrote 'CW0' besides my modified picture, which probably meant she was working at the front alongside Sebastian. Either that or she was making a note of my preference to ensure she had coffee at home for later. *Whatever! You're married – happily so – and have no interest in wrecking your life. Or your family's!*

I looked at my watch and suggested we made our way out to the aircraft, unconsciously thumbing my wedding ring at the same time.

Many years ago airline crew would simply wave at the security personnel, waltz through the metal detector and head out to the aircraft. But then some bearded blokes with a rather big point to make decided to make that point in spectacular fashion. They didn't have guns or explosives, yet they were able to take control of the commercial jet airliners on which they were travelling and ram them apocalyptically into both towers of the World Trade Centre. It was the most shocking terrorist incident in history and it changed the way we travel forever.

Suddenly I was no longer allowed to take nail clippers on board (filthy habit anyway) or my cherished Leatherman multi-tool. Suddenly, should I want to hijack my own aircraft, the authorities believed I would require some minor domestic tools to do so. They assumed I would require a weapon of some kind to take control of the plane I already had under my control.

No amount of intelligent reasoning from me, my colleagues or the British Airline Pilots' Association could convince the authorities that a pilot doesn't need to take anything on board to commit an act of terrorism, and there's a very simple reason why. Strapped up on the flight deck of every single commercial airliner is a lethally shaped fire axe. And the flight deck door is lockable from the inside! Ridiculous.

And then came the 'intelligence' that terrorists were planning to detonate bombs made from dodgy mineral water. So now we can't take liquids, gels or pastes on board unless they're safely cosseted within the apparently explosive-proof plastic of a 100 ml container. Farcically, if confiscated by security, it then sits on a table next to their workstation (brooding menacingly and threatening to explode) until someone decides to drink it!

Next came the hapless chap who tried to blow up his shoes. So suddenly metal detectors were no longer able to detect bombs in your shoes and we have to take them off.

Mercifully, the twerp who tried to set fire to his underpants on a Christmas Day flight to Detroit didn't convince the Department for Transport that banning underpants on aircraft departing the UK would be the only sensible course of action.

Inexplicably, all these events led the various UK Government agencies, and the many airport security contractors, into concluding that your airline pilot is more of a threat to civil aviation than the average passenger. And this belief persists despite our passing criminal record checks, employment and personal referencing, holding an airport-issued security pass, and operating as a licensed professional airline pilot.

That morning, a security agent – who, until recently, might have been serving burgers in a fast food outlet (though he might not have been, I supposed) – wanted me to remove my outer clothing, my shoes and my trouser belt so he could run his hands all over my humiliated body, just in case I might take something on board which I could use to endanger the bloody aircraft!

In contrast, security at airports throughout Continental Europe generally let an identifiable crew member through with barely a glance. You see, so far, there has been no known terrorist incident committed by the pilots or cabin crew of the plane on which they were operating. And the agencies outside the UK recognise this.

There was an incident though, some years ago, when a captain from a country vastly different in culture to any in Europe decided he wanted to end his life. He aimed at the nearest mountain and ended everyone else's life too. Flight data recordings showed that no struggle took place on the flight deck, so it appeared that the first officer didn't think he should challenge the captain's authority. Mercifully, these cultural difficulties have been largely eradicated from Western airlines, though don't try telling a French airline captain that he can't take the new stewardess to the crew rest area during the flight, he'd invoke Clause 69 of the French Airline Pilots' Charter – *Les Droits des Pilotes* – and threaten to go on strike.

I began re-dressing myself, and noticed that the security agent didn't pick on Sebastian – perhaps my senior crew member looked more innocent than I did. He'd make a good waiter, I decided. He was tall and thin, and always looking around at everyone. You just know you wouldn't have to wait all night to attract his attention.

Kelly, though, got the full treatment from the female security agent. I felt a bit pervy watching her modestly exposed body being smoothed over by an older woman, but I still watched. So did Dan. Sebastian didn't, but I expected he was more of a gentleman than we were.

As usual, this mildly lascivious encounter took time and we were a few minutes late arriving at the aircraft. Waiting in her car at the bottom of the steps was a moody dispatcher with a larger-than-life sense of her own importance. She marched onto the flight deck just as I reached for the technical log and started to get stressy.

'What was the hold up, guys; why are you late?' she demanded. I ignored her at first, but could tell she was desperate to ask again. Worried that I wouldn't cope with another attempt to show me who she thought was boss, I muttered something about 'security' and continued flicking through the defect pages of the tech log. She dropped the load sheet on to the centre console and left.

I looked at Dan and shook my head. He told me that I was far too restrained and that I should have put her in her place. Perhaps I should have, but I didn't think it was my job to interfere with someone's personality.

I advised Dan that there were no significant defects in the book, just a few cosmetic issues – flaky paint, worn carpet, that sort of thing – and made a mental note of the captain who last flew the aircraft. I closed the tech log for the time being and flung it back on the combing beneath the front windscreen. Although we've done this for years, the company recently told us not to store the oversized tech log on the combing since it scratches the laminate on the windscreen glass. Perhaps if my hugely profitable company stopped trying to strip away my terms and conditions of employment to maximise profits, I'd be more compliant.

It would no doubt be mildly shocking for many passengers if they were to hear how most aircraft flying around the skies are carrying some form of mechanical or electronic defect. But it's quite legal, and it's quite normal. Aircraft operators are allowed to fly their planes with certain 'allowable' defects according to an aviation authority approved document called the Minimum Equipment List. This document must be at least as restrictive as the aircraft manufacturer's guide, and pilots must ensure that any defect is allowable (according to this list) before signing for the aircraft.

Often a defect will have operational restrictions, for example enforcing a lower cruising altitude if the failure is associated with air conditioning or pressurisation, or limiting passenger numbers if an emergency exit is unserviceable. There are a surprising number of failures that can be allowed for flight, but today the aircraft was tip-top.

Time to get comfortable. I used the flat of my hand to remove last night's dinner crumbs from the captain's seat and wondered how, with a belly like a space hopper, Mike Stover managed to get food on the seat beneath him in the first place. There was some on the floor too, but to be quite honest if it fell from Mike's mouth it could have bounced anywhere. If I smelled toast during the flight I'll assume his bread roll had tumbled off his gut and dropped through the gaps between the pedals and into the avionics bay. It happens, it really does.

I spent a few minutes re-adjusting the seat belt to fit a normal sized person and then reached behind to pull the headphones down from their clip. Using an anti-bacterial wet-wipe, I began scraping the hair, dead skin, and ear grease from the little foam pads, and again urged myself to buy my own headphones. But, at £200 pound a pop, I knew I was more likely to continue with the vomit-inducing cleaning task.

I used the same wet-wipe to clean the consoles and screens (we've been told not to do this because the alcohol eats away at the glass) and then chucked the filthy dried up rag into the gash bag (I'm not being rude; it really is called a gash bag).

With the housekeeping done, I could begin flicking a few switches and prodding some buttons before finishing with a turn of the odd knob. I continued my diligent flight preparations by programming the flight management system with the company route for that day, and then noticed the strong smell of petrol filling the flight deck.

There was nothing to worry about, it was a familiar sensation; just the fuel guy popping up to get my signature for the eight and half tonnes of kerosene we'd asked for. I signed the chit and wished him a good day, followed by a suggestion that he changed his clothes before sneaking off for a quick cigarette.

Now it was time to rifle through the pile of newspapers left from the day before. Since I hadn't been at work and therefore hadn't ready any yet, I knew yesterday's papers would suffice for the trip to Malaga. But I hoped the passengers would leave a new selection behind for my return trip when they disembarked down route – though it was unlikely to be a wide selection.

I stretched my arm out towards the pile behind me – nearly falling from my seat – and silently prayed for something fun to read. Frankly, I was hoping to find a car magazine or similar buried among the news, but it was disappointment all round as my exertions revealed just two Daily Mails and a Sun. A lack of choice is the risk we take with our cheapskate attitude towards the supply of

J.T. O'Neil

reading material. Finally, (the overuse of that word has already started) I decided it was time for a cuppa.

It was now 40 minutes after I'd reported for duty. I sat back in my chair, drinking coffee and scanning the passengers as they walked across the apron below my window, then suddenly the morning brightened up.

'God Almighty!' I said, leaning forward in my seat. 'What a sight! 'It isn't that warm, love. Yes, mate, you do look a complete twat in the Superman costume – And no, of course no one's ever been to Spain wearing union flag emblazoned shorts before; you're the first, mate!'

Dan perked up and peered through the window hoping for an opportunity to shake his head with condescension as I had done.

'No way!' he said. 'What must the Spanish think?'

'Let's divert to Cardiff and tell them it's unseasonal Spanish weather at the moment.'

'Oh, look at that woman,' said Dan, pointing at an elderly lady in a short leather skirt and fishnet stockings. With her long, jet-black hair she looked like I imagined Cher would if she hadn't been able to afford the surgery.

My malicious thoughts began to run away with themselves, so I swivelled my head back to The Sun newspaper and read what Suzie on page 3 had to say about the current situation in Afghanistan. *Fair enough, Suzie, you seem wasted modelling for newspapers, but what do I know?*

Something alerted my peripheral vision and I looked down towards the passengers again. It was the hen parties this time. A group of women wearing pink tasselled cowboy hats and gaudy T-shirts were advertising Leanne's hen weekend. It's a common sight: overweight, underdressed tanning bed junkies, tottering along the tarmac on heels that vanish to nothing as they reach the floor. Some of the women were waving up at me. Caught out, I was forced to smile and wave back. Please don't ask for a flight deck visit, I thought.

And then I saw a group of boys strutting across the apron towards my aircraft. They were clearly bullish and confident, wearing their baggy shorts and preparing to take Spain on single-handedly. Perhaps we should cancel all return flights and just leave these people there.

Kelly appeared on the flight deck holding a plastic cup brimming with chocolates. 'I'm sure you guys are really sweet already,' she said, 'but you can never have too much chocolate, can you?' She vanished before Dan or I could summon up a suitable reply, so we just grinned at each other.

Finally, the dispatcher informed me that everyone was on board, and I sat up ready to get busy. Sebastian confirmed the total on board after carrying out a headcount, and I signed the loading form, retaining the top copy and giving the bottom sheet to the dispatcher.

It was 5.55 am, we were five minutes early, but the previously stroppy dispatcher made no mention of this astonishing achievement. She smiled, though, when she wished us a good flight. I supposed she just had a job to do like the rest of us.

The doors closed and I began to gabble about flight times and pleasant Spanish weather to my strapped-in audience. Hopefully those who had arrived on this chilly morning wearing shorts, T-shirts and flip-flops now felt vindicated by their choice of attire (good job they didn't know how unsuccessful I'd been in predicting the weather so far that morning). It was all rather pointless, though; I knew they wouldn't be listening. It's a speech I give up to four times a day so I know how tired and perfunctory it can sound, but if the passengers can forgive my monotony, I'll forgive them if they're not actually listening.

It was time to get under way and check if the plane would do what I'd programmed it to do during the time it took The Addams Family and their friends to waddle down the cabin in search of a seat.

The doors were closed. Dan and I put our newspapers down and ran through the various checks to make sure we'd readied the plane correctly for action. We even briefed each other on what we both do every single day of our working lives. I told him what we both already knew: the plane was serviceable, the weather was fine, and we were going to perform the same departure routing we always did for a flight to Spain. We also ran through the emergency procedures should an engine fail at some point during the take-off manoeuvre. No questions, said Dan. Then we waited.

We waited until three blokes had finished walking, apparently purposelessly, around the plane. They dragged chocks along the floor, pointed at various bits of ground equipment, and shouted at each other like The Three Stooges.

These people – these service providers – were the ground crew without which no airliner could get under way, and Dan and I were at their mercy. But, unfortunately, they aren't paid or treated particularly well by their company. Worse still, they view pilots as overpaid prima donnas sat on their arses slurping coffee and reading newspapers. Perhaps they're right.

I worked hard at school and earned a place at a private college, helped largely by a bursary for financially disadvantaged students. I should have enrolled at University to study French and English, but at the last moment I changed my mind (I realised I no longer wanted to speak French, and that I could already speak English, so there didn't seem to be any point in going). In the end I joined the Army and became a captain – first time around – in the Royal Signals. Funnily enough, I used to sit on my arse drinking coffee much of the time back then too, but not in quite as much comfort.

I think I've worked hard chasing my childhood dreams and I can't feel bad about what I've achieved every time I appear to be in a better position than someone else. But it doesn't mean I am better than anyone else, including the guy outside. For instance, I bet he goes home to his family every night and meets his mates every weekend. Perhaps he has the stability to enjoy hobbies and pastimes, or secure time off work without having to go sick. There's a lot to be said for the kind of riches he can enjoy every day of his chosen life that I can't.

But with the greatest of respect, mate, tell me what the bloody hell is going on down there! Ten minutes after the doors had closed, we still sat helplessly in our cockpit like a pair of abandoned chicks waiting for mummy to fly home with some tasty worms.

Of course, many of the ground crew are enthusiastic and hard-working chaps who keep us informed when there's a delay, and they approach their work as though sending the plane off on time is the most important thing they'll attempt all day. Then again, many don't, and today that seemed to be the case.

Finally, at 6.05 am, five minutes late already, the head-phones crackled and I heard the sound of someone keying the microphone.

'Cockpit to ground, good morning,' I said.

'Alright, mate?' grunted the push back controller.

'Er, yes, fine thank you.' I replied. 'And you?'

'Yeah, glad when you've gone, mate, and I can get back to my tea. You ready to go, mate?'

'Yes. Er, sorry, could you tell me what the reason is for the delay this morning – just for the paperwork – management will only ask if I don't put something down, you know what they're like.'

I had to choose my words carefully lest our 'service partner' thinks I was having a go at him, or accusing him of failing to get his arse into gear (which I was). Anyone can shout and be rude to me, but I have to tread carefully if I wish to remain out of the Chief Pilot's office. But that's fine; I can do politeness and decorum.

'Er, yeah, mate, headphones didn't work, had to go and get some more. You ready then?'

This was the person responsible for guiding my $60 million dollar airliner on to the taxiway and supervising the engine start up. In days gone by, or in other parts of Europe, the conversation might have gone like this:

> *'Hello, Captain, are you ready for my checks?'*
> *'Hi, yes go ahead, please.'*
> *'All doors are closed and the aircraft is clear of ground equipment. The tug is connected and we're ready to push.'*
> *'Great.'*
> *'Please release your parking brake, sir.'*

I'm not saying that I demand unconditional respect, nor do I ever want to be addressed as Sir or Captain, but it shows the difference in approach to the job that we encounter around the network these days. That's all.

Once everyone was ready, and the comedy troupe outside had settled down, we pushed back and started the engines. Clearly the tug driver had been playing Grand Theft Auto judging by the way we swerved and weaved our way across the apron at alarming speed. I reminded him that the cabin crew were still standing and walking about the cabin, and he replied, 'Oh yeah, sorry, mate,' undoubtedly adding 'tosser' under his breath, but I pretended he hadn't (and there was even a small chance he might not have done).

With the pushback complete I gave him the instruction to disconnect the tug, and we waved jovially at each other before muttering obscenities under our respective breaths.

In his hand I could see the pin that he'd used to disconnect the plane's nose wheel steering mechanism prior to push back. Had he not inserted this pin into the nose wheel assembly, I could have interfered with his directional control by steering the aircraft myself. I wouldn't deliberately do such a thing, that would be childish, and I really didn't need the hassle of him reporting me to his boss for being a knob.

The parting of tug and plane occurred with an efficiency that had been glaringly absent moments before, and the would-be Formula 1 team was back in its garage chatting with some imaginary pit babes before you could say Emerson Fittipaldi.

Dan ran through the After Start checklist: Engines started – check. After Start checks completed, Captain. There is more to the After Start checklist, but not much.

I then asked him to call for taxi (not call for *a* taxi; ATC are just not that obliging), which is pilot-speak for asking permission to drive to the runway. This they granted. They also issued routing instructions; essential in Gatwick, but in Exeter or Bristol, for instance with their single taxiway and single runway holding point, it isn't. This wouldn't stop Exeter or Bristol ATC issuing the full taxi instructions, though, just in case, you know, both pilots are complete numpties. It's the regions; they simply can't afford to take any chances.

How Aircraft Fly

First of all, let me make one thing clear (which perhaps hasn't happened so far): this is not a technical manual for aviation geeks; I am not an aircraft engineer, aero-dynamicist, or scientist. I have never worked for Rolls-Royce, Boeing or Airbus, and I don't eat, drink or dream of aviation. I just fly the planes.

So, if you're looking for a deep technical explanation on the theory of flight then you're going to be badly let down by reading on. That said, I will, from time to time, include the odd technical word and a splattering of mumbo-jumbo to demonstrate some credibility in my chosen profession, but don't get excited – I won't.

If, like me, you've ever stood in a field on a warm summer's day and looked up at a passing aircraft, you might have been struck by one of several thoughts as determined by your proximity to the aircraft's point of departure:

1. The aircraft was bloody noise (you were standing too close to the airport).

2. The aircraft was a bloody nuisance (you live too near the airport).

3. The aircraft made the earth move (you were standing on the airfield).

4. The aircraft really made the earth move (you were near a primary school in Afghanistan, inconveniently located close to an American airbase and you read The Daily Mail).

5. You didn't hear the aircraft but noticed its pretty white cotton wool trails contrasting artistically with the deep blue of our upper atmosphere, and you thought, oh look, that flying machine has two wings.

That's right, modern commercial aircraft design has featured a two-wing layout quite consistently for several decades. Occasionally, it may seem like an aircraft has a single wing with the fuselage (technical word for body) slung under or plonked on top of this single wing. But don't be fooled. Airliners have two wings, one on each side, and it's to do with aerodynamic balance. But how do these planes defy gravity?

Sustained defiance of gravity by aeroplanes on Earth (as opposed to other celestial bodies, such as Mars) is most efficiently achieved by the use of these aforementioned wings. This is because Earth has an atmosphere. Mars, on the other hand, has no atmosphere; so if you were thinking of visiting our nearest neighbour for a night out, don't bother. Book a cheap flight to Amsterdam like everyone else. So, this atmosphere then, how does it make planes fly?

A wing has two important features of its shape: a rounded leading edge which is presented to the oncoming air (unless you're having a bad day, or you're some sort of smart arsed aerobatics junkie), and a thin flat trailing edge at the other end.

Dissatisfied geeks can read about *circulation* and the *Kutta Condition* elsewhere if in-depth science is what you're looking for; I'm all for keeping it simple.

So, in a nutshell, the rounded (or cambered) leading edge ensures a positive aerodynamic angle of attack compared with the angle of the airflow towards the wing (in other words, the wing is at an angle to the airflow), and together with the flat trailing edge of the wing, this shape ensures the air travelling across the top of the wing travels faster than the air which splits and goes underneath the wing. I hope you're still with me.

A popular, and seemingly plausible, explanation for the additional speed carried by the upper air stream is that it has further to travel over the curved upper wing than its mate that goes beneath. If the upper airflow wishes to be reunited with the lazy splitter below, then it must travel faster to meet up again at the trailing edge.

Well, whatever you do, don't suggest this to a fluid dynamicist because they'll fix you a patronising stare and start talking about the *Kutta–Joukowski Theorem*, at which point you'd have to kill them.

The 'equal transit time fallacy' is a convenient layperson's way of accepting the phenomenon of airflow around a wing, even if it's not entirely accurate. Unfortunately the real science is mind-numbingly dull (which means it's too complicated) so we'll just have to leave it there.

Big deal, then, the air flows faster over the top than underneath. Well, imagine air flowing through a tube. Provided that tube isn't shaped like a trombone, then nothing terrible will happen. The air pressure inside the tube would be constant throughout, and this has something to do with a scientific notion that energy cannot be made or destroyed, nor can it simply disappear. Scientific types call it the 'conservation of energy'.

Anyway, shove some kind of wing shaped body into this tube and, as we now accept, the air will split into two streams, with the upper stream travelling faster than the lower stream.

Faster moving air must have more energy, though; after all, faster moving air is more likely to blow your house down – particularly if you were the half-witted little piggy who made it from straw. Well, indeed it does have more energy, but those physicists and their damned laws say we can't just go around creating energy. So we don't. (I say we, but to be honest, I just fly the damned things).

The Dutch born Swiss physicist, Daniel Bernoulli, showed that the total air pressure in the tube must remain the same (pesky laws of energy conservation again), and that the total pressure was made up of static pressure and dynamic pressure:

Static pressure – The pressure we don't normally feel, but is exerted by the weight of the air above us.

Dynamic pressure – The pressure we feel when someone blows in our ear, or when the wind blows.

So it's a simple bit of sums that show if you increase dynamic pressure (the air moving faster over the wing) you must lose a bit of static pressure to maintain the same total pressure. Piece of cake. And indeed this is what happens. The static pressure above the wing becomes less than the pressure below the wing, and the wing is said to generate lift; it is sucked up.

Unfortunately, it took around another one hundred years before anyone thought to apply Bernoulli's Principle to the construction of wings for the purpose of flight. What were they doing all that time?

Eventually, though, someone did get around to hammering together some bits of balsa wood during a school woodwork lesson and, in doing so, encouraged a generation of nutters to endure umpteen painful and often fatal years foolishly attempting to discredit Newton's theory of gravity.

The madness continued until some bloke with a duck's name figured out what adverse aileron yaw was.

Who needs a rudder?

Early attempts at building a controllable flying machine relied on altering wing shapes to steer the plane. If you want to turn left (or actually, in those days, it was more about trying to fly in a straight line) you would increase the lift on the right wing which would raise that wing more than the other one and cause the aircraft to roll to the left. The total lift force, being perpendicular to the wings, would now be angled diagonally to the left and would cause the aircraft to move in this direction. This is a successful way of turning a plane, or preventing a turn, and is still used today. But there's a problem.

By increasing the lift on a wing you also increase the drag of that wing, something racing car designers are always moaning about. Their wings are intended to push the car into the ground to provide grip. But this leads to drag, which slows the car down. Planes suffer the same consequence. The additional drag generated by the up-going wing slows that wing down with respect to the plane's progress through the air. It therefore begins to lag behind the other wing. A situation now exists where the aircraft is banking one way, but yawing the opposite way. This is known as adverse aileron yaw, and moody planes don't like that. If left unchecked this undesirable attitude will result in a spin, stall or spiral dive depending on how bad your day is. In other words, owing to the elementary controls featured on early aircraft, the pilot would find himself hurtling towards the ground with little hope of recovery. Even flying in a straight line requires regular aileron movements, and as soon as these pioneers tried to keep their wings level, adverse aileron yaw would take hold and curtail their attempts at flying with the most unforgiving consequences.

It was Orville and Wilbur Wright who figured out that adverse aileron yaw was causing these crashes and they successfully cured the problem by plonking a rudder on the back of their machine, The Wright Flyer. The result was 13 seconds of controlled flight on the day of 17th December 1903 in a little place called Kitty Hawk, North Carolina. The rest is history.

The first pilot

These early attempts to cheat the great man, Newton, out of his legacy were not actually the first. Long before the curly headed boffin noticed that apples fell from trees, there were a few poorly thought out attempts to head off his theory before he had even been born. And I'm not talking about Icarus and his crackpot father, Daedalus.

A 9th Century Monk called Elmer struck a claim for aviation glory around 880 AD when, covered in feathers, he leapt from the top of Malmesbury Abbey. He survived, but it isn't known if he played for the Malmesbury Bell Ringers ever again. I suspect not.

Now, obviously Icarus lived about a thousand years before Elmer, but come on, the wax holding his feathers together melted when he flew too close to the Sun? I'm not sure we can believe this story, so I'll go with Elmer and his hawk man outfit for first pilot.

The Science Bit

I know what you're thinking: you're thinking how exciting it is when we take off – the roar of the engines, the G-force (no such thing, but that's another story) squeezing you into the seat, and the realisation that you're finally on your way to the Costa del Sol (and you've usually had a few by then). It's the best bit of the flight.

Well, next time you're sat on a plane and the pilot opens the throttles, think of this: it's a 70 tonne Reliant Robin doing 150 mph. Worse still: it's being steered by the pilot's feet pushing on pedals connected to an oversized shark fin stuck on the back of the fuselage. It might as well have 'Trotters Independent Trading' scrawled down the side.

Okay, okay, I can hear some of you murmuring about my earlier comment that there is no such thing as 'G-force', and this is distracting you. It's true: all this pushing and shoving of one's body in one's car seat when we drive around the staff car park too quickly is not caused by 'G-force'. I know you're shaking your head and muttering 'bollocks', so I'll attempt to explain myself and convince you never to say G-force again (did I mention that I wasn't actually a scientist?).

G-Force?

Force is that which a body exerts on whatever supports it. For instance, the force that you exert on a set of bathroom scales is commonly described as weight. Possibly a lot of weight, I don't know. Technically though it's actually force and is measured in newtons.

You actually weigh x amount of newtons (or maybe xx newtons) and not x amount of Kilos, pounds or stones. In scientific circles it is your mass (the amount of matter you contain) that is measured in our familiar units of weight. But I digress.

The force you exert upon an object, let's say the Chief Pilot's nose, is proportional to two factors: the size of your fist (its mass measured in kg) and the speed at which you are throwing it towards the unfortunate nose (measured in metres per second: m s-1). Owing to just such an altercation with a love rival, Isaac Newton was able to work out the following equation:

Force in newtons = Mass in Kg x Acceleration in m s-1

(m s-1 is the scientific way of expressing metres per second, more commonly written as m/s, but once again it's not a science lesson – because I'm not a scientist – so you'll just have to believe me).

The same bit of violent science is true for a car that hits a lamppost after its driver decides to send a text message. The mass is the size of the car, and the acceleration is the speed at which the car is moving.

Going back to our bathroom scales, the force exerted on the scales is determined by your mass (or lack of it if you're a Singapore Airlines air hostess) and gravity, which is pulling you inexorably and unsympathetically towards the scales. Thus, gravity is acceleration and not a force. But I concede that G-force sounds much cooler than G-acceleration, and I even heard a TV scientist calling gravity a force recently, so I'm not going to make a fuss if I haven't convinced you (though the same scientist also reminds us that Einstein decided that gravity was a distortion in space-time so I think the use of the word 'force' is an attempt to prevent our minds blowing up).

Anyway, where were we? Ah yes, oversized three-wheelers storming down thin strips of tarmac. I can just imagine the meeting where they first discussed modern airliner design:

> 'Right, chaps, we don't want every Tom, Dick and Harry flying our aeroplanes.'
> 'Ahem, sir, most of the brave pilots who faced Jerry during the war were called Tom, Dick or Harry.'
> 'Don't get smart with me, Fotheringhill!'
> 'Yes, sir, sorry, sir.'

'Right then. The point is this, chaps: we don't want just anyone flying aircraft, do we? No, it should be made as fiendishly difficult as possible – like trying to race a three-legged horse in the Derby. Now, these automobiles are becoming popular. You, Barrington, what's the trickiest little devil you've ever driven?'

'Well, sir, I drove a damned temperamental little blighter with only three wheels once. A Morgan Super Sports Aero, sir. A jolly fine car, sir, but damned dangerous in the bends.'

'Yes, I know what you mean, ol' boy. Old Taffers had one, damned near killed him. So, three wheels it is, then. The Morgan had a single wheel at the back, if I remember correctly. Let's put it at the front. Should liven things up a little.'

'Yes, sir, and how about steering with the feet?'

'Ah, rather a like a soapbox cart! Sterling idea!'

And so on. Having said that, a plane doesn't have corners so we can't employ a conventional car design and put a wheel at each corner. Planes are also characteristically thin at the front end so it would be tricky fitting two wheels further than a few feet apart, particularly if you wanted to tuck them away after take-off (which we do). So designers are a bit constrained.

Off we scream, then, accelerating to around 150 mph in our giant Reliant Robin, pressing on pedals to keep the thing off the grass, and hitting all the cat's eyes (or centre line lights) with our centrally located front wheel. That's the beating noise you hear when taxiing or taking off; it's not a bandsman in the cargo hold banging away on his bass drum.

Now, a conscientious pilot might think about steering slightly right or left of the centre line, just to stop the passengers freaking out as the aircraft accelerates and the beating noise turns into a drum roll. But there aren't many such pilots left.

More entertaining, though, is if you have two closely spaced parallel wheels at the front (which is common), and you're quite skilful, you can try and sit the two wheels either side of the lights, then gain points for each one you hit. At the end of the day you tally up the points and the pilot with the fewest points wins! It keeps us amused.

Steering with the feet isn't intrinsically tricky, though. What makes it tricky is a howling gale blowing across the runway whilst you're trying to keep the bugger straight.

You're trying to steer the aerodynamically shaped plane using a large fin sticking high into the air, whilst all the fin wants to do is push the aircraft in the direction of the wind. It's called weather-cocking, and it makes things more challenging. So if you're careering down the runway and the aircraft feels like it's wallowing from side to side, then it is, and that's why. Either that, or the pilot's got a trapped nerve in his leg.

Well, eventually you reach a point where, if something

70

went wrong, you simply wouldn't be able to stop without crashing into the spotters (by day) or doggers (by night) who gather around the airport perimeter. But if you've done your take-off performance calculations correctly, and the stressy dispatcher has remembered what her job actually is, there should be enough runway left to get airborne even if an engine fails.

Chapter 3

It's not rocket science. Oh wait …

On the way to the runway Dan and I began multi-tasking; oh yes, we did more than one thing at a time. We performed some vital checks designed to assess if the aircraft would be controllable once airborne, and then we pushed a few buttons. One of these buttons is very important: it makes sure we don't get airborne if, for instance, we lose that previously confirmed controllability.

This important button arms the autobrake and saves me the trouble of stamping on the foot brakes should I decide, for some reason, not to bother flying on the first attempt; I'd have enough to do just keeping the thing skidding in a straight line. So what reasons could I have for not bothering to go flying?

Well, there are many, and I'm not even including a lack of coffee as one of them. The big reason is a failure of one of the two engines. Of course, both could fail, but then I wouldn't be getting airborne even if I had a full cup of freshly brewed coffee by my side. The plane could suffer a number of serious failures whilst we hurtled down the runway, but many of these are suppressed by Airbus's 'inhibit logic.' Basically, the plane decides what to tell the pilot, and since it divulges only information on failures that it believes will prevent controllable flight, the need for the pilot to make a time wasting assessment of the failure prior to rejecting the take-off is removed. If the bell goes ping, we don't go flying. Simple.

With the multi-tasking out of the way, I re-briefed the departure in case we'd already forgotten what we had discussed not ten minutes earlier, and then I asked Dan to read through the Before Take-off Checklist. The idea of the checklist is to ensure that we have done all the things that appear on it.

You may wonder why we don't just do these things as we read the checklist – one pilot reading, the other doing – rather than doing things from memory and checking later.

It's a good point, but clever people have determined that it's far more efficient to do things first and check later since – and this is the cunning part – not everything we have to do is on the checklist. Some of the tasks that don't appear on the checklist need to be done before certain tasks that are on the checklist, but after other tasks on the checklist have been completed. Therefore it would become confusing if we tried to intersperse the checklist items with memory items as we read through the check-list. A further snag with the 'read and do' philosophy, no matter how sensible it appears at first sight, is that you cannot check the flight controls (a memory item on the checklist) until the engines are running (a memory item not on the checklist).

I hope that's cleared things up. But, put more simply, it's a type of memory game for us to play, and an opportunity to take the piss out of each other if we forget to do something that we subsequently read out from the checklist. We just have to hope that if we forget to do something which isn't on the checklist it will be flagged up when we try to do something which is on the checklist – like trying to check the flight controls without first starting the engines. All clear?

Well, it seems to be a fool proof system – which in many ways is quite reassuring – and provides a fun little game to play on the way to the runway.

With drills and checks completed we waited for Sebastian to ring through and give the 'cabin secure for take-off' notice. Once we have that status, I can ask Dan to tell air traffic control that we are ready for departure. This is an important point: we're not ready for take-off; we're not ready to go; we're not ready to hit the big blue. We are ready for departure.

Radio phraseology is very specific in order to reduce misunderstandings, particularly among those whose first language isn't English. The problem is, though, it is very specifically different in each country, and this increases the chance of those misunderstandings, sometimes with fatal consequences. Flying's a serious business.

Anyway. The young fellow in the Tower (well, he sounded quite young) asked if we had the Boeing 757 in sight on final approach. I could see something; a general aircraft type shape: flat protrusions out to the side and a blobby bit in the middle, but to be honest, it could have be a bloody Klingon battle ship for all I knew. However, not wishing to reveal (a) poor eyesight or (b) poor aircraft recognition skills, I told Dan to answer 'affirm' (not affirmative, because this could be misheard as 'negative' – it has in the past, and people have died. I told you, serious stuff.)

The landing aircraft whizzed past. It wasn't a fictitious space ship from a TV show after all, so we lined up and waited behind. We did a few more checks and then switched on all our lights.

The anti-collision beacon had been blinking away since we were ready to start the engines – it's a safety device to alert ground crew and hopefully prevent them from being sucked up by a huge turbo-fanned engine. Now, as we entered the runway, we added strobe lights, take off lights, runway turnoff lights and, bizarrely, landing lights, to the display.

One of the reasons for all these lights is bird scaring; the belief being that birds will see the bright lights and scarper pronto. But come on, if they're not freaked out by the colossal wail of the engines at full chat then I doubt a few shiny lights will attract their attention. You only have to tap on your kitchen window and any garden bird with even a vague sense of self-preservation will instantly fly away as though the grass had just become electrified. But, it wasn't for us to argue with procedures, so we switched on the landing lights and waited for our take-off clearance.

Once cleared, I asked Dan if he was ready. He nodded and grunted something that sounded positive, and so I stood the thrust levers up. Had he not been ready I'm sure he would have been more vocal.

I left the thrust levers in this slightly advanced position until both engines had stabilised at about half power and gave me a strong enough impression that they would deliver the goods when asked. The last thing you want is to rev-up to full power only to find that one engine doesn't bother. But it can happen, and without this precaution one could easily end up asymmetrically thrusting oneself on to the grass.

Confident that we were likely to remain on the tarmac, I shoved the thrust levers forward to the take-off position and we began to scream down the runway. Big Blue, here we come.

The sixty tonne, three wheeled aircraft hurtled along the runway, accelerating towards 130 mph. The wind from the side pushed against the oversized fin sticking up at the back (the tailplane). I dabbed at the pedals, left then right, trying to keep this giant Reliant Robin in a straight line, whilst all it wanted to do was weathercock into wind. It was with some relief that Dan called 'rotate', signalling to me that we'd reached take-off speed. Everything looked normal so I pulled back on the controls and aimed the plane towards the sky. There was a slight jerk as I pulled a little too eagerly (which was unlike me for day one at work) and we swiftly parted company with the tarmac. Dan and I both breathed a sigh of relief, marvelling at how much better the plane flew than it drove.

Just before Dan had called 'Rotate' he called out 'V1.' This is the speed where I take my hand off the thrust levers and commit to the take-off. If an engine failed prior to V1 there would likely be insufficient runway length remaining to accelerate on one engine to the rotate speed (Vr). An engine failure after V1 should not prevent the aircraft from becoming airborne, but attempting to stop because one of your engines is on fire usually ends with a trashed plane somewhere beyond the airport perimeter (followed by a meeting with the Chief Pilot, if you're still alive). But don't worry. Taking a burning engine into the sky is not as mad as it sounds. Pilots train to deal with this eventuality twice a year in the annual bum twitch session in a simulator.

That morning, as usual, Dan and I encountered no such fires or failures during the take-off roll and we found ourselves flying through the air with the greatest of ease. We celebrated with a little whoop then raised the wheels. Our initial routing was west for a few miles, followed by a left turn towards the south coast, but not before a three-dimensional point in space that someone in a white coat had calculated as being sufficiently far from houses to avoid disturbing the local residents.

Regrettably there was a dark mass of menacing-looking

water droplets hanging in the air ahead. We checked the weather radar and correlated the nasty cloud with a red blob on the screen, so Dan asked air traffic control for an immediate left turn. Sorry residents, this is your early morning wake up call.

We weren't being deliberately cruel to the sleepy week-enders of West Sussex when we made the early turn. Flying into a thundercloud or other seriously tall and heaped mass of suspended water is potentially deadly. The force inside can be great enough to tear apart any size of air-craft. That said, at that time of day it was unlikely such a violent cloud would have developed over West Sussex. Can't be too sure though, especially if it gets us a short cut.

Passing three thousand feet we started to clean up the aircraft. This doesn't involve getting the dustpan and brush out, or spraying kitchen cleaner all over the place, it means retracting the flaps and slats (droopy bits on the wings). Failing to do so would severely limit the speed at which we could fly, whilst drastically increasing our fuel consumption.

In an age when aviation is under attack from climate change worriers, Guardian readers and polar bears, we wouldn't want to do anything unnecessary that could draw attention to our lack of green credentials. No, it makes much more sense to clean up and go sleek.

If we'd departed from a sleepy regional airport in the UK such as Exeter (I suggest, through gritted teeth) then we would probably be fairly relaxed, admiring the over admired scenery of the familiar countryside, and slurping the remains of our coffee, or in some cases, dozing off. Oh, yes, dozing off.

If, however, we were departing a busier environment – or anywhere around the Mediterranean – we would probably be concentrating hard to compensate for any lapses in air traffic control competency that might threaten our enjoyment of the scenery. Gatwick was a familiar environment for Dan and me, and the local controllers were excellent. No need for excessive vigilance.

By the time we've changed frequencies once or twice, there is usually sufficient distance between us and the ground – and other aircraft – to relax a little. That's usually a good time to start thinking about another coffee and some grub. We may also be tempted to reach for a newspaper if the other guy is a bit dull. We're supposed to wait until the cruise phase of the flight before mentally adjourning to the drawing room, pipe and slippers at the ready, but for many pilots this tends to be the case only when being assessed by a training captain. Today, it was just Dan and me and we were already in feet-up mode.

Being close to the south coast meant it was not long before we were saying Bonjour to the French air traffic control chaps and being given a direct routing to a way-point at the border with Spain. In other words, *'Sod off, Monsieur, and don't bozzer me again.'*

We cruised along at 38,000 feet, zipping through the thin end of the atmosphere at 500 mph, with an outside air temperature of -57 degrees Celsius (which is why the windows in modern commercial airliners don't open). There was the occasional control input to make; a little bit left, a little bit right, even a bit of up and down, although that's usually only necessary if we get in the way of an Air France jet that wishes to use the sky. The French can get ever-so-slightly partisan when one of their own planes comes on the scene, and it's something we just have to put up with. We're skilled pilots, though, and we can fiddle with the autopilot all day without losing our place in the newspaper, though a DVD might need to be paused. Other than that there's little air traffic control can do up here to ruin our day.

The time, according to the on-board GPS controlled clock, was 6.40 am and I could see a red band of light stretching out around the curved horizon in the east. Soon the Sun would climb into view, peeking over the horizon and poking at my left eye. At 38,000 there's very little atmosphere to attenuate the Sun's intensity so I rolled down my window blind in anticipation of the Sun's appearance.

The cloud had broken up leaving clear skies below. Dan and I had a stunning view of Paris to our left, but to be truthful, I've seen Paris countless times from every angle (including through the slatted windows of an apartment in Montmartre, but that's beyond the scope of this book) so I didn't get excited. Dan and I barely looked up from our laps, though I did consider pointing out the view to my passengers. However, since I was only part way through a scandalous article about a former X Factor finalist, I held off making the announcement. By the time I'd finished reading, Paris was way behind so I decided the moment had passed and carried on flicking through the creased pages of the Sun newspaper. Dan, I noticed, was being a little more company minded: he was reading the aircraft manual.

'What are you doing, Dan?' I asked.

'Oh, I've got my sim coming up.'

I understood completely. Every six months all pilots spend two days in the flight simulator being tormented by a training captain with a fetish for sweaty, nervous pilots. It's the only time we get to practise handling emergency procedures in an attempt to avert disaster, and it's an inescapable part of the job. After all, shutting down an engine during flight to practise the failure drill is likely to distress the passengers unnecessarily, and distressed passengers don't spend money on board. Now that would be a disaster.

The doorbell sounded. I strained around to view the monitor, brilliantly positioned to necessitate frequent chiropractic treatment, and visually confirmed that my breakfast tray of Full English was indeed carried by Sebastian and not a full service terrorist. I unlocked the door and Sebastian entered.

'Hi, guys, how are you both doing in here?' he asked. Sebastian seemed to be in a breezy mood, and there was a faint Scottish accent in his voice that I hadn't noticed earlier.

'Yeah, good thanks, Sebastian.'

'You're the hot one aren't you, John,' said Sebastian, and before I could query this apparent compliment he placed the hot breakfast on my tray table. I silently mouthed my understanding.

'And here's your cold, Dan,' he continued. 'Rice Krispies okay?'

'Cheers, yeah,' replied Dan, and he immediately began rifling through his breakfast box.

I grinned. Rice Krispies, though a fine breakfast cereal, are just air in crackly little sacks, so I reckoned the hot option was likely to be more filling. Dan, though, appeared to be the kind of guy who looked after himself. He was about my height, but more athletic and about fifteen years younger. He seemed the kind of healthy guy that would never eat the hot breakfasts. It's worth pointing out, though, that the healthy appeal of the cold breakfast choice deteriorates rapidly beyond the little box of cereal.

I watched Dan prodding gingerly at a shrivelled tangerine that looked more like an orang-utan's bollock than a nutritional piece of fruit. Disgusted, he turned his attention to something paler than his own blanched face: a starch-filled bread roll. He let it drop from his fingers then offered me the little foil of butter, but I had nothing to put it on.

'Ooh, where's that down there, John?' asked Sebastian, peering through the window.

'La Rochelle, a really stunning part of France's Atlantic coastline, well worth a visit in the summer–'

'Oh right. What time are we landing?'

'Eight twenty five – ten minutes early.'

'Ooh, I'd better get on then.' And with that he was gone.

There was another little doodle from Kelly; this time it was on the lid of my breakfast box. The devil's horns from the sign-in sheet photo had grown a body to match, complete with forked tail. I showed Dan, and noted there was just a smiley face on his box.

'Aren't you the chosen one!' said Dan with a grin.

'It doesn't mean anything – just a bit of flirting.'

'It's a bit forward though, she's never met you before.'

'Yeah, it is a bit unusual,' I agreed.

I began to wrestle the foil lid from the hot tray; my attempts punctuated by plosive cursing, and then spent the next few minutes blowing on my fingers to cool them down. When finally revealed, the contents weren't particularly appetising: congealed lumps of scrambled egg, a few mushrooms which looked as though they'd been squeezed out of someone's arse, and a lump of sausage meat in a condom. Good job I was starving.

We ate in silence like we were doing something unspeakable, but which we both knew had to be done.

By the time Dan and I had packed away our trays we'd reached the airspace border with Spain. The French controller hadn't called to hand us over to Spanish ATC (which was the only thing he had to remember to do) so Dan discreetly prodded him by asking for a radio check.

'Read you five,' came the reply, which is radio speak for loud and clear. But this didn't prompt a frequency change

to the next controller because that would have been an admission that he'd forgotten us. Thirty seconds later he called us back and handed us over to the Spanish.

'Call now Madrid on 1 3 5 3 5. Au revoir!'

Dan and I smiled; it happens all the time.

With breakfast over and the crossword going nowhere, I picked up the PA handset and began telling the passengers that we were now in Spain. There was no cheer from the cabin, but I carried on regardless … *We've just passed between Bilbao and St Sebastian on the north coast …* I told them … *And we're heading towards Madrid.* We were at the opposite end of the country to where the passengers wanted to be, but so far so good.

I've always wondered, every time I pass Madrid, why you would build your capital city in the middle of a desert. It's freezing cold in the winter and baking hot in summer; and then there are the colossal thunderstorms. I imagined the Muslims trekking up the country from North Africa back in the eighth century and meeting the Sistema Central mountain range that stretches across the landscape north of Madrid. They probably thought 'Bugger this, we're not climbing over that, let's just stop here and set up camp.' Not exactly Hannibal.

The Spanish controllers were no longer offering direct routes (little shortcuts to straighten out the jointed airways network) due to industrial disputes, so they simply cleared us to continue along our flight plan route. That was fine; it made things easier.

Just over half way; time for something healthier to

nourish my fat-poisoned flesh. I reached for the bag of snacks behind Dan's seat and rooted around for some fruit. The first apple I picked out – part of my five a week (one a day every day, with a break at weekends) – was so riddled with soft patches it felt like a detached boob. The others weren't much better so I grabbed a chocolate bar instead.

Dan and I chatted casually, trying to ignore the damaging effect this crew diet of fat, salt and sugar was having on our life expectancy. He had been flying a long time, and recently turned down his command again because all new captains would be based overseas and he wasn't ready to leave his family behind. I realised my own situation wasn't so bad: I might have been forced to leave my family, but at least we were in the same country.

I felt sorry for Dan, though, and suggested his family could move with him; it could be great growing up in a foreign country: the language, the culture, the adventure. But his wife had a good career and the kids were settled at school with all their friends. It simply wasn't an option for him; he would remain a first officer to preserve his quality of life.

Dan revealed that he'd got into flying after working as a City trader for four years. He graduated with a First in Aeronautical Engineering but, with a head for figures, had found that bond trading provided the kind of income that would help pay for his flying licence.

These days, pilots and cabin crew come from an amazingly diverse set of backgrounds. Sure, there are pilots who started straight from university, and pilots who were ex-military aviators, but the majority have previous careers, and it's this factor that makes our employee group so fascinatingly eclectic.

The week before, I'd flown with a Dutch first officer who used to be a policeman, a Welshman who'd played rugby for Neath, and a local girl who had been a biologist. The senior cabin crew member on a recent flight to Geneva had once been a teacher, and another was a qualified oceanographer who spoke three languages. We meet the most interesting people in this job, and it's the reason many of us enjoy our work.

Dan, like me then, had self-financed his commercial pilot's licence. Unlike me, though, he'd found work as a flying instructor for a few years before getting his big break with an airline. It's a well-worn route for aspiring pilots pursuing their dream.

Traditional paths to an airline career include a cadetship with a national carrier, or risking your life flying for the military. Mind you, you're also risking your life if you choose to teach people to fly.

These days, though, cadetships in the UK are rare and, where available, require the cadet to stump up close to £100,000 for the training, or to bond them to a particular airline. Worse still, they are made to work through their training provider for less than half the average salary – not much good when you have a mortgage sized loan to pay off and no house to show for it. These cadets may never see a permanent contract, and some are forced into bankruptcy. Market forces, or greedy airline bosses taking advantage of those who follow their dreams?

My own aviation career had started twenty years earlier when I was lucky enough to ride on the jump seat of a Fokker 100 flying between Bangkok to Phnom Penh. It had been the most amazing thing I'd ever done (which is saying something considering I was living in Bangkok) and it left me determined to return to the UK to start work on a private pilot's licence.

'Troubled pilots pampered by hostess?' I asked out of the silence.

Dan looked up from his book. 'Eh?'

'Four down, six letters,' I explained.

Dan gazed through the window for a few moments. 'I dunno, mate. Not my thing, crosswords.'

I poked the top of my pen into my mouth and tapped my teeth. It seemed such an easy clue, but it just wasn't coming.

I told Dan about my pre-airline days. We'd both built up our flying time in the United States; it's considerably cheaper than the UK, with better weather and a more favourable attitude towards general aviation. Over there, a private pilot can get airborne, fly around the sky for a while, then pluck an interesting destination from the map. He or she can land – free of charge – and taxi up to a general aviation terminal where full lounge facilities awaited – and yes, free coffee. In Europe no pilot can simply turn up unannounced at most airports, big or small. Prior permission is required at nearly all airports, and substantial landing fees are levied, too. But what about free coffee? Better bring a Thermos flask – if you can get it past security.

Dan explained how he'd worked as an instructor at Coventry Airport before nailing a job with a small regional airline based in Norwich. My own journey had skipped this traditional route. Instead I'd ended up in Africa flying missionaries and medicines around the bush. Occasionally, my cargo included the very things that made it necessary for these medicines to be flown around the bush, but it's pointless quoting The Carriage of Dangerous Goods bit from our operations manual when some guy's holding an AK47 assault rifle to your head.

Troubled pilots pampered by hostess. Come on!

The aircraft gently rolled left overhead a waypoint and steered towards our next target. I had to reposition the sun visor since our new heading had allowed the Sun to exploit a small gap between the blind and the pillar.

I was bored now. Glancing over the top of yesterday's Daily Mail at the navigation display, I could see that our descent point was creeping up. *Come on, Troubled pilots …*

Too late: the Spanish controller told us to descend. It was a little early – must have been some Spanish planes demanding to use our little patch of sky.

One can often sense when it's time to descend and land: the passengers are getting restless, the cabin crew are bored – *Are we there yet? Are we there yet?* – and you've finished the crossword, usually. That day, though, the crossword was going to have to wait.

Chapter 4

A spanner in the works

In an ideal world of aviation – that is, one not ruled over by air traffic controllers – we would wait until the last moment before commencing a descent. It has always been understood that an aircraft is most efficiently operated by blasting away at high altitude until reaching a point where it can glide to the runway with no further application of power. Air traffic controllers, aviation regulators, and airline safety managers prefer that we employ far less efficient techniques. It's all to do with safety (and not cost on this occasion).

So, generally, the point at which we would like to commence our descent and the point at which ATC would like us to do so are in two different parts of the sky. Now, wherever that point is, it is hoped that both pilots have briefed the arrival specifics, completed any checklists, and successfully returned from a quick nervous pee break before winding down the engines for descent (it has proved to be unsettling for the passengers if the pilot dashes into the lavatory just as the engines run down and the aircraft pitches towards the ground).

One of the most important tasks during the descent and approach (besides not hitting other aircraft or the ground) is managing the energy of the aircraft. Aircraft are bursting with energy, often nervous energy, and this needs to be managed. Failing to manage this energy would mean it was unmanaged, and this usually leads to embarrassment and a meeting with the Chief Pilot.

So we manage the energy of the plane to make sure we don't end up too high or too fast (or both) when what we're actually trying to do is put the thing on the ground. 'Putting the thing on the ground' is an accepted term for landing, and a successful landing usually ends with the aircraft on the ground with zero energy (technically it always has energy in one form or another, but I'm not a scientist so I wouldn't really know about that).

Unfortunately, our attempt at managing energy puts us in direct competition with ATC, and the result is our repeated requests for 'further descent please, further descent please …

Now, quite often at UK airports, a pilot will be told how many miles he or she will be forced to fly before being allowed to land. This is good; it allows us to manage our energy. But if you're in a Mediterranean country, you will have no idea; anything could happen and this is less good. If we dive our height off we can be assured of a long and protracted arrival routing. If we try to manage our descent profile based on reasonable approach procedures, they will cut us in short and leave us embarrassed for height (and I'm not talking about dwarfism). We can't win.

Nevertheless, we usually overcome all these challenges and wrestle (or manage) the aircraft on to final approach safely and calmly. At some point on the final approach we will deploy the flaps, the slats and the landing gear, to configure the aircraft for landing. We call this dirtying up – remember we clean up after take-off? Well this is why. So much filth in aviation.

To improve the chances of a safe landing the aircraft has to be in the correct configuration, at the right speed, on target and with appropriate thrust levels by 500 feet. In other words, we gotta be in the groove. If not, it would be considered so unsafe to continue that the only way to avoid certain disaster would be to perform an under-rehearsed, passenger scaring manoeuvre called a go-around, then come back for another crack when we've burned into our reserve fuel.

We can fly the approach visually (at least, some of us can) or we can use a ground based radio aid to guide the aircraft down. Such technological marvels are essential on cloudy days, but we tend to use them even on gin-clear days too. It means we can keep the autopilot hooked up, and alternate our visual scan between the aircraft's instruments and the local scenery.

The most accurate ground based aid is the ILS - Instrument Landing System. Even without the autopilot, we can use this device as guidance to fly the plane down to two hundred feet above the runway without looking out of the window. With the autopilot engaged and latched onto the ILS, the system will fly the plane all the way to touchdown.

A diligent brief is essential if we are to ensure a safe and efficient approach. However, this wasn't our annual flight check and both Dan and I had been to Malaga a million times before; It was irrelevant that we hadn't been there together, that's what standard operating procedures are for – though quite frankly I thought it was a little too early in our relationship to be discussing going away together. So I gave Dan the shortened arrival brief.

'ILS 31, weather's fine, any questions?'

'No, mate.'

'Cool.'

A hundred and twenty miles to go, just passing flight level 300 (more or less 30,000 feet above mean sea level). In the groove, man. Dan and I were monitoring the aircraft carefully. It was doing a brilliant job of flying the approach, but we were keeping our critical eyes on it as though we could do a better job.

The truth is we couldn't do a better job. Provided we had inputted the correct information, the plane would continue doing a brilliant job itself until we intervened. So, the further truth is that we were monitoring the aircraft in case we had told it a load of old guff in the first place. Sometimes we wonder whether the system ought to be reversed: we do the flying and the plane monitors us. But that sounds like hard work.

Troubled pilots pampered by hostess. Damn!

We were getting close to the ground now. No need to check minimum safe altitudes when you can see out of the window; I'll know if I'm going to smack into the rocks in much the same way as I'll know if I'm going to drive into the garden wall at home, although I have actually driven into the garden wall at home.

ATC had told us to be below flight level 150 at a point 60 nautical miles from the airport. This was quite a lot below our optimum profile and it raised the possibility of a more expeditious routing.

The approach to runway 31 in Malaga is notoriously long winded and could be shortened by about 15 nm (nautical miles – slightly longer than a regular mile) with ATC cooperation. Unhappily, such cooperation has been lacking in recent times after the Prime Minister told his controllers that the country was skint and they would have to earn only four times as much as every other controller in Europe instead of six times. Who can blame them for being upset?

'Hey, what's this?' I shouted, pointing at the little TCAS symbol on my display. 'I bet that's a Spanish plane, and I bet he gets vectored in before us.'

'Guaranteed,' said Dan.

'Iberia tres dos cinco, a th th th th th th th ke...' said the controller, or at least, something similar.

'That's him!' I said to Dan, gesticulating out of the window as though marking a target for my gunner.

And then we were told to turn right 20 degrees to allow our fellow aviators at Iberia to sweep in ahead. It's how it works.

We were both seething at the blatant show of favouritism by Malaga ATC even though we had encountered such envied patriotism countless times before, and knew it wouldn't be the last. But it fired us up.

Finally (there we go again) the controller steered us back in the direction of the airport and gave us further descent. No chance of a shortcut now since we were following another aircraft. So I opted to reduce my descent rate and conserve fuel.

We passed downwind at about nine thousand feet and resigned ourselves to following the long-winded and environmentally unfriendly approach. I peered over the combing and through the windscreen at Torremolinos sprawled out along the coastline. It was probably a bit early to be thinking about a glass of Sangria, so I turned to look through the left window and checked the progress of the new highway which runs to the north of the airport. From my privileged position high above the Spanish landscape I had noted the rapidly growing road network around the country. Either the Spanish transport ministry was expecting an increase in caravanners in coming years, or it had plenty of money it needed to spend in a hurry.

The sky was hazy that morning so I couldn't see the Rock of Gibraltar out to the west. But I did wonder how the Spanish could complain about the British presence on a piece of land attached to their coast when Spain occupies more than one chunk of coastline along the Moroccan mainland. But that's politics for you.

Troubled pilots ...

Suddenly the controller gave us a left turn onto base leg - 8000 feet with twelve miles to run. *Bitch!* Couldn't she work out that we needed twice the distance to lose eight thousand feet? Did she care, or had she done it on purpose?

The plane rumbled as I raised the speed brakes to dump some lift. Sneaking a few more miles downwind before turning in would give us more space to lose the height. She wouldn't notice. As the plane rolled left I wound a few more knots on to the speed. The nose dropped to attain the new target and our rate of descent increased too. We intercepted the ILS localiser above optimum height profile but we could recover that with ease – unless, that is, she slowed us down.

'... *reduce speed 160 kts to 4 miles*,' said the lady operating Malaga Tower.

Typical. Reducing speed reduces our rate of descent dramatically. The aircraft almost levelled out whilst it concentrated on reaching the new speed target (it's not one for multitasking). By the time the speed had reached 160 kts we were much closer to the runway and much higher than we should have been for a controlled approach.

I asked Dan to lower the landing gear – lots of drag from those stubborn lumps of rubber – and then called for more flap when the speed crept within limits. I watched the ILS glide slope sliding further down my screen; we were getting higher and higher, and further away from being in the groove.

Finally we reached the assigned speed. Now we could dive as fast as possible to get after the glide slope. The rate of descent was much higher now we had the wheels and partial flap extended, and importantly, the speed was just where we wanted it.

We passed one thousand feet. Ideally we should have been fully configured with landing flaps, but we still had the final stages to extend. We were clear of cloud and we had the runway in sight, so I was happy to continue the approach for now. The glide slope indicator was nearly where I wanted it. Just inside 3 miles, another mile would do. Sebastian rang through with cabin secure, he was just in time too, another two hundred feet and the inter-phone buzzer would have been inhibited. Seven hundred feet: the glide slope captured; I called for flap three, then immediately flap full and the landing check list. I needed the thrust to power up by five hundred feet otherwise we would have to throw away the landing and come round for another attempt.

'Five hundred' shouted the American hidden in our avionics bay. At that point, Dan, as the pilot not flying, had to say 'stable', or 'not stable, go around'. We both looked at the thrust lever indicators on the centre screen and noticed with relief that they were increasing. Dan took a breath.

'Stable.' Skin of our teeth, but we were in the groove at the right point. We were cleared to land and I disconnected the autopilot.

A good landing nearly always needs to follow a good approach. This had not been a good approach. To say my landing lacked decorum would be most gracious. To say it was like God dropping a giant sack of spuds onto the runway would be closer to the truth.

Dan bent double with laughter. He rubbed his spine, crying 'Oh my back, my back.' Bastard! As the aircraft began to decelerate we both shook our heads in disbelief at the standard of controlling.

'I should have told her we needed more track miles,' I said to Dan. 'I let her rush us.'

'Yeah, but it would have been fine if she hadn't slowed us right down. You weren't to know she was gonna do that.'

'I suppose. It would have helped if we'd known that the Iberia was actually a small turbo prop. I mean, why the bloody hell did she put a slow plane in front of a damned jet!'

'Because it was an Iberia,' said Dan simply.

'Patriotism is their number one priority,' I agreed.

The controller handed us over to 'Ground' with a cheery 'Bye-bye.' I wondered if they were high-fiving each other in the tower.

There was a yellow Séat waiting on the apron to escort us to our gate. It's the same at most Spanish airports: little yellow cars storming around taxiways marshalling aircraft to their stands, but it really isn't necessary. The one place in the whole of Spain that could benefit from this service is the one place they stopped it – Madrid. Baffling.

When he reached the gate the marshaller – also clad in yellow – jumped out and watched me drive the plane in a straight line on to the stand following the illuminated guidance system. When I had successfully achieved this simple task the marshaller turned around and gave me the thumbs up. Fair enough.

We had pulled up alongside the little turbo prop that had wrestled its way in front of us on the approach. It reminded me of my days in Africa all those years ago. The aircraft looked tiny beside our Airbus. Just twelve seats and a modest cargo hold. I had about two thousand hours on this aircraft type, but I never got to park it beside anything bigger than a Land Rover. Its two underpowered turbo prop engines were barely capable of lifting the plane off the ground if all the seats were occupied – unless you skimped on the fuel – and its performance was further sapped by the heat of the African summer.

I'd been promoted to the twin when the single engine plane I'd started on had been blown out of the sky.

It had been my day off. There were rumours in the bush that one of the local militia groups had acquired a rocket mounted grenade launcher to help protect the villages from air raids. I'd discovered that the rumours were true and that the group was practising their technique by firing at trees and abandoned Jeeps. It was inevitable that, before long, they would need to try out their new weapon on a target more akin to its real purpose. I had lost three colleagues that day.

I set the parking brake and shut the engines down before switching off the anti-collision beacon. That was the ground crew's signal to approach the plane. Within seconds someone had plugged into the ground interphone socket and called me.

'Good morning, sir, chocks in position. Do you need fuel?'

'Hi, yes, thanks,' I said, scribbling the flight times into the tech log.

The air bridge was slowly looming in my side window, getting closer and closer then, bump! The aircraft rocked gently as the air bridge snuggled up to the side of the fuselage. The young lady who'd spoken to me moments earlier was now waiting patiently on the air bridge for the cabin door to open. When it did, she made her way to the flight deck.

'Hello again, Captain, welcome to Malaga. Here are your passenger figures, and the fuel is on its way.' She gestured outside with her mobile phone then disappeared leaving a promise to return soon.

My former passengers were now well on their way to the nearest bar. I could see the back of them though my side window as they walked up the air bridge, but it was still too early to venture out of the flight deck. I used to stand at the door bidding everyone a pleasant day, but not any more. I don't like shaking hands with cocky young lads who are using me to impress their buddies, nor do I want to listen to some kid saying 'Cheers, mate!' It happens all the time, so I tend to remain hidden away until the senior crew member shouts that everyone's off. Finally, Sebastian did just that.

'Thank God,' I said, sighing and climbing out of my chair. Sebastian told me how rude some of the passengers were, and how the words 'please' and 'thank you' were missing during the in-flight service. However, the words 'mate' and 'what' had been thrown around as though they had become the most popular words in the English language. Perhaps they had.

And then I walked through the cabin to the back of the plane. *Oh ... bloody ... hell!* I'm not kidding, I think some passengers get up in the morning and think: we're going on a flight today, better empty the bins and take the rubbish with us so we can dump it on the cabin floor. And then they tell their kids, 'Come on, you're not making nearly enough mess – grind those crisps into the carpet.' And not forgetting the fun game for all the family: see who can stuff the most sweet wrappers into the seat back pocket. Despite the cabin crew making several passes through the cabin with a gash bag – and specifically asking for any rubbish to be placed in it – the amount of crap that gets left behind is appalling. It's one of the last things they do before securing the cabin for landing, but still people don't respond. Undoubtedly those passengers who leave rubbish on the floor or in the seat pocket know that the crew has to pick it up – the same crew who might have saved someone's life during the course of that flight.

Sebastian told me that a life jacket had been stolen, but we had spares so we just tut-tutted and moved on.

Since Dan would be doing the flying on our return to Gatwick it was my turn to stroll around outside and kick the tyres. But before I could risk stepping foot on Spanish tarmac (actually it was more like a patchwork of concrete blocks separated by chasms of air) I needed to don my fluorescent yellow vest known colloquially as a hi-vis. Everyone who walks about the apron must wear one of these hi-vis vests, except passengers whom are clearly regarded as being visible enough. Well, who could miss Leanne in her pink cowboy hat and bright T-shirt?

It was a pleasure to spend a few moments in the sunshine topping up the vitamin D. I gave the aircraft the customary once over but, quite frankly, it was a good landing (by my standards), we hadn't hit anything during the flight, and nothing had fallen off. The passengers couldn't see me from the gate, and no one important was parked next to us, so I didn't really need to spend too much time assessing the plane's continued fitness to fly. Had we been parked in, say, Amsterdam, all the passengers would have had an unhindered view of my walk-around and so I would have been forced to wear my serious face and appear more conscientious. But we were not in Amsterdam and it was time to get back on board.

I chatted with the crew whilst they cleaned the aircraft. At one time most pilots would have helped them with this rotten task, but then management suggested we helped them with this rotten task and so we stopped helping. Besides, the aforementioned mess and the shockingly disrespectful attitude that some passengers have towards the crew discourages me from wanting to clear up after them. It's not why I became a pilot, and I would hate to think that passengers are throwing food on to the floor and stuffing snotty tissues into the seat pocket knowing the captain might be clearing it up. It's bad enough that the cabin crew have to do it; they're on board to save lives, not clean up an unholy mess.

The two guys at the back were at opposite ends of their careers. Simon told me it was his first job and he was 'loving it.' Derek had recently been made redundant, which had also cost him his marriage, so he thought he'd try something different and ended up working as cabin crew.

It's a false cliché that all male cabin crew are gay; many are, but certainly not all. One of the attractions of this job for heterosexual men is the chance to work closely with so many young girls, but I thought Derek had left it a little late for that. As though defying my private thoughts, Derek began talking about Kelly.

'Hey, John, Kelly's blouse could do with a bit more material, eh?' he said.

'Could it?' I said, looking down the cabin to the front of the aircraft.

'I would, wouldn't you, mate?' he asked, grinning. I wondered what they'd been talking about down in the rear galley during the flight, but I made a joke about her not being my type (which was true) and walked back down to the front.

On the way I scanned the seats for newspapers and other reading material. There were a few Daily Mails –

always the Daily Mail – and a couple of Mirrors. I never expect The Times or The Independent on a Malaga flight, but what was this? The Guardian! Perhaps it had been left behind by a student going on a weekend bender.

Back at the front both Sebastian and Kelly had finished their turnaround tasks and were chatting with Dan. Kelly thought there might be an FHM magazine in the rear galley, did we want her to take a look? I was about to shake my head, but Dan appeared more eager. The two of them disappeared down the back, returning moments later empty handed. Dan pulled a disappointed face at me and shook his head.

'They must have chucked it.'

'Derek's probably claimed it,' I said. 'Pull rank and search his bags.'

Kelly laughed – *at me or with me?*

'Never mind, Dan,' I said. 'FHM is for teenage boys – and perhaps older men.' I glanced up the cabin then at Kelly, but she didn't appear to be listening.

She sucked on a straw, both hands clasping the side of a little juice carton. Her eyelids lifted and she stared straight at me. I noticed how small her hands were, and how huge the carton looked; no wonder she was using two hands to hold it. I looked away, terrified that I was going to make an inappropriate comment – *and what, ruin my chances? Stupid fool.*

Sebastian broke the silence. 'Cabin's ready for boarding, John, can we get them on?'

'Er, yeah, let's go home,' I said, stealing a glance at Kelly before dashing back into the flight deck. Kelly dropped her eyelids and watched her juice sliding up the straw and through her puckered lips. *I'm not interested in Kelly!*

I settled down into my seat just as the priority boarders approached the door. Priority boarders on a Malaga flight? Why would you pay a tenner to get on the aircraft first? If we'd been on a remote stand then they would have paid a tenner simply to be first on the bus! All the seats are the same and they all arrive in Gatwick at the same time. If you're exceptionally tall and need a bit more leg room then fair enough, head for the emergency exit row. But if you're just an ordinary Joe then save your money and grab an aisle seat; it's only a two and a half hour flight.

I'm not complaining, merely mystified; the priority boarders help to pay my bonus and keep me in whiskey, so cheers everyone!

It was Dan's turn to have a go at the controls. He would be the 'pilot flying' back to Gatwick and I would be the 'pilot not flying'.

These are official terms and they reflect the modern approach to multi-crew operations.

To say that I am the Captain and Dan is the First Officer could suggest that Dan does bugger-all but read the map and move whichever levers I ask him to. It doesn't allow for the occasion when Dan is flying the plane. When he's manipulating the controls – whether it is with great skill and artistry or jaw dropping incompetence – he is still the First Officer, but now we need to describe his operational status. We therefore use the terms PF and PNF to clear up any misunderstanding should there be a Board of Inquiry following one of Dan's landings. *Dan was pilot flying, Your Honour.*

The situation gets more complicated in airlines that employ a 'monitored approach' philosophy. With this baffling wheeze the pilot flying hands over control to the pilot not flying at the beginning of the approach phase of the flight. The pilot flying, now not actually handling the plane, monitors the pilot not flying who is handling the plane. This situation continues until shortly before landing when the pilot not flying – but currently handling the plane – hands control back to the pilot flying, who once more becomes the handling pilot. You couldn't make it up, and I haven't.

Fortunately the monitored approach isn't employed by my airline so for the trip back to base I was the pilot not flying (unless Dan screwed up, in which case I would have to reassert myself as the pilot flying, but that's quite straightforward – unlike the subsequent paperwork.)

One of the duties of PNF is to call for ATC clearance. My first call went unanswered. My second call, with slightly more weariness in my voice, did get a response.

'Station calling?'

Now, I don't have a thick regional accent. A few people over my lifetime have said I sound posh, which belies my working class Irish roots, others say I'm just well spoken. Either way, I strive to speak clearly and intelligibly, and I believe my pronunciation is pretty close to the phonet-

ics used in English phrase books. So what was so fucking
unclear about my radio transmission? I took a calming
deep breath then repeated my request for clearance.

'What stand are you on?' came the reply.

The same one you put us on ten minutes ago when we
last spoke, I thought. Then took a deep breath and told
him the stand number.

'Okay. Go ahead.'

'Er yes, I'm requesting clearance to Gatwick, please …
again.' I finished the sentence after releasing the transmit
button.

'Call you back.' I waited, and I waited. Several minutes
went by before I decided to call him again. This always
risks incurring the controller's wrath since he had clearly
told me he would call back, and by calling him first I
indirectly accused the man of forgetting to do his job. But
I couldn't wait all day so I pressed my transmit button
once more and prompted a response. He wasn't angry.

'Station calling?'

Agh! I told him my call sign again.

'Yes, go ahead.'

'I was wondering if you had my clearance yet.' I heard
my voice rising at the end like an Australia soap character
– or most of our cabin crew.

'What stand number?'

'34'

'Let me check.'

I held my breath.

'I don't have your plan yet, I call you back.'

I let out a throaty yell and threw the microphone to my side. Dan was laughing; we'd both been through it before.

Finally (there we go again) we got our clearance to Gatwick. It was the same clearance as any other day. I filed away the flight plan and waited for Dan to offer me his riveting departure brief.

PF (pilot flying) sets the aircraft up, either upon entering a cold aircraft (one that has been electrically de-powered), or during the turnaround. Once all preparations have been made, PF briefs PNF (Oh, come on – pilot NOT flying!) to make sure the aircraft has been set up correctly and that the departure routing was the one given during the clearance. PF reminds PNF of any defects that could affect the operation of the aircraft, or any special procedures we may need to perform that we don't normally do. These could include things like starting the engines with external power if the on-board auxiliary power is unserviceable, or de-icing the aircraft.

Since, in our case, we were in Malaga the latter was unlikely. PF also raises any NOTAMS (notices to airmen) that are relevant, such as closed taxiways or changes to ATC frequencies.

With the 'non-normals' out of the way PF methodically works through the flight management computer. He, or she, points out that the correct departure and arrival airports have been entered, and that the routing is the same as the flight plan. PF shows PNF that the expected fuel burn is as predicted on the flight plan, and that the arrival fuel is as expected.

We look at the alternate airport in case we can't land at our intended destination, and mention any other 'alternates' that could be useful (if, in this instance, Gatwick closes for some reason, everyone would try to divert to the same few alternates and they tend to get full very quickly).

Next, PF points out any radio navigational aids that might be used on the departure. Generally the Airbus uses GPS as its primary source of navigation, but some old fashioned chaps like to back things up with ground-based beacons. Finally, PF runs through the main emergency procedures that could crop up should we have offended someone high above, and I'm not talking about the Chief Pilot.

Once both pilots are happy with the set up and with what's about to happen, they can go back to reading the paper until someone comes along and tells them it's time to go.

Dan asked how much of a brief I wanted. In reply I quickly looked through the flight management computer and scanned the various buttons and bobs to see what he'd done, then told him 'No questions' (as I said earlier, this wasn't a flight check!).

With the brief completed Dan called for the Before Start checklist. Don't forget, this is when we check that we've correctly remembered to do lots of things from memory.

As on most occasions it turned out we had remembered everything, but we refrained from mutual back slapping since that would be far too American.

Since our work was completed, for the time being at least, Dan and I chilled out with our feet up on the combing. Only Sebastian's voice in the cabin infiltrated our peace.

'Hello, sir, welcome on board … Hello, sir, welcome on board … Hello, madam, welcome on board … Hello, sir, welcome on board. It's free seating, sir, sit anywhere … Yes, sir, really … It's always been like that … Since the company started … Well I've been here ten years and it's always been free seating … There are plenty of seats at the back, sir; my colleagues there will help you.'

Suddenly the dispatcher reappeared.

'Ok, Captain, I need to off-load one male and a female. With bags.'

'Oh, what's the problem, did they see the weather forecast in England?'

'Er, no, the lady is scared of flying and her husband has walked off. They had an argument.'

'Are you looking for the bags already?' I asked.

'Er, yes …' she replied, waving her telephone vaguely towards the window.

'How long do you think it will take to find the bags?' I asked pointlessly.

'Just a few minutes, Captain,' she lied, but with the best intentions.

I'd already spotted that the hold doors were now closed, and ten minutes later our indications showed that they were still closed. It may take 'just a few minutes' to locate the bags (though I doubted it) but that assumed they had actually started to look for them.

The dispatcher, Maria Inmaculada Concepción Ramirez Jones, according to the load sheet, made the last minute changes to the paperwork and wished us *adios*, still promising that the bags would be found in 'just a few minutes'.

Kelly popped in with more coffee; there was a smiley face on my cup with my name beneath. There were no devil's horns, but there was a small x beside my name. I couldn't see Dan's cup so I imagined it just had his name written there.

Kelly performed a mock curtsy, turned, and walked back into the forward galley without speaking. Dan caught me leering after her.

'She's a bit confident isn't she?' he said.

'Yeah, she's put a kiss on my cup, look.'

'You're in there, mate!'

'I doubt it; she's not going to be interested in someone my age, is she?' It was a question, more than a statement. 'Anyway, I'm married, and not looking for trouble.'

I don't look like the stereotypical airline pilot (often depicted as tall and debonair, with immaculate uniform and Ray Ban sunglasses) and I'm probably not how Jane Austen would describe an airline captain had she lived more recently. However, I think I scrub up quite respectably for my age, even if I'm not exactly Mr. Darcy. I did once climb out of a hotel swimming pool late at night with my pilot shirt clinging to my sopping chest, but I was drunk and ended up tumbling back in, so I probably didn't have the same impact as Colin Firth.

'John,' Dan continued, 'when a girl shows you a little more attention than usual you shouldn't ignore it.'

'Perhaps, but she's far too young for me,' I insisted. But what if she were older, I wondered. *Stupid!*

'You would though, wouldn't you – you know?' he asked grinning.

'Oh yeah, she's definitely give-one-able, but ...' I glanced around nervously when the corner of my eye spotted a shape in the doorway.

'Right!' said Sebastian. 'It's such a nightmare! Nobody wants to pay to put their bag in the hold, so we have to find space in the cabin.' It was a familiar complaint, and one with which I sympathised. But you can't argue with policy. He disappeared back into the mêlée of bodies and bags.

Finally, Sebastian came back and he was able to confirm that the headcount matched the paperwork and I cleared him to close up. I reached for the PA handset and warmly welcomed my passengers aboard. *Blah blah blah,* I said, then handed over to Sebastian *who is going to take you through the safety features of this Airbus A320 ...*

It was now twenty minutes since Maria Inmaculada Concepción Ramirez Jones (I wondered if she'd married a Welshman) had assured us the bags would be found within 'just a few minutes.' But I didn't blame her; the baggage handlers find it very disheartening to rifle through and off-load bags they've only just loaded.

We continued to sit and wait with patience. We had coffee, we had newspapers and we had privacy. We could wait. I looked down again at the little turbo prop parked

113

beside us. Parking next to a smaller plane is like walking into the Gents' toilet and grinning smugly as you look down at the guy next to you. But we also park next to bigger planes, in which case we don't look. None of this applies to women pilots, obviously – they're far too grown up for that sort of envy.

Finally (as always) the door monitor display on our screen indicated that the cargo doors had been closed. There was a little whoop of joy from me and Dan before we sat up in our chairs ready to get under way. Maria blah-blah Jones shot directly into our ears as she re-greeted us from below.

'Hello, Captain, we have the bags and we're ready to push. Please confirm the parking brake is set.'

'The parking brake is set,' said Dan as PF.

I called ATC again and asked for 'push and start'.

'Station calling for start-up?'

I called him again.

'What is your stand number?'

I told him again.

'You have missed your slot.'

I told him – with barely concealed irritation – that we didn't know we had a slot.

'Ah yes, your slot was at time 45, time check now 45.'

'Okay, but we have the standard ten minutes grace on that, we can make it in ten minutes,' I assured him.

'You will not make it, there is a traffic behind you, and one at the holding point.'

'But surely we have priority if we have a slot,' I insisted.

'One traffic is an Iberia ... er ... I think he has a slot ... er ... before yours. You will not make it. You need to contact your company.'

I was seething! Not only had he failed to tell us about the slot, but he was blatantly delaying us so that we couldn't meet the ten minute window. I switched on the company phone and dialled operations. I recounted the episode to my colleague in Manchester, where our headquarters is based, and he admitted that it was par for the course these days; part of Spanish ATC's on-going industrial dispute.

The chap in HQ pulled a few strings, or whatever they do, and a few minutes later we had a new slot. Fortunately there was only a short delay. It could have been so much worse. I called ATC again to prompt him to look out for our new flight plan, and he promised to call me back 'in a minute'. I'd heard that one before!

He did call back, though. He had stuck to his promise and it even felt like a minute. It was as though he'd spent the whole minute watching the second hand tick around his watch face, then pressed the transmit button on exactly sixty seconds. He'd had his fun, now it was time to let us go. Besides, there was probably an unsuspecting Lufthansa about to call; they're always good for a wind up: *'Ja, zis vould never happen in Germany ...'*

Air Traffic Control

In an age when commercial aircraft can depart an airfield in one part of the world, navigate to a far flung exotic destination (Glasgow, for example), avoid other planes en route, and touchdown gracefully – or otherwise – on blessed tarmac with no help from anyone but the pilots, why on Earth do we need air traffic control?

It's a good question. We don't need ATC for the process of flying the planes; we don't need ATC for the art of navigating across the globe; we don't even need ATC for the purpose of avoiding other planes. We have the on-board technology to accomplish all of these tasks and we are clever enough to allow the plane to get on with them. So what exactly do we need ATC for?

Well, ATC force us to fly along narrow corridors in the sky called airways (imaginative, I know), which consequently become overcrowded. Euroflow (the belgian based overseers) are then obliged impose restrictions on their use. These restrictions are commonly called slots and are responsible for holiday misery all around the world. There are other reasons for the imposition of slots, but let's not talk about French air traffic control strikes just now.

Another consequence of forcing so many planes to use the same narrow stretch of sky is the increased risk of two aeroplanes being in the same place at the same time. So actually it's a good thing that we have air traffic controllers to ensure that two planes don't, therefore, collide.

With aircraft noise a sensitive issue for the many people who have chosen to live close to an airport, air traffic controllers do sometimes issue instructions to pilots with the local residents in mind. The following conversation between a Boeing 747 pilot and his air traffic controller is alleged to have taken place somewhere in the US:

> *ATC: Turn left 40 degrees for noise abatement.*
> *Pilot: Noise abatement? We're at 40,000 feet!*
> *ATC: Have you heard how much noise two 747s make when they collide in mid-air?*

Funny guys, these air traffic controllers, but why not? If you sit staring at a radar screen all day trying to prevent a literal clash of egos, you'd probably want to get creative, too.

Getting Serious

Okay, let's show some respect – for a moment, at least. Air traffic controllers don't make the rules, nor do they draw up the airways system. They don't even regulate the number of aircraft that are granted permission to fly in their airspace at any particular time. In short, an individual controller is forced to manage a portion of sky as best as he or she can after politicians, bureaucrats and managers have sought to maximise revenues. Oh yes, we pay to use the big open space in the sky.

So, if you're going to charge airlines for flying through God's air then you have to employ someone to provide a service. This is why ATC exists. Once again, it's all about cost.

Okay, let's accept, for now, that we just can't go flying around the skies doing our own thing. The services we are paying for begin before we've even started the engines.

ATC at Airports

If we're going to fly from one strip of tarmac to another then we need a plan, a flight plan. This document tells ATC how we intend to find our way from, and to, our chosen airports. Provided they agree – and sometimes they don't – then an airport based controller will provide a clearance confirming what we already know: the way we intend to find our way from, and to, our chosen airports.

We already know this information because the company tells ATC which routing we intend to fly when they file the flight plan in the first place.

Some airports – mostly the big ones, but even the small ones in France – have a dedicated controller called 'Ground'. Other airports might combine this indispensable

J.T. O'Neil

role with that of 'Tower'. Particularly wealthy airports, such as state run or subsidised airports, have a dedicated controller called 'Delivery'. He, or she, reads out the clearances and then 'delivers' the bad news: a slot in two hours. Perhaps it should be called Deliverance after the harrowing movie of the same name.

Once our slot time is nigh we need to taxi out to the runway. Of course we can't just set off to the runway like you would in your car to the shops; we have to be told when we can get under way and which route to take (even if there's only one).

In the UK we're given a taxi route (even if there's only one route) and a runway holding point (even if there's only one runway holding point). Instructions must be total.

In France, Spain and Italy, however, we are more likely to be told simply to 'taxi to the holding point', even if there are several holding points and several routes to take you there.

You may have noticed that planes tend to be nose-in to the terminal when parked up. This requires the use of a push-back team to reposition the aircraft such that it can be driven away under its own steam (though to be honest steam is rarely used as a source of power on modern commercial aircraft – it's a weight thing).

Obviously, being poor-sighted, push back teams are unable to see any other aircraft within a few miles of their own, therefore they are forbidden from liaising directly with the pilot to perform a safe push back. It thus falls to the decision-making skills of the Ground Controller to coordinate movements on the apron (parking lot) and taxiways to avoid the inevitable taxi-rage. Unhappily though, this coordinating of movements is the chief cause of taxi-rage!

You see, not all countries approach this responsible job with an impartial sense of fairness. Sure there are rules, but rules mean nothing to a controller with a selective sense of national pride.

Once we're sitting pretty at the holding point, and preflight checks are complete, we lay at the mercy of the Tower Controller. This service clears each aircraft to land and take off. It's considered poor manners simply to line up and take off without permission. Worse still, it's rather embarrassing if you try to take off at the same time as someone else – unless you happen to be the Red Arrows.

It's simply not true that tower controllers sadistically spray aircraft into the sky and then sit back chuckling as the radar controller attempts to catch them in some kind of metaphorical net. I know this because the number of times my departure has been delayed due to 'coordination with Radar' is annoyingly high.

Once safely unleashed from terra firma, we attempt to fly our standard departure route that had been given to us in our clearance.

These routings are designed by men in white coats and black rimmed glasses, drawn off scale on little charts called 'plates', and given made up names by a bored scrabble champion. It's all rather pointless since within seconds of becoming airborne, an underemployed radar controller begins employing him or herself by cancelling the cleared routing and telling you to fly on various headings. Often, this radar vectoring follows exactly the same routing as the standard departure!

But I'm being unkind. There are minimum separation criteria for aircraft navigating under their own steam (or petrol for modern airliners, as previously advised) that can be reduced if navigating under direct radar control. This is a good thing because it permits closer spacing and more efficient use of airspace. Furthermore, some departure routings are over-lengthy and radar controllers may offer shortcuts by giving out headings to steer. In other words, we don't mind if the radar controller decides to get busy.

Having been steered away from our point of departure and kept clear of aircraft arriving to the same point, we join the motorway traffic higher up in the skies. The main purpose of en-route controllers is to ensure we all fly just closely enough to each other to make them essential for our safe passage through their airspace. They give us speed restrictions to make sure we don't catch up and fly into the back of other aircraft, and, in France, they take us off route for ten minutes if we've just beaten their national team at football or rugby. Mind you, they tell us it's for spacing, and while it may be, the following conversation took place over the Bay of Biscay during the Rugby World Cup in 2003:

> *Me ('xxx') to French ATC: Do you know who won the rugby today? (England had beaten France, which I knew.)*
> *French ATC: Non.*
> *British charter airline a few minutes later: Do you know who won the rugby today?*
> *French ATC: Non.*
> *Another British charter airline a few minutes later: Do you know who won the rugby today?*
> *French ATC: Non.*
> *Me: England beat France 23-7*
> *French ATC: xxx turn left 60 degrees for spacing.*

You can't win. It's like heckling a comedian: enjoy the moment, but accept your fate.

Spanish ATC

Spanish is an official language of ICAO – the International Civil Aviation Organisation – which means they get to speak their own language to any airline who decides to register it as their language of operation (mainly the Spanish and South Americans obviously). Fair enough. Unfortunately it means that Spanish controllers might not get sufficient practice in English to make them proficient in the global language of everything. In fact, it seems that some of them can't speak English at all, but simply know the relevant aviation terminology as laid down by their authority. And that's a bit of a problem.

You see, the standard phrases used by the Spanish are not necessarily the same standard phrases used by the French, the Germans, the Italians, or anyone else for that matter. As a native English speaker I have only minor trouble understanding some of their instructions, but for a non-native English speaker communications can sometimes be like haggling with a straw donkey seller up a back street in Barcelona.

If the controller's command of English is confined to these proprietary phrases then non-standard conversations become impossible. A Dan Air flight to Tenerife in 1980 crashed into the side of a mountain partly through the misinterpretation of some very non-standard and unclear instructions from the local controller. It wasn't entirely the controller's fault, and there were lessons to be learned from the actions of the pilots, but it was the controller's poor use of English that triggered the fatal course of events.

The precision and clarity of British, German, Scandinavian and some Eastern European controllers are often missing from the transmissions made in Spain: call signs are missed out, read-backs ignored, and excessive information passed in a single transmission. These are just some of the reasons why pilots flying to Spain are forced to up their game. That said, there are good controllers in Spain, too – controllers who speak excellent English and provide a decent service. There are always exceptions and the Spanish can be friendly and polite – even when screwing you over in favour of an Iberia!

I think it's also important to acknowledge that Spanish ATC has improved considerably since the arrival of low cost airlines. EasyJet, for one, consistently pressured AENA – the Spanish ATC authority – with safety and operational matters during the time the airline had a base in Madrid.

The French

Like the Spanish, the French efforts to provide clear and efficient air traffic control services are severely handicapped by language.

French is also an official language of the International Civil Aviation Organisation (ICAO). The others are Spanish, Russian, Chinese, Arabic, and of course English. So why does everyone think English is the only official language, and why do we only complain about the French speaking their own language?

Let's play safe and discuss the first point first. It's probably unreasonable to expect every pilot and air traffic controller around the world to speak all six official languages of aviation. When an Air France plane arrives in Cuba the pilot is unlikely to be greeted warmly, and given clearance to land at José Martí International Airport, if he launches into his Gallic haw-haw-haw.

Similarly, it would be thoroughly unimpressive if an Iberian A340 poked its nose into Chinese airspace with the words, *"Hola, podemos entrar en su espacio aéreo por favor?"* The response may quickly include the use of some MiG derived fighter planes, and the Spanish Airbus could easily end up scattered across a few hundred acres of paddy fields. At the very least, the pilots may find themselves dining on noodles and rice for the next umpteen decades. So what's the solution?

The problem was solved when a German member of the ICAO went on holiday to Thailand. He noticed how young boys would attempt to entice him into their darkly lit premises by speaking English. Why did they shout out to him in English, he wondered, and why didn't they speak German to him, instead? And how did they know he could speak English, anyway?

It was all very confusing until Herr Burger remembered what had happened in 1945 and, contrary to accounts in some French history books, realised it was largely the English speaking nations around the world that had won the Second World War. Herr Burger was stunned by a brilliant flash of inspiration and dashed over to Montreal to announce to the ICAO delegates that there is only one global language, and these days it happens to be English.

Okay, so this little tale might not have happened quite as I described, but the end result remains valid. English is the 'mandated language' of aviation, and all controllers working international routes must achieve a minimum level of proficiency as set by the ICAO. But this does not stop the French *et al* from legitimately using their own language with their countrymen. And this causes a few problems.

If you're regularly switching between two languages – and two sets of phrases – during the course of your job, then the harder that job is going to be. Since these 'conversations' involve issuing instructions for the safe navigation of commercial, private and military aircraft, wouldn't it be so much easier if the controller just speaks one language? The Germans, Scandinavians, Dutch, Italians, Eastern Europeans and others seem to think so.

Chapter 5

Captain Cool

The flight back to Gatwick was business as usual. No direct routings from the Spanish, which was fine, and fabulous views over central Spain. The plains were brown and arid, with small towns scattered far apart, seemingly in the middle of nowhere. During the winter it's quite common to see snow covering the landscape around Madrid and on the mountains to the north. Madrid residents can spend their mornings skiing if they fancy; the nearest resorts are within an hour's drive of the city. By the time lunch is over the city's fashionistas can be back in their pavement cafés and shopping malls, giving the Parisians a run for their money.

During the cruise I lifted a couple of drawing books and a packet of crayons from my bag. They had been a present for my youngest child, but I'd forgotten to give them to him when I was last at home. I asked Dan if he wanted to do some colouring-in, then waited for his reaction. But my jape backfired when he grabbed the crayons and revealed his artistic side. Dan skilfully created a fabulous drawing of a little monkey juggling coconuts and smiling cheekily.

The doorbell chimed and interrupted Dan's masterclass. It was Kelly. She was looking up at the camera, sticking her tongue out and waiving daintily. I released the door lock and she stepped onto the flight deck.

'Hiya, guys, can I hide in here for a while? The passengers are doing my head in.' She pulled the jump seat out before we could nod enthusiastically, and sat down. Her knees pointed towards me, but I resisted the temptation to look down. A longer skirt would have removed the temptation altogether.

'How long have you been flying, Kelly?' I asked.

'Six months.' She was polishing an apple with a paper towel and didn't look up.

'Great. Good. Cool.' Can a forty-five year old say 'cool' without sounding, well, uncool?

'And are you enjoying the job – when you're not being harassed by strange captains?' I added stupidly.

'Yeah, it's different, but it's also fantastic experience – coping with emergency situations, medical problems, fire fighting that sort of thing. Not to mention dealing with troublesome passengers!' She seemed articulate.

'So what do you think you'll do when you're bored of all this?' I asked, genuinely interested.

'Go back to uni – I'm on a gap year at the moment. I decided not to follow the herd around the world and go trav-er-lling.'

I got the impression she didn't consider lying on a beach in Australia as proper travelling.

'So, what are you studying?' asked Dan.

'Law.' She took a bite from her apple and looked away through the side window.

Dan and I looked at each other and raised our eyebrows. It was a reminder that we had some talented and highly accomplished people working in the cabin. We sometimes forget.

'Don't you get bored sitting in here staring at those screens?' she asked.

It was a fair question. 'Sometimes,' I said, 'but we're doing some colouring-in at the moment. Do you want to have a go? I handed her my book.

Kelly looked appalled. 'You're not serious!' she said. It didn't seem to be a question.

'Yeah, look at Dan's little monkey.' It wasn't sounding any better, but I couldn't stop myself.

'I've done a little girl with a pony – messed her hair up a bit, just there ...' I trailed off. Even Dan stared at me now. I realised the conversation was going badly, but I still couldn't stop talking.

'So, do you live near the airport, Kelly?' I asked. 'I'm in a B&B near Handcross. Do you know it?'

'I know Handcross,' she said matter-of-factly. 'But I live in Crawley with my boyfriend.'

Was that bit about the boyfriend absolutely necessary? 'What does he do?'

'He's a Lawyer.'

Ha, beat that, old timer. 'Oh right … he … er … works in Crawley then?' I was floundering now.

'God no! He works for a Portuguese investment bank in The City, so commutes between London and Lisbon quite regularly.'

Lisbon. Portugal. The little flag on her badge; there we are. 'Cool.' I said – uncool.

'Not really, he's been away for a few weeks now, and I'm getting bored of my Rabbit.'

Dan was staring open mouthed, but I'd obviously missed something.

'Understandable,' I said. 'Cuddling a little rabbit is no replacement for a handsome boyfriend.'

Dan and Kelly stared at me for a few seconds, then at each other. What? What did I say? I didn't say anything about sleeping with her rabbit, I specifically avoided that trap.

'Ah, bless,' said Kelly, pulling a sad face and tapping her hand on my shoulder. I was still looking confused when she rose to leave.

'Well, it's been lovely chatting, but I'll leave you little boys to your crayons now. I think Sebastian wants to do another service.'

She left and I turned to Dan for an explanation.

'Mate,' he began, 'a Rabbit – a Rampant Rabbit is a–'

'Fuck!' I screamed. 'No!' I looked at the monitor to see if she was telling the other crew members but the door camera had switched off. I sat cringing in my seat like a teenage boy whose mother had just walked in on him unexpectedly.

'Nicely done, mate,' said Dan. 'Captain Cool!' He was pissing himself.

We relaxed a little as we passed from Spain into France and received our first direct routing of the flight. It didn't last long though, since a couple of Air France planes wanted to use the wide open sky, so Dan had to show mastery in the art of twizzling knobs to the tune of ATC.

We were vectored off course to allow an Air France Boeing 747 to cross our flight path. The Bay of Biscay is a regular crossing point for aircraft travelling from South America, and we are routinely moved out of their way.

We watched the Jumbo pass about seven miles ahead – I'd like to describe it as lumbering but it's actually a graceful flyer for its size – before being given a direct routing again. The controller had tried to judge our separation with great accuracy. I looked at Dan and pulled a face.

'That's a bit close,' I said.

'Too close, we're gonna pass through his contrails,' said Dan, pointing at the puffs of cloud trailing behind the Jumbo. He was right; moments later we flew straight into the big plane's wake.

Wake turbulence feels markedly different from the atmospheric kind. With the familiar latter there's normally some gentle rumbling to begin with, hardly likely to spill anyone's cocktail (cocktail? On a lo-cost? Ha!), and this can either vanish or build into something horrific.

Usually, in Europe, turbulence rarely builds to threatening levels; it's just uncomfortable at worst. Wake turbulence, on the other hand, hits you immediately as though you've just flown into an asteroid belt (which isn't common, to be honest). It can be quite shocking. Luckily it only lasts a few seconds. I reassured the passengers … *nothing to worry about … Quite normal … French air traffic control etcetera …* And then turned my attention back to my crossword. *Troubled pilots pampered by hostess.*

We arrived back in UK airspace and whoop-whooped when the British controller told us no delay for Gatwick (which can mean up to twenty minutes delay).

Clear, concise and unambiguous instructions guided us down our constant descent approach and into the world's busiest single runway airport. When 'London' advises the number of track miles to touchdown, a pilot can have a good stab at managing his or her descent. The aim is to descend constantly from 6000 feet without levelling off and thus avoiding large applications of noisy thrust from the engines.

Dan did a superb job landing our little Airbus. Bastard! The touchdown was so smooth we barely felt it; the six wheels merely licking the smooth tarmac like a lesbian tipping the velvet. We only realised we were down when we felt a light rumbling as the aircraft gently transferred its weight from the wings to the undercarriage. It happens, but not very often. And although such an unnoticeable touchdown is contrary to the aircraft manufacturer's guidance (something to do with tyre wear and landing distance calculations), it's what every pilot strives for (otherwise the cabin crew take the piss, and there's always one passenger who disembarks saying 'Did we get shot down?'). It's the same kind of feeling as hitting a golf ball long and straight (unless you're quite good at golf, in which case it's like being asked on a date by a hot young flight attendant). Just for the record, I'm rubbish at golf, so I don't need to worry about being asked out by any hot young flight attendants.

It had been a good day out. We were late thanks to the shenanigans down in Malaga, but satisfied we'd done a good job. The aircraft's technological wizardry had succeeded in making our jobs seem trivial. I can see why airline bosses think we're overpaid. Today, I have read three newspapers, done a crossword – almost – *Troubled pilots* ... flirted disastrously and inexplicably with a young flight attendant, had coffee handed to me, admired some scenery, and soaked up a few minutes of Spanish sunshine.

Perhaps intense repetition has made me blasé; aircrew in the past flew a fraction of the hours that we do now. It's possible I just take for granted the decisions we make and the skills we employ, and fail to recognise that the job is only easy because this repetition has made us good at it.

It may seem like we'd only messed around all day, but we took over a hundred passengers on a jet airliner down to the bottom of Europe and another lot all the way back. And we'd done it safely.

Pilots have always said that we get paid for the occasions when something goes wrong, but airline bosses point out that things don't go wrong as often these days, so we should earn less. It seems a reasonable argument.

Newly qualified pilots are now unlikely to gain employment unless they pay all the airline's training costs – and this is on top of the exorbitant costs to qualify as a commercial pilot in the first place. They then work for several months without pay, or just measly expenses. Some young pilots even pay airlines for the privilege of flying their planes! Can you imagine paying National Express umpteen thousand pounds to drive their coaches? But, incredibly, there is no end to the queue of hopefuls willing to sell their future for their dream job. And airlines bosses know this.

Cabin crew are now paying for their training. They are forced to buy their uniform, which I suspect makes the company a small profit, and then they work on temporary contracts. They are bullied from day one and can be dismissed for taking more than the average number of sick days. If you're exhausted, frequently cooped up in a metal tube with hundreds of passengers, suffer disrupted body rhythms and are subjected to several pressurization cycles a day, then you will become ill more often than the average worker. These talented people are trained to save the lives of passengers, they're the front line customer facers, and they make millions in on-board sales. So why treat them so badly?

When accountants run businesses, everything and everyone becomes a cost. So, to the accountant, it makes sense to pursue ways of reducing that cost down to bare minimum. Freelance pilots, paid only when they fly, are placed randomly around the network wherever they are needed from one day to the next, and laid-off when volcanoes – or the French – strike. It makes sense to an accountant and there's only one thing that would change his or her mind: a crash. Pilots might be expensive, but an accident is more so. If you want to squeeze your aircrew until they stand shoulder to shoulder with the National Express coach driver, then don't expect to retain the skills which currently help make commercial air travel the safest form of transport in history.

The rapid exit lane was coming up rapidly. I stamped on the brakes harder and vacated runway 26 Left, crossed runway 26 Right and onto taxiway Juliet. The controller told us to take taxiway Romeo next, so I reached for my airport chart before Dan reminded me that Romeo meets Juliet at the tower – it really does. We headed up Juliet and turned left onto Romeo as we drew level with the control tower. Thanks, Shakespeare, for keeping the romance in flying.

Troubled pilots pampered by hostess? Come on, not long left! I thanked Dan for a nice day, but stopped short of inviting him on a weekend break somewhere. I mentioned that it had been a successful day, and despite the Spanish controller with a sense of humour, the turnaround had been pretty good.

We both wished there were more dispatchers like Maria Inmaculada Concepción Ramirez Jones, and we joked childishly about how we could remove the 'Inmaculada Concepción' from her name.

If only I hadn't tried to impress Kelly! What had I been thinking? What had I thought would happen? That she would invite me around for coffee and ask me to get my crayon out? Besides, I was married, had never been unfaithful and I hoped I never would be. So why was I getting so bothered about a girl half my age with whom I didn't want to cheat, and who absolutely certainly had no sexual interest in me?

Whatever the reason, it had left me feeling embarrassed and worried. Worried because I feared she may choose to spread stories of my pathetic attempts to chat her up – which would be untrue – and that rumours would abound concerning some predatory nature that I don't have. Worst of all, such rumours could get back to my wife; she may not believe them, but mud sticks.

I was jolted from my thoughts by the ground controller who gave us our stand number: 57 Left. I followed the green taxi lights up Romeo then across to the apron. The guidance system beckoned me onto the stand where we finally (and this isn't the last appearance of this overused word) parked up – without a little yellow dressed man watching.

The passengers disembarked along the glass sided air-bridge and I watched them go. Hopefully they had enjoyed the flight, but more importantly I hoped they were a few quid lighter. It's how it works these days. Like the airports, we make a considerable portion of our revenue from selling stuff on board. Unlike the airports, however, we offer you the courtesy of a seat whilst we fleece you.

Finally (I told you), the plane was empty and, a little later than scheduled, we handed the aircraft over to the next crew. They were bound for Paphos on the island of Cyprus. The crew looked tired before they'd even started. After eight hours flying and a 10 hour duty I suspected they'd look downright haggard.

My crew and I prepared to leave, but as we stepped onto the air bridge, a young dispatcher came up the steps with a bee in his bonnet.

'What fucking time d'ya call this, mate?' he said. Dan and I simply looked at each other and walked away.

We stood in silence as the crew bus took us to the building that housed our crew room. I was pleased the weather had brightened and warmed since this morning, because it meant my meteorological prowess had been sound after all. I was just a little out with the timing – but that's no worse than the professionals.

Dan and the rest of the crew were busy tapping away on their mobile phones; we've been told not to switch them on until after checking out, so I pulled mine from my pocket and wondered whom to text first. Kelly eventually broke the conversational silence.

'So, Captain John, have you got any pets at home?' she asked with a straight face. Dan looked up, but the others remained fixated on their phones. Mercifully it seemed she hadn't shared my naivety with the rest of the crew. But I still felt my cheeks warming and my skin beginning to prickle beneath my shirt.

'Just a dog,' I said, thinking quickly. 'But he doesn't need any batteries.' It was meant to show that I knew what a Rabbit was, but it was all the others needed. Everyone was now staring at me. It was Kelly's turn to develop a crimson complexion, and this appeared to rouse her for a knock-out blow.

'I hope he brings you lots of pleasure, Captain.'

I was down, out, and on the medical stretcher to the nearest morgue.

Chapter 6

Finally

The crew room fizzed with dozens of uniformed girls and boys jostling for elbow room and chattering about their lives. It's not a particularly big room, and for most of the day it doesn't need to be. But the airline schedules around forty flights, all leaving within an hour of each other between 6.00 am and 7.00 am, and again around midday. So, as with the morning, finding a working computer was going to be tough.

A further consequence of this concertina style schedule is that the airport facilities struggle to cope with the rush, too. There are long queues at check-in and security, and standing room only in the departure lounge. Furthermore, the ground handlers resent having to dispatch forty planes in an hour, though they sometimes do their best, and then have dozens of workers sitting around until the next rush a few hours later.

I eventually found a vacant computer and, as I attempted

to log on, wondered why we didn't stagger the departures a little more. But I knew better than to suggest a change to the scheduling.

There used to be a suggestion box in the crew room, but it was withdrawn after most of the suggestions were found to be anatomically impossible and quite unnatural. Any bright ideas that are fed back to management are invariably rejected with the famous words, 'You don't see the big picture.'

Well, after all these years I reckon this excuse is the company's equivalent of the Catholic Church's 'God moves in mysterious ways.' In other words, don't ask us any questions we can't answer.

So I put such thoughts from my mind and continued with the happy business of getting out of there. Unhappily, though, the computer was being tortuously slow again, and I was forced to wait what felt like my whole lifetime. Again, for most of the day, the IT system works just fine. But since we all tend to use it at the same time across the network, it becomes drained of electrical enthusiasm and grinds to a halt just when it's most needed.

I stared at the little blue bar at the bottom of the screen. It had stopped moving a few moments ago and seemed to be stuck about a third of the way along. If there had been another computer free I would have had two on the go.

Suddenly, after stealing half my day, the blue strip leapt across to the right and I was in.

I stared at the red writing as though it were a matador's cape.

You have changes to your schedule

Bollocks! These are the words we dread when checking in, and as usual I could feel a shafting coming along. I began making myself feel worse by trying to second guess the changes in store whilst I waited for the hamster inside the company's IT system to get its arse into gear. *Come on: pedal!*

Finally (it doesn't end yet) the computer presented my 'refreshed' roster to me. 'Oh, that isn't bad', I thought. My Lanzarote the next day had been changed to a home standby. Great, I could probably have a lie in – maybe even a few extra drinks that night. I glanced involuntarily around at Kelly and then chastised myself for not learning my lesson. Then I thought again about my changes.

A straightforward day out to the Canaries watching DVDs and reading my book had been replaced by a day in the B&B. Furthermore, I stood to lose over a hundred pounds in flight pay. I wouldn't mind losing the money if I were able to spend that time with my family instead of loafing around in a B&B. I was right the first time; I had been shafted.

Being sneaky, I looked up the crew to see who had bumped me off the flight. The Base Captain's name glared out at me. I angered myself by supposing that he had put himself on the flight in order to get out of the office, and that he had chosen the Lanzarote because it pays well for little effort. Bastard.

The week before, when I'd wanted to swap with someone so I could go home and watch my daughter singing in the school concert, I'd been told 'We can't just disrupt someone else's roster to suit you.' Bastards.

I logged off with force, the mouse squeaking beneath my aggressive fingers, and I said farewell to Dan. I looked around for Kelly, trying to avoid her in case she thought I fancied her, but she appeared to have already left. There was still time to say thanks to Sebastian, though, for looking after me and dealing with the passengers so expertly.

'I'll probably see you at the bus stop,' he said.

I was still pissed off with my roster change, and about what had happened with Kelly, but I knew I could do nothing about the former and should be less pathetic about the latter.

As I left the building it became clear that bad luck attracts bad luck: the car park bus was just pulling away. Kelly sat by the window on the back row with her head bowed. Dark locks of glossy hair had fallen forward covering the left side of her face. She was probably texting.

I waited about ten minutes for the next bus and, sure enough, Sebastian arrived just as the bus pulled up. We stood together near the middle doors and enjoyed a last chat.

'Is that you then, John?' he asked, but I had no idea what he was talking about.

'Have ye finished for the week?' Unmistakably Scottish now.

'No, just starting. Home standby tomorrow, what about

you?'

'I'm on leave tomorrow. We're off to Greece for two weeks – trying to get away from this weather.' Less Scottish now – it seemed to depend on what he was saying.

He spotted someone he knew and gave them a loud 'Hiya' accompanied by that cheery face and a little wave of the arm.

'Oh, that'll be nice,' I said, 'Just you and a friend?' I ventured, not wanting to assume anything.

'Och, no. It's just me, the wife and the kids.' I raised my eyebrows; I hadn't expected that at all.

Finally, finally, bloody finally, I made it back to my car. It was fifty minutes since we'd arrived on stand, and eight hours I left the car park that morning. But I was lucky: at other bases they usually have to fly a further two sectors after a Malaga flight. It would most usually be a domestic or short European flight, but to be blunt: a flight is a flight. A quick Paris and back extends the duty time to about ten and a half hours and, after that, I for one would be struggling to drive home let alone land a passenger jet safely.

My crookedly parked neighbours were still there beside my old Škoda, long haul guys probably, but I resisted the temptation to open my door carelessly.

I pulled my seat belt around me and grimaced slightly at the thought of spending another night listening to Mrs Butler complaining about her sciatica. Just five more nights and I'd be back with my family for a few days. It's a job, but it's not a life.

As I started the engine I caught the blur of a red car approaching from my right. I waited for it to pass but it didn't; it stopped directly behind and I heard the horn sound twice. Kelly?

A *frisson de peur* struck my belly like someone tying a knot in my stomach. I considered the hazardous implications of any conversation with Kelly – of any actions with Kelly. I really didn't want this.

My body twisted easily in the seat, but my neck hadn't yet acclimatised to Mrs Butler's plump pillows and resisted my attempts to look through the rear window. I turned my body a little more and spotted the occupant of the red car. It wasn't Kelly, oh thank the Lord, it wasn't Kelly! It was better than that.

Julie and I go way back, perhaps as many as twenty years, and it was a delight to see her hanging out of her car window. I jumped out and rushed over to give her a hug.

'Hey, Tiger, it's been ages!' she said with a beaming face. Julie always called me Tiger, she was the only person in my life who knew of my old nickname.

'I know; it's great to see you. Who are you working for these days?'

'Uh, don't ask! You're looking well, babe, is life treating you good?'

'Yeah, not bad.'

'I'm just finishing too, New York Red Eye – delayed three hours with a technical problem. Passengers decided it was all my fault. But, hey, that's the job!'

'I don't know how you can put up with some of these

146

people, Jules, I couldn't do it.'

'You know me, babe, I just smile and – you know, babes – on with the show! Are you still in that B&B?'

'Yes, I don't see us moving down here, to be honest.'

'Right then, dinner tonight?'

Julie was the most sexually tantalizing woman I had ever known, but frequently and inexplicably single. She was one of the nurses I used to work with in Africa, and although there was no time for dating, let's just say we made sure everything was kept in full working order during our time in the bush.

She knew I was married these days, although I'm not sure if I've ever mentioned Julie to my wife. It was only dinner, two old friends just catching up. That's all right, I thought, I can do that.

'Sure, I'd love to,' I said, 'Usual place?'

'Definitely! My treat.'

'Thanks, Jules, but I can't allow that!' I protested. 'You've rescued my night so I'm taking you out.'

'You've always been a gentleman, Tiger, but I'm sure you've got plenty of opportunities to spend the evening with anyone you choose.'

Was Kelly an opportunity? Is that why some men cheat and others don't? Perhaps infidelity is just a matter of opportunity.

'Not really, Julie, to be honest I try and keep away from opportunities.' More accurately, opportunities tended to keep away from me; and for that I was grateful. I looked at my watch and smiled.

147

'Have you got an appointment?' she asked, nodding at my raised wrist.

'Thankfully, no,' I replied.

'Whatever, Tiger! Good looking, bloke away from home, pampered by young hosties; that's the trouble with you pilots – you're spoilt for choice.'

Spoilt! Troubled pilots pampered by hostess. Finally!

Volume Two

Airlines are where marriages go to die

Chapter 1

Bend over and take it like a man

At some stage in life, most people will take a flight on a jet plane. They will squeeze into a narrow tube alongside hundreds of other passengers where mere centimetres separate everyone from death. Beyond that flimsy tubular wall of aluminium awaits an environment so bereft of warmth and oxygen that it stakes a compelling case to be one of the least survivable places on the planet.

Carving through the thinning edge of Earth's atmosphere at 500 mph, the commercial airliner remains aloft thanks to two or more fiery jet engines burning through an average car's tank of fuel every minute. Would these unwary passengers, travelling on the safest form of transport of our age, sit back and relax with their favourite drink and enjoy the flight if the pilot had an adrenalin junkie's attitude towards risk?

I suspect the answer would be no. Pilots are meant to be risk averse, and most are. I have always considered myself among that enduring group of cautious aviators; I am neither old nor bold. One day I hope to be old, but I doubt I will ever be both.

So, as I sat in a taxi en route to our head office, I puzzled over my decision to go on a date with someone other than my wife.

Taxi drivers are a curious lot. I sat in the back of the Volvo for three hours listening to the driver explaining all the incredible things that had happened to him during his remarkable life. A life of adventure and heroics, it seems, if his career as a racing driver was anything to go by. Then, after a serious accident (testing Ayrton Senna's new Formula 1 car, no less) he launched a successful second career as a stunt driver. He owed all this skill, he claimed, to the training he received whilst 'working with' Special Forces in Iraq – but he couldn't talk about that.

It had been a fascinating tale, and for some reason part of me wanted it to be true. But the rest of me puzzled over how he coped so casually with the utter monotony of driving airline crew up and down the motorway six days a week. Sadly, I couldn't get a word in to find out.

At last he pulled into the drop-off zone outside Manchester Airport (soon to be renamed Gary Barlow Manchester Airport to upset John Lennon Liverpool Airport down the road) and it was time to shake and walk. I had my own tale to tell now, so I thanked him for getting me there without rolling the car in a fireball, and headed off for my meeting with the Chief Pilot.

There's a schoolboy feel to standing outside your boss's office waiting in line to receive a verbal spanking. I thought back to my youth when I was first summoned to the headmaster's study. I had waited outside with the other boys, squashing my ear up against the panel-wood door, listening to the groans coming from within. As the door creaked open we all jostled back in line before a sobbing boy limped out. He was clutching his buttocks with one hand and wiping the tears from his flushed face with the other, moaning that he wouldn't be able to sit down for a week. I remember praying that the headmaster wouldn't fancy me, too (it was a boys' school, after all).

None of the chaps summoned to head office had an ear to the Chief Pilot's door; corporal punishment has long been abandoned as a way of disciplining naughty airline pilots.

Thirty years ago a captain might have rapped his co-pilot's knuckles for touching the controls, or bellowed with pompous authority at any attempt to question his decisions, but times are different now. We're all meant to be super friendly and cooperative these days; at least that's what they tell us in our annual friendship class (to give it a less formal and completely made up name). My next friendship class love-in was set for later that day, but first I had to answer a charge of bringing the company into disrepute.

The door to the Chief Pilot's office swung open and a red faced first officer walked through. He wasn't clutching his bottom, which was a relief, but he did wrench the black clip-on tie from his neck as though he'd just been screwed by Barcelona Air Traffic Control. Things didn't look good, and I was next in line.

I'd had an eventful week. It had started six days earlier when a young cabin attendant, half my age, began flirting with me on our flight to Malaga. I'm no oil painting (more of a preliminary sketch) so I was mystified as to why a hot twenty-three year old – with a lawyer boyfriend – was showing so much interest in me. In the unfamiliar excitement I'd overlooked the golden rule for middle-aged blokes: when one reaches the point in life where the bartender wasn't even born the first time you drank in that pub, flirting with those half your age is likely to end in disaster. Granted, it's not a snappy rule, but it's an important one. Sadly, it hadn't been any giddy disregard for the Golden Rule that had found me in the queue for a bollocking. No, that moment had come later in the week.

I felt a nudge against my arm. The chap beside me pushed me towards the door, probably worried that I would scarper, leaving him next in line to face a career-ending meeting with our lord and god. I ambled through the doorway trying to disarm the Chief Pilot with my fake nonchalance, but I gave myself away immediately the door clapped shut behind me. I'm sure it was only a breeze from the open window, but I couldn't stop my body jolting on the spot as though I were in a haunted house. The Chief Pilot gave me a smile – not a lasting one – but a smile at least.

'Sit down …' He paused and raised his eyebrows to

invite my introduction.

'John,' I said, holding out my hand with a blagger's confidence.

His expression didn't change so I guessed there was probably more than one John in the queue this morning.

'Reilly? Captain John Reilly?' I said with a questioning intonation as though I wasn't sure myself.

'Ah, right. Sit down,' he snapped. I wondered if he still didn't know who I was.

My working week had begun on Saturday, and I'd enjoyed a fairly carefree start, but by Tuesday it had become clear that my life was about to make an unscheduled departure.

A day earlier I found a note in my drop file; a few elegant lines of curly script informing me that I seemed like a nice bloke. The author of this unexpected message went on to ask if I fancied a drink sometime. There was a name and a mobile number at the bottom, but I doubted this curious invitation could possibly have come from the flirtatious hostie. Why would she be interested in a bloke who had failed to show any composure or maturity when confronted with female attention?

Kelly was smart, articulate and hot. She was absolutely not the kind of impressionable air hostess who fell for the first captain who 'seemed nice,' or for any pilot for that matter. She was more the kind of flight attendant who would say 'My boyfriend's a handsome international lawyer, and we have a villa in Portugal' (which she did). Yes, the note was obviously a wind up.

I had stuffed the small piece of paper into my pocket, telling myself I was hiding it to prevent discovery by others who may draw the wrong conclusions.

I was happily married, had two cherished children, and lived a blessed life in the country (well, the West Country). There had never been anyone else in our marriage and I'd always intended to keep it that way. But on Tuesday, a small seismic murmur had wobbled the domestic ground beneath my feet.

Tabitha, my wife, had announced that whilst the children were still off school after Easter, and since I'd be working away in Gatwick, she and the children would be spending a few days with her mother. The issue was that she wasn't planning to return home until Sunday – the last of my days off. If your working pattern forces you to spend six days away and only three days at home, surely you could expect your family to make the most of the precious time you have together. I thought so.

Worst still, this worrying news had arrived by text message late Monday night, long after I had gone to bed, and it wasn't until I got up for work at 5.30 the next morning that I had been able to read it. Since that was a clean two hours before Tabitha awoke, my day's work was set to begin without my discussing the news with her. I worried that an anxious, distracted captain might not be in the right frame of mind to make sound decisions. And so it proved.

I glanced down at the newspaper lying on the Chief Pilot's desk. Seeing my interest, he reached out and turned the red-topped tabloid towards me. It was only a minor news item, but the headline was eye catching:

Pilot lands in trouble with chiropractor joke

I could see what the journalist had done there, and I smiled at his tabloid creativity; it hadn't been my best landing. I had been tired at the end of a long duty. We'd taken Polish plumbers to Gdansk (bringing replacements back with us – they were like a tag-team), then stag and hen parties joined us for a trip to Ibiza. I could barely focus my eyes on the touchdown point by the time we arrived back in Gatwick. Worse still, the wind was gusting from the south – right across the runway – and the plane clattered onto the tarmac like a heavyweight boxer hitting the canvas in the twelfth round. We've all done it (more than once) during our flying careers, and we've all survived. There had been no danger, no breach of procedure – just not a graceful arrival, that's all. So my slam-dunk wasn't the reason I was in trouble; even my boss doesn't castrate pilots for crap landings. Well, not yet anyway.

I had been receiving treatment for a back ailment from a local chiropractor, and had a number of business cards in my bag to leave in the crew room. Sitting in an airline seat all day, every day encourages poor posture and everything that goes with it. So it had seemed a good idea, at the time, to make light of my temporary skill deficiency by handing out these business cards to passengers as they disembarked. It was funny; they laughed, they made jokes of their own 'Are you on commission? Can I book an appointment now?' they shook my hand, and they enjoyed the contact with their otherwise invisible pilot. It had all been good fun, but you never know who's on board – until you read it in the paper.

The bollocking was over quickly. The Chief Pilot handed out a formal warning, and I vowed never to be funny again. Of course, as a grown up professional, I wasn't scared of the Chief Pilot. Obviously not. If he sacked me I would shout 'unfair dismissal' and claim millions in lost income, then retire to spend time with my family who live two hundred miles from where I'm forced to work. No more consecutive early starts; no more B&Bs; no more constant testing and regulating; no more grubby hands smoothing over my half stripped body in the name of 'security'. I'd be out of there and on the motorway home before you could say Dan Dare, Pilot of the Past.

It was a short walk from the sprawling purple Portakabin that served as our headquarters to the similarly liveried training building. The company insists on calling it the Centre of Excellence, but to the thousands of crew members who squeeze, sausage-like, through its garish corridors every year, it is what it is: a cheap, badly painted building used to carry out mandatory training. And if the Civil Aviation Authority trusted me to remember how to open an aircraft door, or how to put a life jacket on, I wouldn't have been swiping my pass at the main entrance of the former aircraft hangar within minutes of my disciplinary meeting.

Annual recurrent training is vital for cabin crew in the same way as biannual simulator training is for pilots. First aid, evacuation drills, and passenger placation are all important skills for the crew who work in the cabin, and these skills need to be refreshed and polished every year. But for pilots, well, these days we don't even need to practise opening and closing the doors: all the CAA requires is that we watch a video of someone else doing it.

I spotted a group of casually dressed blokes standing around the coffee machine; one was banging his fist on the slot where I assumed he'd just deposited a coin.

'Thieving bastard!' he snarled. 'Fifty bloody pence. That's worth another Kit-Kat from the on-board bar.'

'Here, Pete, have a coffee on me,' offered a captain stood beside him.

I walked over, coins at the ready, and introduced myself.

We stood around asking all the usual questions: which base are you from? What's it like there? Where did you work before? Do you know so-and-so. It doesn't pay to show too much imagination when chatting within spitting distance of the management offices. Breaking free of one's programming is forbidden in an industry that enforces conformity through standard operating procedures.

Before long we'd moved on to more intellectual matters, still within the confines of predictability, and started moaning about being there again. We made all the usual comments.

'Why do I need to know how many fire extinguishers

there are in the cabin? I'm not allowed out of the flight deck,' complained Steve, the coffee machine mugging victim.

'I know,' said Lars, a Dutch first officer, 'it's crazshy. All we need to know is what shtuff we have in the flight deck, and we check that every day.'

'Well, it gets us out of flying,' I said, 'which means we can't screw up and get our names in the paper.' I smiled to myself as I remembered my moment of fame, and Pete suddenly made a connection.

'I thought I knew your name – you were the guy handing out the chiropractor cards!' Pete looked around at the other guys, 'Did you see that in the paper?'

Of course they had; it's all we do all day – read the papers.

'Brilliant,' said Steve, slapping my arm. 'Loved it!'

'Unfortunately our Chief Pilot didn't,' I said, smiling. 'I've just come from a bollocking – official warning not to be funny ever again.'

'Fuck off!' spat Lars, demonstrating linguistic mastery of his adopted country. 'That tossher hash only been here six monthsh. I would have told him to shove his head up his arshe.'

I wondered why the English (and Anglicised Irishmen, like me) were so much more compliant than other Europeans. I'd accepted my bollocking without even a murmur of protestation. Perhaps I just didn't care.

Two more pilots joined us, both women, and the conversation returned to the beginning: *where are you based? What's it like there …?*

Eventually a cabin crew trainer burst into the room like someone who had just lost her child in a busy shopping mall, and informed us that we should have been in the classroom fifteen minutes ago.

It seemed as though a lifetime had passed since I, Pete, Lars and the others had stood beside the coffee machine, but the first session of our annual recurrent training had lasted just an hour. It was 10.15 am, and we now knew that we still knew what safety equipment existed on the flight deck. During the next hour we would get to try on a life jacket, a smoke hood and a portable oxygen mask. There are no portable oxygen masks on the flight deck so the only time I'm likely to wear one is when travelling as a passenger, or if I faint during flight, but in that case the cabin crew would take care of it. Still, at least I could now say I'd know if they were putting it on correctly. Then again, I'd probably be unconscious, so perhaps I wouldn't. I can't dress this up anymore: some of this refresher training seems to be a colossal waste of time.

At some point during the morning we would even get to pretend to put out a pretend fire. Once again, though the cabin crew would extinguish any real fires since I'd be flying the plane.

I slurped my coffee and looked around the room. When you've worked for a company for ten years, even one as widespread as mine, there will always be someone you know, wherever you go in the network. But this year I struggled to recognise anyone. All the cabin crew sharing our day of dullness were new entrants, such is the turn-around of staff these days. And they all seemed to be so young (middle aged men, bar staff; remember the rule). My hand clutched the note still concealed in my pocket, and I remembered that I was going on a date that night with someone who wasn't my wife.

Christ! What was I thinking? I knew I ought to phone my wife and talk about things. I'd texted her on Tuesday, but I hadn't heard back. Sometimes, if Tabitha doesn't reply straightaway, she forgets. Perhaps there was a reasonable explanation for why she was spending my days off at her mother's. But then again, she could have called me. If I spoke to her now, though, what would I say I was doing that evening?

My struggling thoughts were halted by the sound of my phone chirruping its brief message alert. Aha! An explanation from my wife, I thought. Dilemma solved. I dragged it from my jacket pocket, along with the inner lining, and checked the screen. My cheeks burned: it was a text from Kelly.

Another hour and a bit had dragged on in the classroom. We'd watched a few videos of people tumbling down the escape slides, and one showing a girl operating the aircraft doors. Then (in the way of a test) answered a few questions at the end. We'd all passed.

Sat in the canteen, I scoffed a sandwich in the untidy manner of a hungry homeless man. It had been seven hours since I'd slammed my fist down on top of the detested alarm clock back in Handcross, and sixteen hours since I'd last eaten. Even a crew meal would have vanished down my throat in slippery haste.

The other guys had heard the declaration from our trainer that it was lunchtime and disappeared in the time it had taken me to tap out a text to Kelly. To be fair, the text had taken quite some time to construct, and bored pilots don't hang about when they're not imprisoned in a locked cockpit. The pub didn't appeal to me, anyway, since we can't have a proper drink whilst on duty – even during classroom training – and the bar staff have been known to grass-up crew members who order anything stronger than a ginger beer. We may not be flying but we still can't drink alcohol whatever duty we're doing. Perhaps our managers are worried that we might pass out whilst in charge of a classroom chair. Then again, they don't seem worried that we frequently pass out with fatigue whilst in charge of a $60,000,000 jet plane filled with passengers. And that's unlikely to change as long as the regulators allow airlines to roster consecutive twelve-hour days.

The alternative to a dry lunch in the pub with the other pilots was a sandwich in the canteen with a bunch of young flight attendants. I'd opted for the latter. Naturally, I wasn't part of their conversation because I had no idea what they were talking about. The bits I did catch, though, suggested the girls had some kind of perception filter obscuring my presence. The topics were partly fascinating and partly shocking. For example, I couldn't imagine Kelly having a piercing where few would ever see. Given the lewd nature of their conversation, any unexpected contribution from me would have been on a par with getting my knob out and slapping it on the table. Which I hadn't done since the *last* Chief Pilot bollocking. Just kidding. Really.

I kept quiet and absorbed as much girly gossip as I could without taking notes (because that would have looked unusual). In ten fascinating minutes I'd been updated on all the main soaps and celebrity news, and felt adequately briefed for my date that night – though I planned to steer clear of genital piercings for the time being (conversationally or otherwise).

Chapter 2

Close enough for jazz

Flight crews are selected by employers for their unri-valled social skills. That is, we get on with each other. It's important that any team, when faced with mortal danger, can gel together and work effectively. 'Getting on with each other' is the key ingredient in our gel. But every year we must sit in a classroom and practise what our intrinsic talents allow us to demonstrate every single day of our lives.

We gather in groups discussing a variety of docu-mented aviation incidents, and suggesting ways we would have dealt with them. We get into role-playing to better demonstrate how well we all get on. And we agree that, actually, we have no idea how any of us would react if the wing fell off our plane and spiralled to the ground like a sycamore seed. This is what I earlier referred to as the annual friendship class, but the industry calls it Crew Resource Management (CRM) and believes that it invented it.

The truth is that the aviation industry invented only the name, and for many years there was even confusion over what the letters actually stood for. Once, pilots believed it stood for *Cockpit* Resource Management until someone pointed out that the crew who work in the cabin also play a vital role during your average flight to Spain and back.

Whatever the letters stand for, and whatever aviation thinks it invented, CRM is all about working together to have a nice day out.

So, after lunch we regrouped outside the classroom – fellow pilots with their bellies swishing with ginger beer and cabin crew still catching up on the latest gossip – whilst we waited for the CRM instructor to turn up. After several feet-shuffling moments, which we filled with more moaning about being there, a tall, suited man appeared from inside the room.

'Wait here,' he ordered. 'My team and I are re-arranging the furniture to improve your learning experience. I will inform you when I wish you to enter.'

There was a swivelling of heads and a few puzzled expressions before Lars spoke for the group.

'Fuck! What a fuck. Who da fuck ish he?'

I thought it was well said and didn't feel the need to add anything more.

'Fucking CRM?' Lars continued. 'Not with that attitude. Arsehole!'

He had a point. The guy didn't even have the courtesy to greet us politely, but instead addressed us like we were still at school – a boarding school. In the 19th Century. What could someone like that tell us about CRM?

'He should have recruited us to move the furniture around,' I said. 'Wouldn't that be a good exercise in team-work, you know, just to warm us up and get us in the mood?'

'What the fuck dush he know about teamwork, man?' Lars was clearly setting himself up for a very un-CRM session with this guy, but at least it should liven up what can often be a tedious waste of 0.008% of the average pilot's life.

The thing is, you either know how to interact with other humans or you don't; sitting in a classroom talking about it isn't going to change any personalities. Sure, decades ago some captains believed they were god-like, and must be obeyed and never questioned. But those days ended at the same time as the Black and White Minstrel Show, and a new way of thinking dragged along a gradual improve-ment in cooperation between crew members. It has had a profound effect on safety. These days pilots are all cuddly and lovely, and since we know it's the cabin crew who are first aid trained, we are most cuddly and lovely towards them – sometimes too much.

Eventually the door opened and our instructor (or 'facilitator', I think they prefer) dapper with cravat, waved us in.

The desks had been banished to the walls – along with our personal possessions – and the chairs positioned to form a semi-circle. Our man took up a commanding spot in the middle of the floor, flanked by two other men.

None of them smiled.

As we jostled for a seat the facilitator's two flankers took their own seats behind a desk that lay at the focal point of our semicircle. I slumped down on the end chair and stretched my legs out, crossing them at the ankles. With my arms folded close to my chest I probably gave the impression that I couldn't care less. I couldn't.

'Right,' shouted the dapper man clapping his hands together. 'CRM. What is it?'

His head revolved from side to side as he eyed each one of us, hoping to intimidate someone into a response. It was a steady sweep, almost machine-like; I wondered if he was about to raise a forearm and then bend at the waist before turning his head again. All we needed was some Eighties disco music and we could all have jumped up and danced The Robot.

Eventually, frustrated by the blank faces of his indifferent audience, he settled his eyes on me (since I sat in the end chair) and concentrated hard – the kind of concentration a baby shows when taking a dump.

Alright, mate, I'll have a go. 'CRM is a bit like jazz,' I said. 'If you have to ask what it is, then you'll never know.' The room erupted with laughter, but I could see from his scowl that our facilitator was strictly ballroom in his musical tastes.

'Well I disagree,' he snapped, once the laughter had died down, and turned to someone else. What a cock.

We decided not to help the facilitator and his chums

return the room to a traditional classroom layout before we left, but rather scrambled through the door like kids at playtime. It had been a tense and combative session, and the main thing I learned was that I really wouldn't want to meet this guy again, let alone fly with him. And we never did learn who he or his mates were. So much for CRM.

The rest of the day groaned along like a clock with fading batteries, and after listening to an ex-copper telling us that bad people, usually wearing beards, wanted to blow our planes up, we heard the sweetest words of the day.

'Thank you everyone – see you next year,' said the retired policeman.

Thank the Lord!

Moments after these simple words had brought forgotten smiles back to all our faces, my own mouth snapped back into place as though I had suffered muscle failure. I was that much closer to my date with Kelly, as a tightly knotted stomach was eager to remind me. Part of me wanted out of the rendezvous, that was for sure. The last time we met I'd blabbed on like a starry-eyed school kid meeting his idol. Even my first officer had been embarrassed. That kind of thing never happened to me, and I feared that much the same would happen next time. But part of me was angry with Tabitha, and that part wanted in, which is why I'd accepted the date.

I didn't have the confidence to believe that Kelly had an amorous interest in me. Apart from her being half my age, her glamorous lawyer boyfriend, and my clumsy conversation, she knew I was married. I considered that our date was simply a get together between two people who were absent from their partners. It was all above board – and if came to it, above the waist only – but I was still nervous.

The door to our Centre of Excellence was stiff but it jerked open under the strain of a hefty shove, and I stepped into the daylight for the first time in eight hours. Even the industrial air of Greater Manchester tasted fresh when compared to the recycled air from the underpowered air-con I'd been sucking in all day. As I exhaled like a smoker denied a fag for half a lifetime, the gobshite taxi driver from this morning waved at me from inside his Volvo. Bollocks.

Chapter 3

Horses, and one hound

When I'd packed for my usual six days away, I failed to consider packing some smart party gear for a hot date with a twenty-something beauty. Worse still, as I gathered my meagre clothing collection for its week of usage, it hadn't crossed my mind that such a date (however unrealised at the time) would occur at the end of the week when all my clothes would be clambering for the washing machine.

It was with increasing panic, then, that I rummaged through my bag, shaking out anything that I considered vaguely appropriate for a night out with a young lady, and despairing that everything I found was more suited to a night out with my mother. That was an omen, I thought: a sign that I was doing the wrong thing.

My wardrobe malfunction had begun a week earlier when I'd awoken on day one of early shifts to find all my clothes still stuffed into my overnight bag. I'd gone to work looking like a man in desperate need of an iron. I went out only once during the week, and that had been with an old friend who, quite frankly, wouldn't care if I came dressed as a chimney sweep. She's seen me looking worse. Considering how packed with incident my week had been, I felt I'd had more important things to think about than my clothing collection.

Kelly was a law student on a gap year. She was the kind of girl who preferred to spend her study break working for a lo-cost airline instead of serving beer to Aussie surfer dudes in a beach bar somewhere Down Under. I had to assume she was either career focused or mad. On the evidence so far, and I include asking me out on a date, I had to think the latter. But whatever Kelly was, surely she was smart enough to see past the shabby outfit, and home in on my mind instead. Whether that would impress her remained a whole new area of doubt.

I pulled on a plain blue T-shirt and tried to smooth down the creases with my palms. It didn't work. Looks like I'll be leaving my jacket on, I thought.

There had never been a time when I played the field, even during my youthful days as an army officer. There had been opportunities, of course, but my work always came first. That isn't to say I was some kind of robe-wearing, bread-making monk. I had my encounters, and I had my heartbreaks, but I's always been a one-woman guy.

Maybe this fidelity during my earlier years was the problem. Maybe I hadn't got enough back then, and now I'm facing the rest of my life with the same woman: a woman I loved and found beautifully attractive, but a woman who had decided to spend my cherished days off this week at her mother's.

The thing is, I am still a one-woman guy. This idea that my night out with Kelly was some kind of date was really just the fantasy of a married man in his forties, and the product of a rebellious, if not childish mind.

If I took the car to my 'date' with Kelly it would stop me drinking and making a fool of myself. I was still thinking about that brilliant idea when I jumped into a taxi outside my B&B.

'Crawley town centre, please,' I asked the driver, and he performed some kind of reverse nod of acknowledgement.

The rear seat of his Toyota was infested with grey hairs, and I eased myself down like a man forced to use a public toilet on New Year's Eve. It wasn't the plushest cab I'd ridden in that day, but at least the driver was quiet (obviously he had no James Bond background to talk about).

I spotted some dried mud on the seat beside me and without thinking I brushed it away with my hand. They looked like little footprints. On the floor was a round plastic bowl surrounded by more mud and hair.

'Do you have a dog by any chance?' I asked the driver. There had been no conversation other than my destination request, and I felt the silence was coming between us.

'Oh, he's not gone and crapped on the floor again has he?' replied the driver stretching up to see through the rear view mirror.

'Hopefully not, but he has left his little paw prints on

your seats.'

I wished the driver would stop trying to see the floor through his mirror; it simply can't be done without straying into oncoming traffic (unless you're a trained stunt driver).

'Oh he's a bugger, ain't he? Do you like dogs, mate?'

I'm always someone's mate, especially passengers: *it's all cheers, mate! Nice landing, mate* (admittedly I heard that last example only rarely).

'I quite like dogs, but they don't seem too keen on me. My wife has a dog – he just growls at me most of the time.'

I could hear the driver talking back to me but his voice bounced off my ears; my looming date with Kelly barred all distractions.

I looked at my watch, the Breitling my wife had bought me some years ago, and the stiff finger of conscience jabbed at my belly. I had no idea why I was doing this or what would happen during the evening. What I did know was that Kelly was the kind of girl that gets between a man and a happy ending. Still, there had been no word from my wife, and she was spending my days off at her mother's. Stuff it! I paid the driver and strode into the bar.

Kelly was already there. She sipped from a glass of red wine, her mobile phone poised in the other hand, probably mid-text. I wondered if she'd just prepared a 'You're late' message and was giving me the time it took her to take one more quaff of her drink before pressing send. She looked up as I walked in, which I expected she'd done each time someone came through the door. I checked my watch again to make sure I wasn't late (which I was), and held my wrist in place a fraction longer to ensure she noticed.

I couldn't help but choke out a 'Wow!' With her glossy black hair and perfect white teeth she looked like a piano. Shame I couldn't play. I would probably find a more flattering vision to compare her to when I sat down, or just keep my mouth shut for safety. She smiled and patted the chair beside her at the table. It was good of her to save a seat for me, so I did the proper thing and sat down. I could see that Kelly was a confident and assertive young lady. If she wanted, she could probably get me to rob a bank for her.

'Blimey, you look stunning out of uniform,' I blustered. 'Like a thoroughbred horse.'

She raised her eyebrows – was that good?

'Majestic and ... groomed ...' I added.

Her eyes widened slightly and I felt encouraged.

'I'm not saying I'm trying to groom you ... or that I want to ride you ...

Her eyes widened even further and I floundered, searching for a way out of my conversational hole.

'Er, actually, I can't ride,' I said, trying to avoid further faux pas.

Kelly's expression sagged so I thought it best to end on a positive note.

'But I'm eager to learn,' I said.

She smiled, one of those cocky smiles that precedes a killer comment. 'Perhaps you should get some practice in on a few old nags first,' she said.

'I have,' I admitted eagerly. 'Obviously … I mean, well not today, in the past, you know … Sorry, just a bit flustered by how great you look.' *Come on, fool! Get yourself together.*

'Put your tongue back in, Captain John, and explain why you're late!' She flashed another smile, the type that usually comes with a wink, though it didn't on that occasion.

'Couldn't find anything to wear,' I said, only half joking.

'I can see that. At least you're not wearing trainers.' She took another mouthful of red wine, but didn't put the glass down. 'Let's hope your conversation is better than your dress sense.'

Aha, a chance to redeem myself.

'Aren't you going to get a drink?' She asked, looking puzzled.

'You told me to sit down …' *Bollocks!* I was a grown man – twice her age – and I'd followed her signal without thinking. Worse still, my lame reply made me look as though I had no mind of my own.

'Ah, bless, I'll save your seat for you. Off you go.' So I went.

At the bar I was desperate to turn round and look at her, but I knew her dark brown eyes were locked onto the back of my head like she was trying to see inside. She had stolen control of the entire encounter without challenge. I wondered if she had a balaclava and a sawn off shotgun in her bag.

I paid the barman and turned back to the table. I was

right about the eyes. She watched me walk back across the room, only looking away when another guy entered the pub.

'I didn't think you'd come,' she said simply.

'Me neither when I saw the contents of my suitcase. What's the problem with trainers anyway?'

'We won't be allowed into a club if you're wearing trainers.' She raised her glass to her lips and drained another inch of wine. It was good job I hadn't been sipping my drink when she announced this plan.

'I'm not sure I'll be awake that long, Kelly, I've been up since four-thirty. I was thinking of a quiet drink and off to bed.'

'Not on the first date, Captain!'

'No, no, I mean, off to my own bed – alone, just me. And you to your bed alone, well, not together anyway. I mean, you can go to bed with someone else – not that you would–'

She reached out and pressed a finger against my lips. It was the single most erotic gesture I'd experienced in years. And it worked instantly.

'I get it,' she said.

I really wanted to go home, but standing up now was not an option. Hopefully it would be safe to do so by the time she needed her glass refilling, though that seemed imminent.

Our evening continued in a similar manner through two more drinks and three packets of crisps. It was unlikely to be the most sophisticated dinner date she'd enjoyed but at least it wasn't costing me a fortune. I watched the last cheese flavoured crisp disappear between her lips and meet a violent end. Her jaw slammed shut with an aggression I hoped she reserved for crunchy snacks. We'd started with prawn flavour, followed by roast chicken for our mains. Now, after the Cheesy Wotsits, I wondered if we should order some coffee.

The sound of her crunching rose above the Friday night din of the pub. I was surprised she had that power, then I realised she was sitting closer to me now. It was a relief she ate with her mouth closed. I remembered a girl I'd dated briefly years ago; she chomped on everything like a toothless old man trying to eat a toffee. I couldn't stand the noise so she had to go. That had been just before I met my wife. Oh yes, my wife. It was the first time I'd thought about her for two hours. Now, after a number of glasses of wine, I found it hard to understand how I should feel.

'Is it your bed time, Captain?' Kelly waved a hand in front of my eyes, giving me that 'Ah bless' look again.

I realised I'd been staring at nothing. 'Perhaps it is,' I conceded, and put my hand on her leg. It was a friendly gesture, nothing more, and it was only meant to be there for a brief moment – a kind of affectionate pat. I hadn't planned it. Now I couldn't move it. Her hand was firmly resting on mine. *Bollocks.*

There was a time when a guy could gallivant around the world (or simply go on a weekend bender) and be completely unreachable. He could be lost, gone to ground, hidden. One didn't need to be an expert in communications to evade those wishing to keep in touch. All you had to do was neglect to mention the name of your hotel. Any guy could disappear without trace in the time it took his wife to say Alexander Graham Bell.

Twenty years ago, whilst serving with the Royal Signals, I had been sent to Thailand to provide communication expertise to some blokes working for the Foreign Office. One weekend I took a break and spent a few days up country riding on elephants. I didn't mention this to the Embassy because I wasn't sure about their policy on elephants, and because I went with a girl from the Hungarian Embassy, though that would probably have been fine. When I rolled up to work the following Wednesday it emerged that some poor clerk had rung every hotel in Bangkok searching for me (he should have made a trunk call). But this was all before the most pervasive creation in human history found its way into our lives: the mobile phone. And as I sat in the back of a cab with Kelly, my phone rang.

'Hi, Tabitha, how's your mother?' I asked. It felt like I'd been punched in the stomach. My heart rate doubled in an instant. I'd been desperate for a phone call from my wife over the last few days, but now she'd finally called I blushed like a posh tomato.

The intimacy in the bar had inspired a rousing recovery from my long trip up north, and we'd stayed until the final bell at 11.00 pm. After a too-short ride, our taxi journey was over and I fretted about what would happen next – what Kelly expected to happen next. Perversely, my wife held the key to that.

'*Fine, why?*' Tabitha's voice was dismissive, as though her mother's welfare was far from the most pressing subject of her belated phone call.

'Well, that's where you are so I wondered if she was okay–'

'*Yes, that's where I am, the question is, where are you?*'

It was hard to glean from her tone if she was being playful or serious. I feared the latter because I shied away from confrontation – especially with loved ones – but Tabitha was normally a humorous lady so I responded to the former.

'I'm safe. They haven't hurt me. Did you get the ransom note?' It was daring, but I'd had a few drinks. Besides, people can be prone to saying ridiculous things when guilt swills around the mind like slop in a bucket.

'*Don't make jokes, darling, not when Woofy is probably eating his own legs by now.*'

Bollocks! She'd left the dog behind.

'*Steve from number 26 fed him this morning.*'

'Oh, I'm sorry, darling, I thought you would have taken him with you – I'm so tired after my trip to Manchester, I couldn't face the drive back. He'll survive the night and I'll be home first thing. After all, I've been on earlies all week so I'll be up by six tomorrow.'

Our brief call ended. She hadn't mentioned why she was at her mother's, but that didn't matter anymore. I felt like shit. Which was ironic since that's exactly what

Woofy would be busy leaving around the house right now. I imagined an unholy mess if he couldn't contain himself until the next morning. Then again, it wouldn't be the unholiest of messes made that day; I think I could trump the dog on that score – which takes some doing.

I thanked Kelly for a lovely evening and stepped out of the taxi without looking back. Her warm hand slipped from mine and I heard a gentle thud as it fell onto the back seat of the car.

Chapter 4

Out with the new, in with the old

To say I was up by six, as I'd promised Tabitha, would be a flagrant misuse of words. I was still awake at six. Despite my exhaustion from the fifteen-hour trip to Manchester and the late night with Kelly, I hadn't slept a second.

Now, as I drove back to Devon, my mind flitted between the stomach wrenching mess probably left by Woofy and the stomach turning mess currently being made by a middle aged man with a girl young enough to be his daughter.

At twenty-three Kelly was half my age. If I'd stayed in Cork with all my school mates I may well have had a daughter that age, probably with children of her own. Christ, I could be a grandfather! But my actual daughter was only seven and my son was still settling into his first year at primary school. They were adorable children, polite and well behaved – courtesy of Tabitha's skills as a mother – and I loved them dearly. No way would I allow Kelly to split my family apart.

I enjoy the journey back to the West Country: the rolling hills of Salisbury Plain, the little airstrip at Popham with its rickety microlights bustling about in the breeze, and the increasingly silly names of the towns and villages. You know you've left behind the thrusting capital and its earnest suburbs when you see the sign for Middle Wallop in Hampshire. There's an airfield there – part of the Army Air Corps – and each time I pass I always smile at the association of 'Wallop' and the less successful efforts of a bunch of soldiers learning to fly. After all, you don't see the Royal Air Force buying a job lot of tanks and storming across the desert towards Bagdad. As a former army captain who became a pilot I should know better than to ridicule the Army Air Corps, but to be honest, if I'd wanted a military flying career I would have joined the Air Force (if they'd have me) or if I had a penchant for baggy trousers, the Navy.

By the time you see the signpost for Huish Episcopi you know you are well and truly in straw chewing country. I skirted around Yeovil and continued along the A303. The road was unusually quiet for a Friday, particularly so close to the summer season. Perhaps the tourists had been put off by warnings of April showers over the weekend. I didn't care about the rain; as an airline pilot I would rather be at home on the sofa when the weather cranks up a notch. There's nothing worse than sitting on the flight deck staring at the life-ending storm clouds on the weather radar screen – except, perhaps, flying into those life-ending storm clouds. It's one of the most horrifying experiences you could have in a plane.

I got caught in a thunderstorm once flying a light twin – a Piper Seneca – out of Germiston Rand Airport near Johannesburg. There were no passengers on-board, just medicine for missionaries over the border in Botswana. The plane and I somehow survived the encounter; the medicine, and the patient waiting for it, didn't. There is an old saying among pilots: it's better to be on the ground wishing you were up there than being up there wishing you were on the ground. It frustrates my wife to the point of depression that I stare out of our living room window at the wind and rain and express how glad I am to be on my days off. All she wants to do is make the most of my time at home by going out for the day. Or at least that was the case until that week.

My old Škoda and I ended our three-hour journey by pulling onto the drive beside the family home. It wasn't as impressive a house as many of my colleagues boasted but, with four bedrooms, it fitted my family well.

After leaving the army I used all my savings – and then some – qualifying for my professional pilot's licence. The two years I spent flying missionaries in the African bush were unpaid, though my expenses were covered so my debt didn't increase. My first paid job in aviation came when I worked for Viktor Voblikov in Moscow. But, despite flying his corporate jet around for five years, I ended up worse off. By the time I started my airline career my debt had doubled and it took three years of frugality before Tabitha and I could buy our first house. That had been eight years ago, a year after we married. The house had been an enormous financial overstretch because I'd gambled on higher future earnings as a captain, but the decision had been vindicated; we were now comfortable, though not wealthy.

I sat in the car for a few moments listening to the last part of an interview on the radio, but I soon saw the dog's head sneering from the dining room window. My neglect of him wouldn't have done our fractious relationship any good whatsoever. It was frustrating to think that my late return had probably undone all the progress I'd made tossing him treats and walking his ungrateful little butt around the park. I switched off the radio, grabbed my case from the passenger seat and headed into the house – vomit bag at the ready.

And there it was, smack bang in the middle of the hall. Wallop indeed. It was still glistening, and I'm sure there was a trace of steam rising demon-like from the conical tip. Bastard dog! It looked like one of those whirly ice-creams you get from the bloke in a van, only it was the colour of the chocolate flake rather than the whippy treat itself. I imagined it squeezing from his arse and curling round and round onto the floor (though I don't know why I did). He must have been storing it up for days.

I put my hand into an empty poo-bag and looked down upon the task ahead. Had he done it yesterday it would have been a dry, hardened lump by now. Instead, I found myself choking as my fingers sunk into the soft and slippery pieces of Woofy's undigested Pedigree Chum.

It was early evening before Tabitha called on the landline. I guessed she'd rung the home number to make sure I was actually there. It was a short conversation, mostly to announce that she would be home 'sometime on Sunday,' and also to ask if Woofy still had all his limbs. 'Yes,' I said, 'but he's lost some weight.' After explaining the crude joke to her, she bollocked me again for leaving him locked in the house for so long, and mentioned something about ridding the place of foul smells before the children came home. I asked her if that meant she wanted me to move out, but clearly I was alone with my humour. 'Not you, the smell of Woofy's faeces,' she said after a moment's hesitation. I laughed out loud, and alone, then Tabitha said her goodbyes and hung up. It was hardly a cheery phone call. I was due back at work on Monday afternoon, and since keeping one's children off school in order to chill-out with them was discouraged, Tabitha's 'sometime on Sunday' meant little time with my darlings.

Tabitha had told me that her mother hadn't seen her grandchildren for several weeks and, owing to her volunteer work at the hospital, had only the weekends to spend time with them. 'What about me?' I asked, but she told me that her mother didn't feel the same way about me. Some of my own unfunny medicine, it seemed. At least I assumed so.

There was no doubt that Tabitha showed signs of stress. Normally she was an easy-going lady; someone who giggled at my humour and indulged my forgetfulness. Menopause, I concluded, and dialled the Indian take-away.

I sat stretched out on the sofa pondering whether dogs blinked. Woofy's eyes had been locked on mine all evening, closing only once when the effort to stare me out overcame him. I wondered if that meant I'd won, but the instant I reached forward to finish the last of my whiskey, his eyelids sprung to attention like a couple of guardsmen caught napping, and he redoubled his efforts.

But that's the odd thing: he's not a guard dog, and as far as I know, has no trace of snarly Alsatian or vicious Doberman in his blood. In fact, Tabitha – the dog expert – described him as 'a mix', some kind of crossbreed, but didn't offer any combination to satisfy my curiosity. To me, he was part collie, part whippet and part suspicious bugger. You can tell he's part whippet because whenever he sees a bloke with a flat cap he's off before you can say 'Aye-up, lad'.

During my night at home alone I managed to get many things done. I got through most of the television shows I'd recorded in recent months, finished off a delicious Chicken Biryani, and emptied the top half of a bottle of whiskey. It was like being single; I could do whatever I wanted. No noisy kids to get ready for bed, no questioning wife wanting to know what I was doing now, and no one telling me I was drinking too much (which I wasn't). Bliss. That said, I couldn't decide what to do first so I just watched the TV.

Then a chirrup from my phone jolted my lolling head upright. It was late, gone 10.00 pm, and I was already falling asleep on the couch. Rock and Roll. I looked at the large window on the front of my phone and read – then re-read – the name displayed in the middle. Kelly. A text. I opened the message and, despite my anger at her texting me at home, gave in to a little smile.

Don't forget to delete my texts! x

I hadn't thought about that. With reluctant participation comes reluctant planning. And then a second text arrived.

... and don't forget to change my name in ur address book to Kelvin! Night night xx

Bloody hell! She was way ahead of me. I wondered if she'd done this before. And then my thoughts escalated. Perhaps she did this sort of thing all the time; flirting with older men, and getting her kicks out of exposing unfaithful husbands. She probably wasn't interested in me at all. The thought riled me, and I started to imagine all manner of skulduggery. Perhaps she intended to blackmail me. She was a hustler, a home-wrecker, a plant. Yes, that was it, she was a honeytrap. Well, I can play games, too. I could sleep with her then dump her, denying any involvement whatsoever. All I had to do was play the game more skilfully than her, and I'd be home and dry.

I stewed for a while, staring at the TV but not taking in what I was watching. There was no way I could be so foul and devious, not when other people were involved. Besides, such selfishness would betray myself just as much as it would betray my wife. It wasn't what I'd intended when I accepted the date, and it wasn't what I wanted to do now. No, Kelly or Kelvin, I have a better idea: delete your name and your number altogether. And with a press of my thumb she was gone.

My wife arrived home with our children shortly after 6.00 pm on Sunday. I'd had a few beers with my lunch at the local pub, mostly worn off by the time Tabitha turned up, and the freedom to do so without question had contributed enormously towards a relaxing afternoon. But I was glad my family was finally home.

The front door flung open, cracking hard against the stop, and my children thundered down the short hallway towards me. They grabbed a leg each and clung on like the ground had disappeared beneath their feet. But this show of affection lasted no longer than it took the dog to poke his bony little head through the kitchen doorway. Suddenly they found the floor again and I was relegated down the hugging order. My children fled as quickly as they'd arrived. After their desertion I was free to walk up to Tabitha and greet her warmly.

She wore tight jeans that accented her long legs, and her blonde hair hung freely around a face that seemed slightly flushed. As she flicked her shoes off she dropped a couple of inches and I stooped to kiss her cheek.

'Welcome home, darling. Missed you.' I said genuinely.

'So I smell,' she replied, pushing me away. 'How many did you have?'

'I just had a couple of beers with lunch–'

'I might have known you'd be straight down the pub.' She pushed past me and went into the kitchen.

'Have you mowed the lawn?' she asked. 'Did you notice the side gate was hanging on one hinge? And I bet you haven't emptied the dishwasher!'

The list sounded as though it could go on, so I jumped in quickly.

'It's been raining. Everyone knows you can't cut the lawn in the rain. And I haven't been through the side gate so I didn't know about that.'

Tabitha looked at me like a woman fed up with excuses. But, if true, it would be unfair; I'm hardly at home, and when I am I do whatever she asks.

'That's one reason I left you alone over the weekend.' She paused as she took in my crumpled brow. 'To give you time to finish the jobs!'

Hold on a minute! Was she making this up? At no point had she mentioned this carefully thought out plan.

'What jobs? Have you left a list?' I followed the roll of her eyes as she looked over at the scrap of paper pinned to the notice board.

'What a waste of time,' said Tabitha, shaking her head. Even the dog seemed to be shaking his head. And as they both followed the children into the sitting room, the bastard dog looked back at me.

I was left confused and upset that my wife's unexpected weekend away, during my precious few days at home, had contrived to make me some kind of useless father and husband – and had left *her* angry with *me*. How do women do that?

Barely an hour later Tabitha ordered the children to bed; apparently they'd had a busy day. I went up to squeeze the last few drops out of their company before lights out. In the morning they would have little time for me whilst they scrambled around getting ready for school.

Joseph snuggled down in his speedboat bed and closed his eyes waiting for me to begin the story about something called a Gruffalo. He always adopted the same sleep-like repose during his bedtime story. I'd read this book a hundred times, but I still didn't know if the Gruffalo was real or imaginary. And because my son had heard it a hundred times, I couldn't improvise even one word without him objecting querulously.

Lucy was a more interactive audience, demanding to see every single picture that accompanied the text. All this took time, of course, and Top Gear was about to start on television, *so come on, Lucy, look at the damn picture and let's get on with it!*

Chapter 5

Gaul strikes, Rome heats up

You know you've arrived back in the South East of England when the volume of cars on the road exceeds the space available. I'd been stuck in a jam on the M3 for close to an hour. My report time at work was way off so I had plenty of time, but it's just one of the many reasons I usually detested leaving my home and journeying up to Gatwick Airport.

But today I didn't mind so much. It had been a pointless few days at home, the only benefit being the pleasure of sleeping in my own bed and enjoying the space of my own house. Tabitha had taken great umbrage at my lazy weekend and mentioned it frequently. I had rattled through my chores in the morning, but ran out of time before I finished the lengthening list. Oh well.

The week away from each other would give us a chance to rebalance our relationship and return to what was, until this week, a happy family.

At last I pulled off the M3 and onto the M25; another half an hour would see me at my home from home, and for once I wasn't depressed about it.

The traffic had thinned as I drove southbound on the London Orbital, and after a four hour journey I pulled up outside the B&B in Handcross. I had an hour to spare before reporting for work.

A cadaverous face popped up above the windowsill in the lounge. It seemed as unwelcoming as Woofy's – and as hairy – but this one was human. The thin ashen skin was stretched over an expressionless face, flanked by fuzzy side burns and topped off with a mess of long black hair. Probably a new Polish cleaner, I thought. But, as I walked into the lounge, I could see that the unkempt head, accompanied by its lanky body, was clearly not the cleaner but a guest at the B&B. His bare form was draped over the furniture like a blanket – a blanket that ought to be draped over his bare form. Only a pair of tatty purple shorts shielded my eyes from a sight undoubtedly worse than Woofy's turd.

'Hey, how ya doin, buddy? Rivers Andersson, man.' The chap jumped up and held out his hand. It was a relief, and a surprise, to see that he was alive.

'Hi – er, Rivers Anderssonman?' I asked, just checking that I'd heard his name right.

'What, dude?'

'Uh? Rivers Anderssonman,' I repeated to clear up the confusion.

'Yeah, man, that's me, not you. Jeez, buddy, you're

quick!' He laughed and offered me a beer.

'So who are you, man?' he asked, and then it clicked.

'Ah, Rivers Andersson, full stop!' I jabbed my finger to emphasise the punctuation.

'Fuck! Don't start that again, man. We ain't both Rivers Andersson, man.'

'No, neither is – man.' I was getting it now, but I was on my own.

'What the fuck's going wrong with you, man?' Rivers smiled so, whilst I was obviously confusing the hell out of him, he seemed to be taking it well.

'Sorry, I was just checking your surname, but I think I've got it now.' I could see relief brighten his blank face, and he slumped back into the chair.

'I'm John Reilly, pleased to meet you.'

'Dude, take a beer,' he offered.

'Sorry, I can't, I'm a pilot and I have to fly to Rome this afternoon.'

'Like the discipline, buddy. Maybe later? I'll still be here.'

'I wish, but I have to go to Prague after Rome so I won't be back until midnight.' It's good to have a beer with someone after work, but I wasn't sure Rivers Andersson-whatever was my kind of guy.

'Like I said, dude, I'll still be here. I ain't flying till Thursday.' And he gulped the bottle in one.

No. Nah. Oh, come on! He can't be a pilot. Surely! Although the airline employed people based on ability and not dashing looks, this guy did come across like a guy who'd spent more time in a commune than a flight school.

'Er, you–' I began, pointing a hand towards him.

'Yeah, dude, just transferred in from Amsterdam, can't work there anymore – I'm not Dutch.'

Ah, I knew about this guy; he must be the Swedish chap we'd all heard about. He was almost folklore among the pilots; a tree hugging, free-living hippy who just happened to fly airliners. A pilot with an environmental conscience – a bit like the tart with a heart.

'You don't need to be Dutch to work in Holland – European Union and all that,' I said, throwing him a quizzical look.

'Dude, the law changed, only Dutch nationals can smoke in their special cafes. Know what I mean?'

My God! Is this guy on drugs? How's he getting away with this?

'Chill, dude, just kidding. I've been clean for five years now.'

'Right.' I was relieved; drug use would have given me a dilemma I could do without. I still didn't think I could get on with him, though; too far out there for my taste.

'So, welcome to Gatwick, Rivers, and to the Blue Mantle Hotel.'

'Cool. We'll have a blast,' he said with the now familiar blank face.

Why did those few harmless words scare the life out of me?

'Well, Rivers, nice to meet you, but I've got to be on my way. Catch you later, perhaps,' though I wasn't sure about that.

'Sure, dude. Jet easy, man.'

Gatwick was by far the airline's biggest base. There were over a thousand flight attendants to populate fifty planes flying about two hundred flights per day. Given that pilot roster patterns are out of sync with cabin crew rosters, the chance of regularly bumping into the same person twice was low; the chance of flying with the same person twice was comparable to lightening strikes. So it was clearly fate that the first person I met at the car park bus stop was Kelly. Bollocks.

Perhaps she sensed me coming, I don't know, but she was already watching me as I came into the shelter, and my step faltered. That was awkward. I patted my pockets as though I'd left something in the car, and allowed my hesitation to linger a few moments more. I then realised I had no time to return to my car so pretended to find the missing item.

'Hi, great to see you,' she said simply. 'Got everything?'

I hesitated, deciding how to play the situation. Was she mocking me? I didn't think so; her question had seemed genuine because there was less boldness in her voice than in our previous encounters. I decided to give her the benefit of the doubt.

'Hello, Kelly, yes. Thought I'd left my phone in the car.' I patted my pocket again and smiled. 'How are you?'

'I'm good, thanks. I'm really sorry for texting you at home – I just didn't want your wife to see my name in your phone, in case she ... Well, I don't know if your wife

199

would look through your phone. Oh, I don't know … I'm sorry, really I am.'

This was a different girl to the assertive Kelly who had almost snared me like something out of Greek mythology. She seemed vulnerable and, bloody hell, absolutely gorgeous.

'It's fine,' I said shaking my head. 'Where are you going today?' I tried to change the subject and appear nonchalant about the text – and about her – but, as she drew in a deep breath and held it for a second, I guessed she had more to say.

'Barcelona,' she exhaled, then took another deep breath. 'John, I don't know where we're heading but I've never slept with a married man, and I don't want to ruin your marriage so …

She was still talking but I wasn't taking any of it in; these were horny words. I imagined her undressing, those plump boobs, that trim body; I could almost feel her breath fluttering past my ear as we made love. Oh my! My fantasy blew away as I became aware of the growing erection lifting the front of my trousers. The last time I'd been so turned on was when the same girl pressed her finger against my lips to stop me talking. Now she was the one who needed to stop talking, particularly since other people had joined us under the shelter. I dug my hands into my pockets and shuffled uneasily from foot to foot.

'… so what do you think, John?'

I'd missed quite a lot and I wasn't sure how to respond.

'Sorry, I've got such a headache,' I said. 'It's really drilling into my head. What was the last bit?'

Oh, that was ridiculous; if I'd had such a bad headache I'd have called in sick.

'Never mind, the bus is here. Tell you later.' And she stepped forward to assert her place at the front of the queue.

There was no opportunity for discreet conversation on the crowded bus, and we spoke hardly more than a stunted sentence on the way to the office block that housed our crew room. I was desperate to know what I'd missed. We joined the smokers returning from the bike sheds and entered the building to begin our working day. Just as I opened the door to our crew room, she clasped my hand briefly and gave it a gentle squeeze goodbye. Almost instantly I felt the need to place it in my trouser pocket again. What the hell was wrong with me?

As usual, the room was throbbing (I knew the feeling) with crew, some just finishing their early shift, others, like me, with eleven or twelve hours work ahead of them. I had my usual battle with the IT system, firstly to tell it I was there, and then to persuade it to print out all my flight documents. It was like a jobsworth security guard manning the front gate of a factory – *Yes I really do work for the company, and yes I want to come to work. NOW LET ME IN!* I imagined it eyeing me suspiciously as I approached the desk.

I glanced around at Kelly, then twisted my head round further as though generally sweeping the room. Ridiculous. There were far too many people in the cramped room to notice, or be bothered by, some anonymous pilot ogling a flight attendant.

The modern jet airliner's navigation system has trivialised the map reading skills of its modern pilots. No more do we need to calculate wind drift and plot courses. No more do we need to fiddle with complicated slide rulers and compasses. No more do we need to look at a map. All we have to do is tell it where we are, where we want to go, and the route someone else has planned. Then press 'play'.

Okay, so there's a little more to it than that, otherwise we wouldn't have to study and train for years to fly the damned things. What all this modern technology has done, however, is make flying safer and less fatiguing, which means airlines can work their crew up to the limit. In doing so we become less expensive to an accountant, and these cost savings have made a significant contribution to the low price of tickets. And this is a good thing, because without these penny-pinching airlines lowering ticket prices and revolutionising air travel, I wouldn't have had the chance to fulfil my boyhood dream of becoming a pilot.

Despite the waning interest I sometimes show towards my dream job, I recognise how lucky I am to have realised that dream. My employer provides the perfect plane – mostly new planes in good condition – a variety of short haul routes, and the friendliest people to work with. But it doesn't mean I can't moan. If, as a race, we had evolved to settle for what we have, however good it may be, we would still be living in caves. I can just imagine some cavechap called Ug coming home after a day in the marshes:

> 'Hey, honey, I'm fed up with living in this hollowed out rock! Let's move into one of those new homes that the Cro-Magnons built by the river.'
> 'Oh, Ug, we can't afford it, not with the new baby coming along. This cave is perfect for us. We have shelter, a place to crap, and it won't burn down every time you light up the barbecue.'
> 'Well, I'm sick of eating Mammoth. A diet of red meat every day isn't good for you. None of us live past thirty. I want a garden where I can grow vegetables.'
> 'You don't live past thirty because you all get killed hunting the mammoth.'
> 'Exactly! Red meat isn't good for you!'

The first officer and I had guided our plane, with its one hundred and thirty four passengers and four cabin crew, as far as the Alps without so much as a nervous glance at a map. Giles, my first officer, was doing the flying on the way to Rome, and he'd barely looked up from his iPad (every pilot seems to have an iPad these days) since reaching our cruising altitude. All he had to do was turn the heading knob once when the French controller decided we might invade the personal space of an Air France 747 coming from the East. My task was more arduous. I had the responsibility of communicating with air traffic control and, as we passed from Switzerland into Italy, that was about to intensify.

I had to sympathise with Italian air traffic controllers; how do you make yourself understood if no one can see your flailing arms? For an Italian it must be like being gagged. So it seems they do what every travelling Englishman does when speaking to a foreigner: they shout. Modern radio equipment is designed to convey spoken words effortlessly; it's not the same as yelling into a conically shaped rolled up copy of yesterday's Corriere Della Sera. Calm down, step away from the microphone and allow the electronics to do the work.

Arriving in a busy terminal area (controlled airspace that feeds one or more major airports) the tension ratchets up as controllers get more excited. It's like they're commentating on a Formula 1 Grand Prix race – *And there he goes, turning on to final approach – and what's this? Oh no, here comes Alitalia – he's overtaking – Wow! That was close!* Anything can happen in Rome, and it usually does.

I wondered how that Rivers bloke coped coming down to Rome; his 'Chill out, dude' approach to life probably didn't sit easily with high octane controlling. Jet easy, man! I'd never heard that before, but I feared I'd hear it again.

We took the chequered flag and arrived on stand in Rome Fiumicino Airport.

'Buon Journo, Commandante,' said the dispatcher, immediately waving his arms about and knocking several switches on our overhead panel. 'Wonandred a toowenty-tree passengers, no speziale, and fuwell is coming. Ow macha do you needa?'

'Seven tonnes, please,' I said, looking at Giles for his

agreement.

'Ok, I come back, ciao!'

'Hang on, do we have a slot?' I asked before he vanished into the terminal.

'Oh, si, I forgot, your departure time is, aaaah, eighteen-twenty zulu.'

'What? That's three hours from now!' I said, almost speckling him with spit.

'Yes, I check for you. Minuto.'

He dragged a walkie-talkie from a clip on his belt and machine-gunned a stream of words into the tiny microphone. The reply, to my ears, was like the noise a TV makes if you remove the aerial from the socket on the back.

'Grazie, ciao,' said Paulo (or whoever) into the radio, then turned to me as though he'd understood the burst of painful static.

'Eh, there issa strike in France, they justa walk out. We see, I don't know.'

And with that, he was gone. I turned to Giles and told him we wouldn't be going to Prague as scheduled, unless the slot came forward. But that was looking unlikely, even at this early stage. If French controllers had just staged an impromptu walk-out, then they wouldn't be turning around and walking back in for a good while yet. Well, not until they'd had coffee, dinner and an early evening nap. No, we would be stuck here for some time.

One thing was for sure, there was no way we were going to board the passengers on schedule (which was the company's policy). I had no intention of spending the next three hours in a confined space with a bunch of moaning travellers who blamed the crew for life's intolerable quirks. I descended into a miserable mood.

Anything unplanned that crops up and unsettles my day tends to have a negative affect on my moods these days. I think the whole crew would much rather operate all four flights and go home early, rather than sit on the ramp in Fiumicino for three hours. And I'm sure such grumpiness isn't confined to me. Whenever there is a long delay, the poor cabin crew always suffer abuse from angry passengers. And if things deteriorate further, then horror of horrors, I could be dragged from the sanctuary of my cockpit to deal with it.

A tickly vibration in the trouser region jerked me from my discontent. My mobile phone was nudged up against my gentleman bits and, as it heralded a text, it felt like someone was gently groping me. I didn't recognise the number, so assumed it was Operations. I opened the message.

> Hi, stuck in Barcelona. Poor Captain was on airport standby at 6am, so he'll be out of hours to fly back. Might have to night stop. What about you? X

Probably not Operations, I guessed. It took me a few moments to remember who had gone to Barcelona that day, and that I'd deleted her number. But why would Kelly choose to text me about her delay? Had she also texted her boyfriend? I hoped not. I liked the thought that she was sharing her misfortune with me. I wrote that we were delayed, too, but should be home earlier than planned having binned the Prague flight due to flight time limitations (not that we'd told the company yet). I held the phone in my hand hoping for a reply.

I never kept Tabitha informed of my activities during the working week; she had told me that my six days away were simply wiped from her life as lost time. Delays, cancellations – bollockings from the Chief Pilot – they were things that just affected me.

I thought of Rivers Andersson. He was probably still draped over the sofa, a bottle in his hand, and one on the floor with my name on it. He would be pleased about my early return, and someone to drink with. The phone buzzed.

> Lucky you. Shame ur not my captain today – tapas and sangria on the beach. How does that sound? Text you later... x

Well, it sounded great, but you're bound to get sand on your tapas, I thought, grinning at my own silent joke. I closed the text programme down and dialled up the company; they needed to know that we would not be extending our flight duty to squeeze in the Prague trip. Working days are long enough. If the company rosters flight combinations that take the crew up to maximum duty hours allowed by law – without leaving a suitable buffer for unforeseen delays – then that's their problem.

J.T. O'Neil

Besides, that's what standby crews are for.

It had been three hours since we'd learned of the delay, and one hour since I'd given in to the mithering dispatcher and allowed passengers to board. By now the French controllers must have moved on from the coffee, quaffed their Cognac, and stubbed out the last of the *Gauloises*, but there was still no sign of French skies opening up soon.

I realised – too late – that the dispatcher's eagerness to board passengers was to avoid providing free refreshments in the terminal. That now became our responsibility. The problem was that, owing to customs regulations, we couldn't open the bars until airborne. That legality hadn't gone down well with some passengers and, before long, I had to call the police to remove an increasingly aggressive family. Still, it entertained the rest of the passengers for a while.

I wondered whether eating my crew meal whilst hungry, fed up, and with fractious passengers sat on board would be a responsible course of action. Probably not, but I hadn't eaten since breakfast, and that had been only a bowl of Weetabix, so I worried my decision making skills would begin to suffer if I didn't eat something. I persuaded the cabin crew to open the bars as a diversion so they could heat up my meal while the passengers were distracted by free booze. The subterfuge could end with me making another trip to the Chief Pilot's office, but not that day, at least.

The cabin crew jumped at my suggestion since it helped them to placate the passengers. As for me, well I was just happy to be scoffing.

Being in a ravenous state is almost a prerequisite for eating crew food. Laden with salt, congealed in fat, and unidentifiable as organic matter, crew meals at my company are not prepared by a celebrity chef. It takes some will to polish off the contents of the small plastic trays – trays that must never be opened prior to heating; *don't look at me frozen, you won't like me when I'm frozen*. It's a mistake I made once, and it was weeks before I could eat another crew meal.

Today it was chicken (processed, pumped with water, and formed in to breast slithers) laid to rest in a bed of lank spinach and brown liquid, with a jumble of mushrooms on the side. *Mushrooms again?* But these were different from the breakfast fungi; large and wrinkled, they looked like gorilla's nipples. When I bit into one, my mouth filled with cooking fat; it was like they were lactating. I'd broken the law for this?

My phone tickled me again. I'd left it in my pocket because the idea of Kelly setting it off and giving me the little thrill made me smile.

> Hi! How are you getting on? We've just arrived at our hotel. Captain's going to bed, but me and the girls are off to find a beach bar. wywh! X

It looked like her predictive text was throwing a screwy – wywh – then realisation hit: wish you were here! Wasn't that normally a question? She was meant to ask if I wished I were there, surely? That's how it was on the old holiday show on TV with Judith Chalmers. But then again, Kelly was too young to know that. I sighed at the thought.

> Still stuck here, passengers on board, everyone fed up. Bloody French!

It felt good exchanging texts with Kelly, sharing each other's predicament, offloading the stresses of the day. That's how it used to be with Tabitha when I still worked from Exeter airport and lived at home. If you live in a B&B it doesn't matter if you're late back.

After four hours on board with no news from air traffic control, I called the company and spoke to one of our Crisis Management specialists. I asked him to consider cancelling the flight back.

'Just wait, we hear the French will be back within the next hour,' said a man, watching Sky News in the operations room.

'Oh, yeah, I'll let the passengers know!' I said. 'They'll be thrilled in was all worth while.'

'And don't forget you can't open the bars until you're airborne due to strict customs regulations.'

Bollocks!

The French did return to work (though not quite within

the promised hour), but the accumulative effect of countless delayed flights, all trying to depart at the same time, pushed us beyond our maximum permitted duty hours for the return flight. We had no choice but to cancel the flight back to Gatwick. By the time we had emptied the plane of riotous passengers it was almost midnight.

Now, at what seemed like the cheapest hotel in Rome, I collapsed onto the bed and stared at the ceiling. My first thought was that Rivers was still speckling the sofa with the dead skin flaking from his bare body, waiting to hand me a beer and shoot the late night breeze. I shivered and feigned a slight retch to myself. My second thought involved texting Kelly to find out what the tapas was like in Barcelona these days. I reached for the phone, still in my trouser pocket.

> Hi, Kelly, stuck in Rome. Fed up, no sangria,
> no tapas!

The reply took no longer than it took her to type the words.

> Hey, John, bet ur exhausted! Had Paella
> and a beer in the end – ice cold. In bed now
> watching the news in Spanish. They say
> flights will be back to normal tomorrow.
> Didn't pack my PJs! Xx

Having a Portuguese mother ensured Kelly was fluent in

that language, but I didn't know she could speak Spanish, too. I guessed she'd learnt at school.

I reread her last line – Didn't pack my PJs! – and quickly updated the decaying image of a partially naked Rivers with this new and entirely naked image of Kelly. Oh my.

Chapter 6

Nurse, we're losing him

It could have been worse, I told myself. My boss didn't need to arrange transport for my trip to Manchester; he was within his rights to demand I made my own way to head office.

Not even a week had elapsed since my last visit. I didn't think there was a 'three strikes and you're out' rule, but twice in less than a week was pushing my luck.

At least this time the driver wasn't James Bond; this one thought he was Sherlock Holmes.

'Alright, mate.' He had said, in his harsh Mancunian sounds – sounds that seemed out of place coming from within the smart grey suit. But that was just my prejudice. I had, after all, once seen a chap wearing a suit on Coronation Street, the long running Manchester based soap. Granted, he had been in court for assault, but a suit's a suit. In any case the character was Irish and that's my homeland, so I silently reprimanded myself for stereotyping and waited to hear what Chauffeur Sherlock made of my situation.

'You up for a disciplinary meeting, then?' he asked grinning in the mirror.

'Of all the purposes I could have coming up here,' I began, haughtily, 'why would you think I'm in line for a bollocking?' So, it was obvious then, I conceded.

'You're in uniform, but no flight case, so you're not flying and you're not training. It must be a bollocking. Am I right, mate?'

'I have a meeting, that's all.'

'It's a long way to go for a one-hour meeting, mate.'

There was probably no point being evasive, what did it matter if he knew? More importantly, how did he know it was only a one-hour meeting?

'Are you driving me back?' I asked.

'Yeah, you can tell me all about it later, our kid.'

Brilliant.

The day after my night in Rome had been business as usual in the sky, as though the previous day's walk-out might never have happened. French ATC behaved as though they had been at work all the time, and spoke to the hugely inconvenienced flight crews with the kind of breezy nonchalance that comes from unswerving belief in one's own cause.

When I'd logged into The System back at base, a red message symbol had flashed up advertising the email that cordially invited me for the meeting.

Kelly had been outraged that I was being 'victimised'

for looking after my passengers and taking the heat off the cabin crew. She had called the management 'mindless fools', and I had been warmed by her support.

When I'd spoken to my wife later that day she had taken a different view: I had broken the rules and the law, and I had only myself to blame. And it was the cabin crew's job to deal with angry passengers – that's what they get paid for, she had said. Not true, I insisted, they get paid to save lives, not take abuse. But it was pointless arguing.

She was right about me, though, and I agreed with her verdict, even if her sentiments were alien. They were the sentiments of someone who has never worked as airline crew.

There was plenty of time in the taxi to reflect on my life so far. I hadn't exactly plundered the sexual resources of our small planet during my bachelor years, but I'd done enough to deplete my testosterone cartridges. And I had done so in the hope that when I finally met my future wife I would have no reason to reload for a fresh rampage. It had worked, too. I'd been happily married for nine years and a proud father for seven. At no time during the eleven years we have been together had I felt any urge to be unfaithful. Sure, I didn't look at Tabitha with the same frenzied face of lust that had fired our early years, but I was still attracted to her.

If my wife's aggressive moods were due to the menopause, how many years would it go on for, or was it only months? I had never thought about it before. Or perhaps it was simply our forced separation taking its toll on the marriage. I'd never thought about that, either. Whatever the reason for this sudden sticky patch, I tried to assess whether I really could have my cake and eat it. And if enjoying the company of a loving family really was incompatible with my commuting lifestyle, should I consider a change of career?

God! Could I really give this up? The vocation I had longed for since childhood, the job I had worked at, gambled on and depended on for so long. What would I do instead? We'd have to sell the house, that's for sure. No way could I land another job on this kind of salary. Perhaps we should just move to Gatwick, but that would probably be Tabitha's least preferred option – and mine. I was beginning to fret, and it hadn't gone unnoticed by Sherlock.

'That bad is it, mate?' he asked.

'Uh?' It took me a moment to catch his meaning. 'Oh, no just thinking about non-work related things.' In other words – mate – mind your own business.

'Women.' He said with no questioning intonation.

Close, I thought: one woman and one girl!

'No, just family,' I said. 'Sorry, I just have to make a phone call.'

'Yeah, alright, mate.'

My lie had worked, but now I needed to find someone to talk to. I flicked through the phone's address book looking for inspiration, scrolling down the screen with little flicks of my thumb. Everyone would be at work, D Dad (dead), Dave, Drew ... E Ed ... F Fiona, Francis ... G

… H Helen … no one in I. J Jenny, Julie – Ah Julie, an old friend from my missionary days. We'd had dinner together the other night after bumping into each other in the car park at work. Julie had known me longer than anyone, but I wasn't sure if it was appropriate to call her. We had enjoyed a great evening, but that's all. Calling her could raise suspicions that I wanted something more – for old time's sake – especially if I mentioned marital problems. No, I didn't want to go there right now.

K Katy, Kelvin … Kelvin! I'd reinstated Kelly to my contacts after the other night. The driver glanced in the mirror. I had to make a decision quickly before he realised I was just making excuses to shut him up. The phone began to dial.

'Hi, it's me,' I said in a whisper as though I was about to divulge a secret.

'Hey, John, how are you?' Her light tone suggested she was just wrapping her legs beneath herself on the sofa and settling down for a cosy chat.

'I've just perked up. What are you doing today?'

'Coffee and cake at the moment, Alicante this afternoon.'

I heard a faint slurp before she continued.

'Fingers and toes crossed for you, sweety. Just take the telling-off and get yourself back to Gatwick.'

'Thanks, Kelly, I'll be back for tea. What time's your Alicante?'

'Two, back for eight. But then Joachim is supposed to be calling, so I'll have to stay in.'

I'd completely forgotten about her Portuguese boyfriend over the last few days. Kelly didn't know when he would be back from his latest business trip to Lisbon, and I didn't know what would happen when he did come back. But it was clear to me that Kelly was far from committed to their relationship.

'I'm going out in Crawley tonight to drown my sorrows,' I said, changing the subject. 'I'm going with a new guy from the B&B. He's a bit weird so I'm not sure what kind of night I'm in for. As long as it involves lots of alcohol I don't mind too much.'

'Stay safe, sweety, it can get pretty rough in Crawley later in the evenings – and watch out for the women; don't go chatting anyone up!' She let out a little laugh, but I knew she was serious. If I was going to cheat on my wife, then it had to be with Kelly.

'No chance, Kelly, I won't be in any fit state to chat to anyone. I've been taken off flying tomorrow pending the outcome of today's meeting. I fully intend tomorrow to be hangover day.'

'I'll dig out my nurse's outfit and come round to administer some special hangover medicine, if you like,' she said softly as though someone might overhear.

'I hope your nurse's outfit is more appealing than your air hostess outfit; turquoise and purple could make my intended condition much worse.'

The airline's colour scheme had been designed to shock; a brash little kid snapping at the heels of traditional conservative airlines. The cabin crew uniform certainly could take your breath away.

'My nurse's uniform is from a different supplier,' she said. 'Don't worry about the colour of the material – there isn't much of it.'

Oh, my word.

There was no way Kelly could visit the B&B whatever she chose to wear. Mrs Butler, my landlady, was a worse gossip than any airline crew. The chance of Tabitha finding out was off the scale; she'd probably know everything before Kelly had even pulled up outside.

I told Kelly that the uniform would have to wait, and I suggested she could save it for Joachim. Her reply was a revelation. Joachim hated sexy clothing, had a low sex drive and rarely made love to her. She thought at first it was his age – another revelation, he was a year older than me – but I stressed to her that I could still sustain a full blown symphony on my old Irish horn, so age was irrelevant. She giggled at this, and asked if I performed regularly, or just polished it. Sometimes she left me lost for words.

After the call I dug a squashed sandwich from my jacket pocket and began to peel away the cellophane. Looking ahead through the windscreen I could see the sky starting to cloud over, becoming murkier. I guessed we were getting close to our destination.

Sherlock chirped up again. 'This meeting,' he said, releasing his casual grip on the steering wheel to make quote marks with his fingers, 'has it got anything to do with the hostie you're seeing?'

His impertinence was staggering, but I put it down

to the friendly familiarity of Northerners and tried not to take offence.

'Excuse me?' I said, wondering if a sleuth-like explanation would follow.

'Low voice, coy grins.' Can only be a woman. 'If she's going to Alicante then it probably means she's crew.' He paused, as though weighing up his next piece of deductive reasoning.

'She could be a pilot, I suppose,' he said, 'but then I'm going with law of averages on that one.'

The cabby grinned in the rear view mirror, waiting for my response, no doubt.

'She's just a friend,' I said. 'Men can have female friends without being sexually involved.'

'Yeah, yeah, true,' he said. 'But then there's the nurse's uniform, of course …' The driver finished with a wink and a flash of his teeth. I was almost disappointed he didn't say 'Elementary!'

'No, I'm afraid it isn't anything that salacious,' I said, with little conviction, and looked out of the side window to indicate an end to the interrogation.

My meeting with the Chief Pilot ended after just a few minutes. There was no discussion, no chance to explain, just a straightforward written warning to follow the verbal warning from last Friday, and suspension from flying for the rest of the week. One more incident and I could be fired. It *was* three strikes and you're out, after all. The only blessing that might come from this disagreeable episode was that being fired would solve my indecision; I could move back to Exeter and re-join my family full time.

Seven hours in a taxi for a minute's meeting. Couldn't he have picked the bloody phone up and called me? Oh no, HR this and HR that, or whatever it's called these days – The Department of People? They couldn't run a bath never mind a business.

The taxi ride home was largely a silent affair. I decided to tell Chauffeur Sherlock why I'd been dragged up for the meeting, but he lost interest almost before I'd finished speaking.

I texted the outcome to Kelly, and she'd told me I was still her favourite captain. That was nice. Next stop, Crawley, and a night with the strangest chap I'd met in a long time. Rivers Andersson, why have you come into my life?

Chapter 7

In for a penny …

If I'd had children in my early twenties, would I now be discovering the nostalgia of my youth by reclaiming a pub-going independence lost to all responsible fathers of young children? Would I, for instance, be capable of drinking more than two pints of gassy beer without complaining of being bloated and calling for a whiskey? Would I be telling a close stranger that I'm on the verge of cheating on my wife?

But that's the thing; I'm not *going* to cheat! Kelly is a lovely girl, and if I were single then there would be no holding me back. For sure. What's the difference, though? I'd gone too far already: thinking about it, longing for it, fantasising about it – getting bloody stiff for it! Twice! Would it be hypocritical to resist after all these impure emotions? Isn't it just as bad as actually doing it? Perhaps, but I'll never find out *(Because you're not going to screw her, you sad old fool).*

Rivers and I were slanted against the bar in a crummy place close to Crawley town centre. It was only Thursday but already the streets were filled with scantily clad girls and raucous boys. I hadn't noticed the name of the bar as we walked in, just the look we drew from the doorman. *What? Are we too old, too smart? Jeans not hanging far enough down our legs?* Call me old fashioned, but my undies are for the sole viewing pleasure of Mrs Reilly (not that she considers picking them out of the laundry as pleasurable).

My scrutiny of the other patrons in this seedy place was fleeting and edgy. It seemed the kind of dump where eye contact with the wrong person could be fatal. Girls wobbling on pinprick heels, guys mouthing off – they reminded me of Alicante passengers, which in turn reminded me of Kelly. She'd be on the phone to her boyfriend, no doubt. I wondered how that conversation was going, then remembered I was supposed to be having a conversation of my own right now.

'Sorry, Rivers, was just struggling with wakefulness,' I said.

'You wanna take something for it, dude?' he asked, not even glancing around or lowering his voice.

'I thought you said you didn't do drugs.' I glanced around for both of us.

'Ain't no drugs, dude. You wanna coffee?' He gave me a stare. I wasn't sure how to interpret it, but it looked like the stare of a man on drugs.

'Oh, I see, no thanks, I'll get my second wind soon.'

'No worries. So, tell me about this hottie,' he asked grinning.

'She's a smart, attractive, mature girl–'

'You mean she's young, right?'

'Okay, yes, twenty-three, not that young, but she has old shoulders – she wouldn't fit here in this bar, I tell you.' I thought for a moment how much I'd love to be in a nice quiet country pub with her instead of this abattoir.

'But yo' married, dude, you can't jingle the jangle, man.'

'What?' I expelled a large puff of air from my chest alongside the word. Sometimes I had no idea what Rivers was talking about, or where he'd learnt his English.

'You can't go around loosin' off your jangling thing and lettin' it jingle with the vajangle, dude.'

I got the message, but the effort needed to decipher it had given me a headache.

'Rivers, where are you from exactly?' I changed subject, partly to avoid further words of wisdom from a mental patient, but mostly to get to the bottom of his displaced personality.

'Yurtaburg, man.' He pronounced the 't' with the soft d-like quality used by Americans.

'Where the hell is that?'

'You say Gothenburg, but to us it's Göteborg.' I listened to his American mish-mash turn into melodious Swedish for the first time, and he seemed a different person instantly, a person I immediately felt more at ease with. It didn't last long.

'Yurtaburg is how they try to say it in the US, man,

but that's cool.'

'You seem more Yank then Swede, I guess you spent a bit of time there.' I was guilty of stating the obvious, but I wanted to lead him into telling me his story – it was better than telling mine.

'Yeah, I went over on exchange with the Air Force back in the mid-nineties. Flew the F-16, dude, one hell of a bitch; stayed there after parting with the mil, and got my commercial license. Flew buckets of shit round the regions, then came back to Europe and joined this lot.'

'You flew, what, for farmers or something?' I asked, joking.

'What, dude?'

'Was it fertilizer you were carrying in the buckets?' I was struggling to keep a straight face, but Rivers was buying it.

'You dumb ass, the planes were shit, man: ATRs and other piss-ass twin turbo props.'

His insult to me didn't carry any intent; it seemed more like a Tourette's type burst of words rather than an attempt to offend. I really didn't think Rivers realised what he was saying half the time.

'Oh, I get you,' I said, 'twenty thousand rivets flying in loose formation. Been there, mate.'

'Right!' he said, looking doubtful. 'Bet you ain't lost all your electrics at fifteen thousand feet over New York – post nine-eleven – and had to use your cell phone to talk to the F-16s who were gonna shoot your ass down.'

'No, but I had a rocket propelled grenade blow a hole

in my tail whilst flying in Angola.'

'Shit, man, well, have you ever flown into a thunderstorm and had your windscreen knocked out by hailstones the size of baseballs, then had to fly blind as the hailstones blasted around the cockpit?'

'No, Rivers, and neither have you!' This was getting a bit childish now.

'Fuck you, dude. Check this out!' He dug out a tatty brown wallet from his back pocket and rummaged inside. Moments later he thrust a photo in my face of a badly beaten cockpit minus its windscreen. The jagged shards of glass still clinging to the window frame made the front end of the plane look like the gaping jaws of a white shark. Staring through this deathly hole was the blanched face of a clean-shaven young first officer. Despite the groomed appearance, the blank look belonged unmistakably to Rivers.

'Shittin' chicken! What the hell were you doing in a bloody thunderstorm in the first place?'

'Squall, man, unbroken line of storms stretching from Kansas down to Arkansas. We were flying St Louis to Oklahoma, thought we'd spotted a gap in the middle. Turned out to be wrong, man. Captain was hit on the head, clean out for most of it.'

'What did you do? I mean, how did you get out of it?' I asked, horror contorting my face.

'Had my head in the captain's lap, squinting up at the instruments to keep control. Tried to execute a straight one-eighty to get out, but ended up in a spiral dive. Didn't know which way I was spinning until I booted the rudder pedal. That made it worse so tried the other. Lost five thousand feet just working out which way I was spinning.'

I was desperately trying to think of some comparable story from my own experience to compete with Rivers, but his tale was too compelling for me to think straight.

'When we were out of it,' he continued, 'I put on my oxygen mask – it was only fifteen thousand feet, but the O2 was way more drinkable than the ice water coming through the smashed windscreen.' Rivers gulped a quarter of his pint in one go, then belched noisily. 'So, big shot, what have *you* got?'

I plundered my memory for something equal.

'Flying two hundred miles with an AK47 held against my head?' My voice rose at the end of the sentence like I was asking for approval.

'Get your shit outta here,' ordered Rivers. 'Where were you flying, Ibiza?'

'In Angola, some local militia commander felt I needed persuading to take his raiding party to the intended scene of their atrocity. At the time I would have preferred money, but looking back, I'm glad I can say I was coerced.'

'So what were you doing – missionary shit?' asked Rivers with his usual vocabulary. Seriously, if he were to spit the words out with more urgency I would be convinced it was Tourette's.

'Yeah, two years ferrying medicine and missionaries around Africa. Best way to build hours – twin time, no cost, no expenses – led directly to my next job in aviation, but the less said about that the better!'

'And here we are, after all our adventures, flying bums to Spain in planes that work: autopilots, weather radar, TCAS, all the shit that takes the fun outta flying, man.'

'All the things that make flying safe, Rivers,' I corrected. 'We're here to carry fare-paying passengers to their destination in safety. We're not here to have fun – the company sees to that.'

'Fuck the company; more beer needed, Captain Dude.'

I was beginning to get my second wind now; it kicked in whilst we were having a discussion about which cabin crew we'd screw if we were much younger, single and if they'd have us. Rivers had flown only once in Gatwick, but already he'd made a mental list of girls who were destined to turn him down.

We were still at the bar, but now the growing clientele had forced us upright from our earlier slouch. It was getting more and more difficult to speak so we decided to move on, which is when the inevitable happened.

Rivers, slower than the clambering crowd expected, began to push away from the bar as two blokes tried to rush in and fill the narrow space he'd almost left. 'Come on, Catweazel, get out of the way', one of them said. 'Fuck you, dumb ass', was Rivers's spontaneous reply, and this time I think it *was* meant as an insult.

One of the blokes grabbed Rivers's collar and wrenched him away from the bar. Rivers tumbled to the floor and the other bloke looked as though he was about to move in on him. Instinctively, I stepped across and put my hand against the man's chest. He didn't appreciate that. He raised his arm above and behind his head, then hammered it down towards me.

A few minutes later the four of us were standing outside. The bouncers had seen everything, and had allowed me to leave by my own effort, even though I'd done most of the fighting. My attacker had been dragged out and dumped on the pavement outside. They hadn't even called an ambulance for him. I crouched down at the man now sitting on the cold tarmac and checked him over.

'Broken nose, and at least one rib,' I said. 'I'll call an ambulance for you, but then you're on your own.' It was the least I could do after causing the injuries, but I wasn't sticking around for the police; any kind of criminal record would put an end to my career.

'Cheers, mate,' said the other man. 'We didn't want any trouble, he just don't think when someone challenges him. Hope your mate's alright.'

Rivers held up an arm and nodded, but said nothing. Moments later we fled the scene and turned the corner.

'Shit, dude, where did all that come from?' gushed Rivers, 'You totally owned his ass, man.'

'If you mean I bettered him in the altercation then, yes, I suppose I did.' And, as Rivers took his turn at not understanding something, I exploded with laughter.

I've spent years suppressing my Irish working class upbringing. Boys from Cork would fight with someone just because he lived in a different street. He didn't need to throw insults at you or kiss your sister, you just fought because you had contrived a difference sufficient to justify the violence.

When I was twelve I won a scholarship to attend a private school. The six years that followed dragged me away from the feral streets of Cork's Northside. They took the edges off my Irish accent and persuaded me that a bright future was mine for the taking; it just wouldn't be in Cork. But however you may try, your formative years are the ones that mould your inner character; the one that lies beneath whatever you dress yourself in during later years; the one you fall back on when under stress.

And then there was the Army. Okay, I was in the Royal Signals, not charging around a battlefield killing people, but training is training, and we all did it.

'Shit, I need a beer,' I managed at last.

'Across the street, look,' said Rivers, showing the way.

There were no doormen at this pub, and the clientele seemed more refined. Gone were the lairy lads trying to impress the totty. The totty was gone, too, replaced by smart young things in clothing that fitted and covered. Best of all, it was quiet enough to hold a conversation without feeling like you were too old for all this.

'Hot shit, buddy,' breathed Rivers, passing me a cold beer. 'That's what I call a smorgasbord worth eating.'

I followed his blank gaze wondering what he was comparing with a Swedish buffet.

'Oh, yes, that's more like it,' I agreed, spotting the table of exquisite thirty-somethings.

'Easy, dude, you already have a wife and a mistress,

don't get greedy.'

'I have a wife, Rivers, that's all.'

'Let's go, Captain Dude.'

He was half way to their table before I even thought about grabbing his arm, so I chose to watch his attempts at bonding from the safety of the bar. What was the point in following him over, only to come straight back again when they took immediate offence to his unique patois of unde-cipherable slang and obsessive swearing? A few minutes went by, then a few more. The women were smiling and laughing. One of them pulled out a chair, and Rivers sat down. *Bollocks!* If I didn't go over they'd think there was something wrong with me. But I didn't want to go over. Then again, they'd soon beckon me over if I waited where I was, and I'd look completely juvenile. Bollocks again.

I grabbed my beer, took a deep breath and walked to their table. There was no spare chair so I just stood beside Rivers, smiling.

Come on, think of something! 'I hope my friend isn't bothering you,' I said. 'He was released only yesterday … Ha, you only turn your back for two seconds and he's gone. Ha ha …' *Oh, bloody hell, what was I saying?*

'Sorry, girls,' said Rivers. 'This is John, he's married so he's forgotten how to talk to women.' He sounded almost normal; no strange words, no dudes or mans, and his accent was distinctly Swedish now.

'Hi, John, I'm Amanda,' said a well-spoken blonde lady dressed in a business suit. 'This is Louise, Kate and Rachel.'

'Hello, everyone, sorry, I'm just with …' *Oh don't say*

friend '... him,' I spluttered, putting a hand on Rivers's shoulder.

'There's a chair over there, why don't you bring it over and join us?' said Amanda.

I was determined not to start jumping to attention again just because some woman was issuing instructions, so I simply said, 'It's okay, I don't mind standing.' Which was nonsense, obviously, but what else could I do?

'It's up to you, but it does look a bit odd,' said Amanda.

Right, I'll just do as I'm told, then! 'Well, if you don't mind,' I said. 'I don't want to impose on your evening.' And off I trundled to fetch the chair.

I was on my second whiskey, drinking and chatting easily. Rivers had dropped in the bit about being pilots but, to be fair, it had been the truthful answer to a direct question and not an attempt to impress. Though whether the women would have been impressed if they knew how perfunctory and mundane the job was remained to be seen. Being an airline pilot nowadays is as dull as being an accountant, but without the obsession with cutting costs and screwing up the lives of those trying to earn a living.

Amanda had a sparkling wit and a low-cut top, and I'd spent most of the last hour immersed in conversation with her to the point where I was struggling to remember what the other women looked like. It was hard enough remembering what Amanda looked like.

I'd explained to Amanda that I was married and just out for a few beers, nothing more. It had worked; she relaxed and opened up her mind to some deep talk about African politics. It was refreshing to meet someone who believed that overthrowing a government was more about seizing power than liberating an oppressed people. Africa was littered with examples, past and present, from the Nile to the Cape of Good Hope. She had also opened up her blouse; something I thought physics would have taken care of judging by how much the buttons strained against her bosom. It had been a subtle move, hardly breaking her verbal stride. Her hand simply slipped up the seam joining the two halves of her flowery top and deftly separated the top button from its hole. Had she not been talking about brutish African dictators at the time, I could have easily misinterpreted her move. Amanda's convivial personality was drawing me closer; each word was like another tug on the rope, her heels digging in with every breath.

By the time I realised that Rivers was jabbing his bony knuckles into my thigh, the pain in my leg had severed the rope between Amanda and me.

'Ouch! What's the matter?' I asked, rubbing the tender spot he had created.

'We're going for a curry, you coming?' asked Rivers, looking first at me and then at Amanda.

I expected Amanda to go with her friends, after all they were on a night out together, so I was surprised when she looked at me and said nothing. Neither Rivers nor I had eaten that evening; my last meal had been a crew dinner on the way back from Rome the previous day, and Rivers's lanky body looked as though it hadn't seen a meal for a month. But going for a curry seemed like a bad omen. It was turning into the perfect night out for a pair of lads: beer, fight, curry, sex. It was the fear of reaching the conclusion to this boys' itinerary that delayed my decision. Amanda was still quiet, and still looking at me. Bollocks.

'Sure, let's stick together,' I said finally, 'I'm starving.'

Amanda smiled briefly, lips together, and reached for her bag.

Outside the pub Rivers sidled up to me and nudged my arm. 'Dude, you're one dumb ass babe magnet!' he said, incoherence instantly returning.

'Explain.'

'She totally wants your jangle, man, and you just blew it!' His second attempt at advanced linguistics was much clearer – given that I already knew what a jangle was.

'But I'm not interested in her, what was it, vajingle?'

'Vajangle, man,' he corrected. 'Yeah, I forgot, you got two already!'

'Rivers, I told her I was married, I spoke about my wife, my children, our home two hundred miles away – she doesn't want my jangle.' My reasoning was sound to me, though not to Rivers.

'Dude, she don't want marriage, she just wants a rumble in the jungle with a dumb ass fuck who lives two hundred miles away. Simple, no bondage, man.'

'Oh, now, wait, I'm not into all that nonsense,' I said, hoping that bondage in Rivers-speak might mean something else.

'No commitment, man, no getting tied down.' I felt I

was getting good at understanding his special language, so I had a go.

'Yes, dude, there'll be no rumble in the jungle with the jingle and a jangle.'

Rivers stared at me for a full five seconds. I would have sworn that he'd just looked deep into the eyes of Medusa and her slithering locks of death, such was the expression on his frozen face. But eventually he roused himself for a response.

'Are you taking the piss?'

'Understood. I'll stick to English,' I said, moments before one of the women turned and shouted back at us.

'What are you two whispering about? I hope you're not ogling our bums from back there!'

'I'm really trying hard not to, Rachel, really I am,' said Rivers back into Swedish-mode. 'But I'm like a rabbit caught in headlights.'

I felt like throwing up, but merely shook my head and apologised for his behaviour.

I've never really understood the attraction to bottoms, not when you think what their primary function is. Okay, some can look attractive as part of the full package, and if indeed they themselves are packaged appropriately, but what are you going to do with one? Just think about how close you are to something very unpleasant. I mean, the amount of bleach I bathed the hall floor with last week after Woofy's deposit was enough to kill even the 1% of germs that bleach can't kill. But I still wouldn't lick the floor where his radioactive crap had been.

I was feeling queasy now. Back in the pub I'd drunk five pints of Kronenburg and two whiskies on an empty stomach – a stomach that was already knotted up by the prospect of an indecent proposal from Amanda.

In the Indian restaurant I added three more whiskeys, and now someone had ordered Flaming Sambucas to wash down the curry. Mercifully I had my third wind by then, because I needed to guzzle a whole bottle of beer after burning my tongue on the fiery cocktail.

The waiters busied themselves around our table trying to clear the dishes in between our rounds of stupidity. One of the girls, not Amanda or Rachel (I knew who they were now) slipped from her chair as she stretched over to slap Rivers. He'd just made an indecent joke about his former girlfriend – something to do with insisting on buying long necked beer bottles instead of dumpies. The woman (Louise?) had made the mistake of asking why, and it had been Rivers's salacious reply that earned him the playful slap – followed by the sight of Louise on her back with her legs in the air.

The head waiter, a parody of a British sergeant major overseeing a parade, glared towards our group as though he was about to suspend our rations. But he was too late; we were finished with food, all we needed was the bill. It arrived before I'd finished mouthing the word across the restaurant.

'Club or casino?' asked Rivers, tossing his credit card on top of mine.

'Bed,' said Rachel with finality, though I wasn't sure

if this was an invitation to Rivers.

'Me too,' chorused Louise and Kate, and again I wasn't sure how Rivers ought to interpret this.

'Cool,' drooled Rivers, which made it clear how *he* interpreted things.

'Louise and Kate are staying at mine tonight,' said Rachel. 'You can jump in our cab if you like.' She looked only at Rivers and he reacted as though she'd cracked a whip.

'See you later, dude, don't wait up!'

I wasn't convinced they were all reading the same book, but that was far from my problem.

'So,' began Amanda, 'that just leaves us two. Come on, this way.'

What is it about me? Why do women insist on telling me what to do in such an irresistible manner? I had no intention of going off with Amanda, but my brain was stuck in mud and my legs were out of control. She bundled me into a cab (at least that's how it felt) and gave the driver an address.

We arrived outside a large house on a modern estate on the outskirts of Crawley. It was the kind of house a family would live in rather than, say, a single woman with no husband lurking upstairs. Or parents. My discomfort grew. She carefully turned the key in the door and held her finger to her lips 'Shhh,' she mouthed.

I hadn't noticed the light on in the front room when we approached the house, but now I could see the glow spilling into the hallway, and the faint sound of voices drifting from the same place. I hesitated, expecting to see some guy in a gimp mask appear at the door, 'Who've you got for us, mistress?' he might say. Or perhaps they were just ordinary swingers, if there were such things. To be fair, anything would seem ordinary compared to a fat bloke in tight leather pants and a gimp mask, struggling to restrain a stud-collared bulldog on a link chain leash. My imagination was guilty of developing a scene wholly incongruous with this sophisticated lady who had, so far, been an absolute joy to be with. But then again, it's always the ones you don't suspect.

'Wait here,' she whispered, and disappeared into the sitting room.

Oh, God! I turned round and looked at the front door, now closed, locked and latched. *Run! Where are your survival instincts?* Even if I did run, it would take too long to open the door; the gimp or his dog would be on me before my panicking fingers could remove the security latch. Amanda reappeared at the doorway and beckoned me in. Oh, shit!

I cringed as I entered the room, body tensed ready for some kind of assault. But the only other person in the room with Amanda was a young girl of perhaps sixteen, sitting on the sofa smiling sweetly. She raised a hand and said 'Hi.' There was no leather in sight except the sofa, and the only animal present was a friendly cat, which wasted no time in wrapping itself around my trembling leg.

'John, this is Vanessa,' said Amanda, and then turning to Vanessa, 'John's a pilot.'

'Ooh, did you bring your uniform?' she asked.

Oh, my. Things *had* turned around. Fear to fantasy in the time it took to say dodgy website.

'Vanessa's my baby-sitter, sorry I didn't mention I had children, hope you're not put off,' Amanda said, with that short smile again.

'No, of course not', I said, but I was concerned about where all this was leading. *Put off what?*

'It's okay,' she continued. 'My husband's in the Royal Navy, won't be back for months, and Vanessa is very discreet.'

That was clear then. Bollocks.

Chapter 8

Strictly a one woman guy

The sign for Middle Wallop hadn't cheered me up. I wasn't sure what could. The traffic had thinned, the car was pointing west, and I was heading home. Even the wobbly passage of an Army Air Corps training plane couldn't rouse any mirth.

Sure, the hangover didn't help. My cells were a battle-ground for a flood of lager, countless whiskeys, and a forgettable quantity of Sambuca, all engaged in mortal combat with a thick Indian curry. Earlier, I sensed the battle had even spilled over into the toilet bowl judging by the angry fizz of the water. But that could have been the bleach.

It wasn't a feeling of shame and guilt that was affecting my mood. It was embarrassment. Let's be clear, I'd had no intention of sleeping with Amanda. I was drunk – no excuse, I accept – and I was strongly seduced by a charming, witty, and large breasted woman. She clearly had every intention of sleeping with me and, it turned out, made a habit of this kind of thing. She was a professional (not in the sense that it cost me money) and I was an amateur – an amateur who hadn't had any activity for quite a while.

But despite this lack of recent sexual experience, I had been unable to field a full side. One indispensable member of the team had called in sick, its head hanging in shame, stubbornly refusing to take part. 'That's okay' Amanda had said in an understanding way, though that short smile of hers suggested otherwise. Moments later the rest of the team deserted, and I fell asleep leaving a sexually charged woman clinging to my disappointing, limp carcass.

I passed Stonehenge on my right hand side. A group of tourists spread around the eastern perimeter. They held cameras to their faces and leant across the rope that prevented pagan worshipers (or whatever) from getting close to the megalithic structure. I had almost as good a view from the road, and I was £10 better off. How ironic, I thought: a collection of solid, phallic-like stones sitting up proudly on Salisbury Plain. And this time, I did manage a slight smile. Thinking more philosophically about my mood, I realised that embarrassment was immeasurably better than guilt.

The forced weekly separation from my wife and the tiredness I experienced at the end of the working week, not to mention her own cyclical moods, meant it had been several weeks since we last had sex. Compounding my pent up frustration was Kelly, a sexually tantalising young woman of stunning beauty, and a young woman who'd nearly had me popping my cork with the simplest of gestures. Twice!

Now, heavily weighed down by overflowing urges, Amanda had led me to the brink of infidelity, and only my alcohol soaked body had saved me. Yes, embarrassment was definitely preferable to guilt.

I pulled up in front of our home and quickly spotted Woofy's resentful face at the window. *Surprise!*

I was a day early owing to my brief suspension from flying and I wanted to surprise the children, so I hadn't called ahead with the good news (not that Woofy would have answered the phone). I knew my family was home this weekend because Tabitha had mentioned something about a Polish landscaper who was going to be there rearranging the garden. His van, still on a Polish registration plate, was on my side of the drive.

As soon as I opened my car door I could hear yelling. Tabitha sounded hysterical. The air crackled with her profanities and I winced at the thought of my neighbours hearing it. She repeated herself several times, slower and louder with each attempt. I guessed she was arguing with the landscaper.

Woofy barked twice as I walked through the door. He stood in the hallway as though he were considering whether to let me in. His bolshiness trailed off into a low growl then he skulked into the kitchen. I could stay, he'd decided. Both children sat silently on the sofa, eyes locked

243

in by an invisible force emanating from the television set. Neither spoke. I made my way out to the back just as Tabitha came storming in.

'Christ!' She blurted. It was an unusual greeting, and it didn't improve. 'What are you doing home?'

'Long story. How are you? It's great to be home again.' I was trying to be happy and positive, though my abused body was putting up strong resistance.

'Well save it, I haven't got time for long stories,' she snapped, but that was good, I didn't want to get into any long stories right now.

'Will you go and sort out the gardener; he's excavated my entire flower bed! I told him the sand pit was going against the back fence. His English is appalling!'

'Didn't you draw him a diagram–'

'Oh, I knew it would be my fault,' she was close to tears.

'Sorry, of course it isn't, I'm just trying to find out if we have any legal come-back on this.'

'Legal come-back?' She formed the words with exaggerated mouth movements. 'Legal come-back? He's from Poland!'

'They have legal – er – things there, too,' I said, feeling tongue-tied.

'John, he isn't insured, and you'll probably find he's not even registered with the Home Office!'

'Okay, I'll go and speak to him, but if he doesn't understand you, then he won't understand me.'

'You speak Russian!' Tabitha said, as though I was overlooking something so obvious.

'Does he?'

'I don't know, but you told me that they were all the same over there. Go and have a go!' She was raging. If I could sort this mess out for her then I would be in favour and in flavour. My needs would be met that night, guaranteed.

My language skills were rudimentary at best. I had learned basic Russian whilst working for the military, and that limited skill had secured me the job I endured prior to joining the airline world. The time I spent working for Viktor Voblikov was one of those experiences that makes a person wonder why unforgettable experiences are often the ones you really want to forget. But if you think more deeply about it, you realise that it's your brain's way of making sure you don't make the same mistake twice. After all, there's no such thing as a bad experience unless you repeat it.

Following the slow and loud conversation with 'Call-me-Chaz' (which I'd guessed was short for something much longer with no additional vowels), it became disappointingly clear that I would be excluded from Tabitha's inner circle later on. There *was* a diagram, and it clearly showed the sandpit against the side fence where the flower bed was (though it didn't specifically state 'flower bed' on the diagram). I would need to get to the bottom of the error (I didn't say 'her' error, and wouldn't be doing so later). She had probably changed her mind, or perhaps forgotten what she'd drawn and then imagined the sandpit elsewhere. I really didn't know, but Chaz was unlikely to rebuild the flower bed for nothing.

And then I had my Eureka moment; nothing inspires cunning like desperation. I would blame it all on Chaz, tell my wife he would make her flower bed more beautiful and impressive than before, and pay the bugger myself. I'd be jingling and jangling all the way to the bedroom.

Should I have been surprised, then, when things didn't go quite as I hoped? The problem with cunning plans based on deceit (however well intentioned) is that fate has a way of scuppering them. Perhaps it's nature's way of discouraging immoral connivance, but then again nature has been known to be bloody selective in its moral governance of the people. Take any Twentieth Century dictator, for instance: where was fate's morality during the overthrowing-the-Government connivance before power, and clinging-on-to-Government connivance in power? All *I* wanted was a shag!

'All sorted, darling,' I said with a smile. Tabitha pulled her face into a quizzical expression.

'Sorted how?'

'He's going to put things back as they were, and do what you asked.' I was starting to spot holes in my own plan as I described it out loud.

'For free?' she asked doubtfully.

'Er, yeah, yeah.' I turned away and picked up a newspaper from the kitchen table. 'He said this was an important job to help get him established. I guess he wants a good reference from you.'

'He's snowed under with work; it's taken me weeks to get him around here. Why would he need a reference when he came well recommended to begin with?'

The questions were becoming difficult to field convincingly. Soon I'd be in as big a hole as the one Chaz had made where the prized flower bed used to be. Next I'd be buried in it.

'Well, you know, it's obviously his mistake–'

'Of course it's not his mistake!' she yelled.

Hang on, time out. I was getting confused now; she accepted that it was her fault so what was I supposed to sort out? Surely making a new flower bed was repairing the error – her error.

'Look, Tabitha, do you want the flower bed rebuilt or not, because I'm–'

'Don't have a go at me; you're not even supposed to be here today!' And with that curious accusation she left the room.

'Fuck this!' I muttered to the empty kitchen. If I weren't in such a fragile state after my night out, I would have gone straight back to Gatwick; at least I had a chance of a leg-over there, and at this stage I no longer cared who it was with. Instead I went upstairs, stepping quietly so not to attract her attention, and collapsed on the bed.

I couldn't sleep – far too much going on in my head – so I stared at the ripples in the Artex ceiling. We needed to sort things out between us, that was plain. She just wasn't making sense at the moment. Okay, I could accept that my flirtations with other women were unacceptable, but none of that could possibly have any influence on her behaviour – because she didn't know about it. The only conclusion I could draw was that my regular absence was wrenching us apart. I had negligible involvement with my family's daily routine, and Tabitha was forced to organise every aspect of our lives. I was just the guy who turned up for three days in every nine and got in the way. She'd had enough, and so had I.

A thud downstairs rattled the house, but I was too lethargic to jump up. It sounded like Tabitha slamming the front door, and this was confirmed when I heard three softer thuds and a car firing up. That didn't bode well. Boy, was she pissed off with me!

I wrestled my hand into my jeans pocket and wriggled my phone free. It was a risk, but I had to talk to someone.

'Hi, it's me.' I said when my call was answered.

'Hey, I'm so pleased you've called, I was worried.'

'Sorry, Kelly, I got really drunk last night and I have the mother and father of all hangovers.'

'It's fine, just glad you called. Where are you?'

'I'm at home, but I wish I were there.'

'So do I. It would be great to see you. I've split up with Joachim.'

I had no idea how I was supposed to react to that – either within myself or for Kelly's benefit. I knew one thing for sure: it was going to complicate the hell out of things now.

'Sorry to hear that, Kelly; what happened?'

'It's fine. He finally admitted what I'd suspected for ages: he's been seeing someone else, and now he's got a permanent job in Lisbon. It makes things simpler, though, doesn't it?'

Bollocks.

The aviation world is littered with broken marriages. Relationships are strained by forced separation, like mine; fathers are left feeling disconnected from their families, like me; and pilots are seduced by hot young hostesses. Almost like me. Airlines are where marriages go to die.

If I ended up with Kelly then I wouldn't be the first middle-aged captain to run off with a younger woman, and I wouldn't be the last. It wasn't Tabitha's fault; she was under pressure to manage the children, the house, our life, all without me for much of the time. I supposed she didn't really need me anymore, just the money I earned – and she didn't need me to get her hands on that. Perhaps we should just end it and start new lives. I could still see my children on my days off, Tabitha and I could remain on good terms, and we could enjoy normal relationships with people we lived close to – almost what we have now, in fact.

My salary and pension would be halved, which I would deserve, and my life split in two. But I'm used to that. I spend money on the B&B and on commuting, and I spend my time in opposite ends of the country from my home. Splitting up wouldn't seem much different to the life I was already leading. With one exception: I'd probably get some sex. Alternatively, I could quit my job.

The conversation with Kelly had lasted as long as my phone battery would allow. She had been in a cheerful mood and this perked me up. I rolled off the bed and straightened myself up in the mirror. As soon as my phone had re-charged I would pop into town and buy myself something that would make my life as a pilot complete: an iPad. All my colleagues had an iPad; they used them for watching movies during the cruise, or reading books and newspapers. I would use mine for something else. I would get myself an account with Skype and then do the same for my children. This technological marvel could help make longer periods of separation from my children tolerable. Granted, it wasn't the same as lifting my five-year old son up in my arms and giving him a hug, but that happened probably only once a week anyway.

I logged on to the family computer and opened up the Internet browser. Skype could wait a few moments. First I needed to find a classy restaurant near Gatwick and book a table for two.

For the first time in the twelve months I'd been making this trip, the sign for the M25 motorway didn't depress me. In fact, if I'm honest, it gave me a small bulge in the trouser department. Tonight I would have dinner with Kelly, and tonight I would stay sober. There would be *some* alcohol, of course, just to help delay the champagne moment; I wouldn't want to disappoint *this* woman.

Back at the B&B Rivers was again draped over the sofa like a slept-in bed. His eyes were closed and gentle snuffles emerged from his angular nose. One leg dangled over the edge, affording me a shocking view up his surfer shorts. He clutched an empty bottle of beer in his left hand but it was just after midday, so fair enough.

'Oi, dude,' I shouted, kicking his leg. He jerked his entire body like a man in the electric chair, and looked around the room through crusty eyes. It was the fastest I'd seen him move.

'Dude!' he managed when he finally recognised my presence. 'Fuck, what time is it, man?'

'Twelve-thirty. Having a siesta?'

'Fuck! I gotta report in thirty minutes.'

'Call in sick, Rivers, you can't fly if you've been drinking.'

'I ain't been drinking, buddy, I've been here all night. Slept-in.' He raised the beer bottle and peered through the green glass.

'Twelve-thirty, man, yeah, finished this baby ten hours ago. Gotta get changed, come with me, dude, need to talk.'

Rivers's room was an extension of his body: untidy, disorganised and pale. The white walls were enough to give anyone snow-blindness, and Rivers was quick to draw the curtains. It was difficult to tell where the bed was since all his clothing was spread out from wall to wall. No wonder he slept on the sofa. And watching him get dressed was like witnessing a break dance competition. I was beginning to like this guy. He was, if nothing else, entertaining.

'Dude, did you do it?' he asked while struggling with his uniform trousers.

'It? Or her?' I asked, just to see if we were on the same page.

'Bird with the boobs, man, bird with the boobs.'

'Oh, no, but we had a lovely evening.' This was not the time to reveal my shameful secret.

'She wants to see you again, dude.'

'How do you know, has she called here?'

'No, man, the three girls, you know, that I went with, one of them was here last night. They all wanna get together with us again.'

'You went with all three?' This was astonishing. Rivers was not a Premiership footballer, and being a pilot wasn't even close.

'Not at the same time, buddy. Notched up the last one yesterday.'

I wasn't sure whether to be disgusted or impressed, but I didn't want to fall out with him, so I tried the blokish response first.

'You rampant cad,' I said grinning.

'You talking in code again, dude?'

'That's rich coming from you!' I said,

'Here's the deal. All four girls are up for a bit of adventure – four girls, two guys, what d'ya say, buddy?'

It was a tempting offer, but no straight man should share a bed with his mate whilst he thrashes a girl with his light sabre. And after the view Rivers had just afforded me I really didn't want to see any more. Besides, I had plans tonight; one man, one woman, no audience.

'Love to, Rivers, but I'm seeing Kelly tonight. Anyway, didn't you tell me not to jangle my thingy or whatever?'

'Shit, man, this is different!' he said, thoroughly convinced by his own principles. 'Doing the hostie would be the beginning of an affair; the orgy is just an orgy – a bit of no strings fun.'

It was logic, but not as I knew it. Rivers's face rarely told any story, but now it had managed to mobilise some of its muscles into a look of expectation. Regrettably, my answer would fail to reward that effort.

'Sorry, mate, I really need to do this thing with Kelly, then we'll see.' We never would, but it gave him hope.

'I gotta go to work,' he announced. 'Shit, man! This ain't over.' And with that promise (which seemed more a threat) Rivers glided from the room as though he'd already taken off.

Crawley is not a name you would hear being put forward as an answer to the question 'Does anyone know a good place to go clothes shopping?' To be fair, I've never asked anyone that question, but for the sake of further unfairness, Crawley would not be the answer to *any* question that asked for recommended places – except, perhaps 'Where's a good place to get beaten up on a Saturday night?'

So it was with good fortune that I found myself in a smart shopping mall handing over cash for a pair of snazzy denim jeans – something called 'boot cut' – and one of those short sleeved shirts that didn't need tucking in. Best of all, neither piece of clothing required ironing. Next on my list was a pair of shoes from a shop where they didn't insist on measuring your feet before selling you some footwear. Finally, underpants with someone else's name on the outside: Calvin Klein.

I sat in Costa sipping the froth from the top of my Latte and found myself cruising the room with my gaze. I noticed every woman who entered, every woman who sat down, and every woman who was with a guy. The only woman with a man who looked old enough to be her father was, in fact, with her father.

I looked down at my bags and began to feel foolish. How would it look if Kelly were here now? Would others see a guy with his daughter? And then if we held hands, perhaps kissed, would they gossip?

The father laughed and joked with his girl as they shared a pastry with their coffees. He was about my age, though fifteen years ahead of me as a father. If he risked his marriage for a selfish affair, the affect on his grown-up daughter might be a feeling of disappointment rather than devastation. Not for the first time, I wondered if starting family life earlier would have made me more settled in middle-age. But it was too late now. There was something I needed to get out of my system; I had to understand if this flirtation with Kelly was just a wobble, or a sign that my marriage had run its course. In my mind there was only one way to find out. And I desperately needed to get laid.

Another girl entered the coffee shop. Wow, she was pretty – about Kelly's age but blonde with long slender legs and discreet breasts: the opposite of Kelly, but equally mesmerising. I couldn't help but watch as she threaded her way through the tables towards the standing figure of the dad with his girl. I wondered if he secretly fancied his daughter's friend. Then, whilst I was distracted by my own loathsome thoughts, the young girl did something I hadn't expected. She tilted her head back and kissed the man fully on the lips. With his hand holding hers, he introduced the blonde girl to his daughter. Oh, man! This was his girlfriend. You beauty!

I took a last gulp of my coffee and left the half-full glass behind. Gathering up the bags containing my future-self, I made my way back to the car and the Blue Mantle Hotel. It was 5.00 pm, two hours before my dinner date.

Chapter 9

Waiter, there's a fly in my ointment

I sat in the soft leather chair with my back to the restaurant and grinned to myself. I'd chosen well. It was going to cost me, but hopefully only money. It would have to be cash, of course, there was only the joint account and Tabitha took care of that. I filled it, she emptied it. Tonight I would do a fair bit of emptying myself, and that needed to be anonymous. A large bill from a swanky restaurant could mean only one thing because married men do not share culinary extravagance with other men.

The maître d' had greeted us quite courteously when we arrived; I knew he was a maître d' by the way he looked down his nose at me after examining Kelly with deliberate indiscretion. Yes, she's young enough to be my daughter but, actually, fuck off!

Someone arrived at the wave of a hand and took our jackets. A third person showed us to our table and asked our choice of aperitif. The table was tucked away because

I'd asked for that, but still I felt like we were being put in the naughty corner. Surely this was a popular place for bosses to bring their young secretaries. What was the big deal?

Kelly accepted the polished courtesy of these tightly suited waiters with the practised ease of someone accustomed to being courted and romanced in the finest (and most expensive) restaurants in Europe. But the multilingual, international lawyer boyfriend was history; now it was my turn.

My sensitivity to the maître d' was a confidence failing. I hadn't done anything like this before. The last time I dated a hot twenty-something I was one myself. Perhaps not that hot, but I was single at least. Kelly hadn't helped with my confidence either. She had pointed out the high performance German cars and other luxury marques decorating the small car park, and quipped that the only other time a Škoda had been here was when the local taxi firm dropped off passengers. She seemed embarrassed. I was surprised she didn't put on dark glasses and run for the door as though the paparazzi were waiting.

And now, as we shared a bottle of house red (which had pissed off the waiter, but was still costing me a fortune), I began to feel intoxicated by her beguiling beauty. Her lips were proud, their fullness emphasised by the rouge with which she had carefully painted them. And her skin, still uncreased by life's endeavours, was smooth and tanned like a Mediterranean girl's. She looked like she'd been airbrushed. But that was only half the story.

Had her dark eyes not been so hypnotic it would have

been impossible to avoid gawping at the tight cleavage that plunged beneath her pale blouse. It too was tanned, and the deep line it formed was clearly intended to lead the gaze somewhere it was happy to go without guidance. The only problem was that she held my attention continuously; she never looked away from me. How was I supposed to sneak a look at those golden globes? Even when the waiter arrived to annoy us she didn't break her tractor beam scrutiny; I was expected to deal with him. But I consoled myself in the certainty that this was the night I would take the irredeemable step which would make me a cheat. By sleeping with Kelly I would do the very thing I imagined I never would. I would be unfaithful to my wife and, in doing so, ridicule the vows I made on our wedding day nine years earlier. But at that moment I didn't care; I would get to see those siren-like boobs.

Kelly laid her hand on top of mine, which immediately brought me back into the conversation.

'John, you know I've really fallen for you, don't you?' she asked, looking erotically serious.

My only decision to make at this point was choosing to reply with glib immodesty or nervously serious. I played it safe. 'I was hoping so, because you've done a great job on me – I've never dated anyone else since I met my wife.' I leaned into the table and lowered my voice as I alluded to my imminent infidelity.

Kelly continued, 'And you know that I really want to make love to you.' She paused and looked down at the table. At last! I looked down, too, just for a second.

Her words drew a flush to my face, and that wasn't the only place blood flow was stimulated. But I was so eager to hear the next sentence that the movement in my trousers was instantly forgotten as soon as she started speaking again.

'I really do, John, I want to rip your shirt off and slide those stupid boot cut jeans down your legs right now.'

So, the jeans hadn't impressed her. I couldn't speak; my throat was drying as fast as spit on a stove. I was enthralled.

'I hope we can spend the night together, it would be so lovely to fall asleep with you.'

Hang on, back the car up. Wouldn't it be so lovely to shag like rampant animals first? Why were we moving on to the sleeping bit suddenly? Again she dropped her eyelids. I stole another peek; I couldn't help it.

'I've got some croissant at home, and what was it, coffee no sugar?'

Whoa! What was I missing here? A moment ago we were making love like French movie stars, now we were eating their breakfast. I really had to get her back on track.

'Kelly, is everything all right?' I asked nervously. 'Breakfast would be great, and I'm impressed you remember how I take my coffee – we only flew together once – but I really liked it when you were talking about us making love.'

'I thought you might, and I can't wait for it, but it won't be tonight.' She lowered her gaze again (get in there, my boy) and placed a hand over her mouth.

I looked up from her boobs as she started to speak – just about getting away with it.

'It's a bit embarrassing, John, but …' She paused again and her chest heaved as she took in more air. 'I've got a bit of thrush and it's as sore as hell down there right now.'

Bollocks, and double bollocks! I thought for a moment that the waiter had just stumbled and tipped a champagne bucket down my back. The situation in my trousers was already back to normal but my cheeks still tingled, this time with the embarrassment of dashed expectation.

'Oh, that's fine,' I managed. 'I thought it was something serious.'

'Well, it is for me, it's fucking uncomfortable!' She flashed an angry glare directly into my eyes. It was enough for me to recognise that I preferred the look of lust that had been there only seconds ago. *Must recover, say something nice!*

'Sorry, it must be awful. I didn't mean it that way. I'd love to spend the night with you just cuddled up. Besides, I could take over when you want a rest from scratching.'

I knew immediately it left my lips that I'd ruined the sentence, perhaps ruined everything. There was silence from the other side of the table, I dared not look up, but instead looked at the remnants of my entrée on the little square plate. Help her out with the scratching! Had I said that? Perhaps I should just get my coat and leave, or perhaps the chair would tip back, Bond-villain-like, and I'd drop into some death chamber beneath the floor.

The silence dragged on, and like an errant schoolboy becoming aware of the teacher's silence, I was finding it hard not to look up. I had to know what was going to happen next.

Kelly's caramel complexion had burnt red and her lips were clamped closed as though holding back a flood of foul language. That was it; I no longer wanted to know what would happen next, and so lowered my face once again.

And then a few guttural sounds emanated from her side of the table, like someone beginning to clear their throat of phlegm. Was she going to spit at me, I wondered. Like an idiot I looked up quickly, providing her with the perfect target. But she wasn't going to spit, at least not intentionally. Her face exploded in raucous laughter. Some saliva did end up on my face and, as I wiped it away with my hand, she apologised as best she could whilst roaring her gorgeous little head off.

She eventually calmed down, glancing around the restaurant at the disapproving diners, and lowered her head.

'Don't worry about them, I said. 'They can't throw you out for having a good time.'

'The maître d' is staring at me,' she said, and snorted out another giggle.

'Fuck him!' I looked around at the staff as though I were about to play rugby against them.

'He's not on my to do list, John. Give me your hands.'

I held out my hands and she grabbed them with hers, turning them palms down. She took a moment to scrutinise their appearance then thrust them both back at me.

'You're not coming anywhere near me with those finger nails!' She said.

We both fell about laughing, louder than before, and other diners started to point. I turned round and saw the maître d' cocking his ear towards a crusty old bloke. The man jabbed his fork in my direction and shook his head. People laughing – he'd probably never seen anything like it.

The maître d' asked us to leave. He even stamped his foot. Had he been less effeminate I'm sure he would have physically thrown us out. I suggested to Kelly that he would make a good flight attendant, and that boosted our guffawing to new levels.

In his hurry to rid the restaurant of 'behaviour ill-suited to the class of clientele' he waived the bill and offered to call a taxi. I told the maître d' not to bother since my Škoda was parked in his car park, and Kelly announced loudly that I was a taxi driver. As I followed her through the door, I felt a shove on my shoulder. It seemed that the maître d' was getting physical after all, but I didn't care, I was too busy pissing myself with laughter.

Kelly and I jostled each other all the way to the car where we fell into a close embrace. It was a warm May evening; one of several recently that suggested summer was arriving this week, so we both wore only light clothing. I could feel her breasts pushing into my lower rib cage and she held her hips against me. Her arms tied themselves around my neck, tightening like a boa constrictor every time I moved. She had me in her grip.

And then her cheek slid against mine as she moved her lips into position. Oh my! Her tongue slipped in and out of my mouth like a starved kitten lapping milk. It was everywhere; for a moment I thought she had two of them. My new jeans were helpless to prevent the growing interest beneath, and Kelly could feel it. She pressed her hips closer and closer with each pump of my heart, her arms tightening around my neck to the same beat.

At last she peeled herself away leaving my lips tingling as though she had sucked the oxygen from my body. I wondered how much lipstick had been crushed into them during our snog. Quite a lot, I worried.

'Come on, Captain John, let's get a burger and go to bed.'

Kelly's right hand had rested on my left leg all the way to Burger King, and then all the way to her house. Occasionally she would stroke the inside of my thigh with the tips of her fingers and, to be quite honest, it was hard to ignore. In fact, strike off the last two words of that sentence, and leave it there. The side of her hand had edged closer to my crotch during the second part of our car ride, until it rested casually against my left bollock. Mercifully, the rest of me pointed the other way, so I hoped she wouldn't feel the extent of my arousal. After all, I wasn't a teenager.

Back at her apartment I lay in bed listening to running water, cupboards closing, products being used (anti-itch ointment?) and other ritualistic noises wafting from the bathroom. I snuggled beneath the duvet – not entirely naked since I wasn't sure of etiquette – with my legs crossed at the ankles and my hands supporting my head. Such casualness was an attempt at calming my nervously excited body into a grown up *sangfroid*. The bottle of Cape Pinotage, which she'd opened when we arrived at the house an hour earlier, helped, though I'd just belched up the taste of gherkin, so I started to panic about kissing her again.

Suddenly, the noises from the bathroom stopped. I imagined her appearing at the bedroom door wearing a silk chemise, a finger at each strap ready to brush them off her shoulders, and then walking the last few steps wearing nothing more than a smile. In reality, and owing to the untimely dose of fanny fungus, I supposed she would actually be wearing cosy pyjamas – probably with Winnie the bloody Pooh on the front. My decision to hide behind a pair of boxers was probably a wise one.

I heard soft footsteps, and then she appeared in the doorway. Shittin' chicken! She was naked. Absolutely naked. Nothing on, not even the smile. Bloody starkers!

She stood for a moment to unfasten her necklace. Even if she was looking at me I reckoned this was as good a time as any to stare agog at those breasts. Man alive, she was inch perfect. The caramel smooth skin was tight over her boobs like it had been painted on. Her entire upper body looked as though it had been carved from oak and then varnished with coffee and cream. Everything was tight, and her boobs sat high and firm on her chest.

Then I dropped my eyes to the obvious place. Had her boobs not been so magnificently crafted it would have been the first place I looked. There was probably only a split second to go before Kelly curled her necklace up and placed it on the sideboard. Within a moment she would be in the bed and out of sight. There were no white bits, no strap lines, and no bikini line. Just a narrow strip of black curls creeping upwards from the top of her folds, like smoke rising from the flame of a candle. It was my birthday.

She slid into bed and pulled the duvet around her. She hadn't spoken since making her erotic entrance moments ago, and I was frightened by how nonchalant she was. It seemed like her entire body had managed to press against mine. From toes to lips we lay motionless until Kelly realised I still had my pants on.

'Ah, bless, are you a bit shy?' She was back in charge.

'I just wasn't sure what would be appropriate, you know, considering, the situation down, er, with you.'

'Let me help you,' she said, pushing down on my pants and sliding them over my knees.

'That's better,' she whispered. 'There are other things we can do.' And her body closed in on mine once more.

Chapter 10

Loaded, cocked and fired

The last few days had been as thrilling as any I could remember. Hardly an hour passed without an adulterous exchange of texts with Kelly, and hardly a minute passed without a thought of her magical, naked splendour. Only during the cruise to some miserable place too far from her was I prevented from sending her a lustful message or loving sentiment. But during the turnaround – even whilst taxying out to the runway – we shared each other's thoughts by text. True, mobile phones could interfere with aircraft systems, but I've never noticed, and my forget-fulness means my phone is regularly on during flight. I suppose if everyone decided to call their wives, bosses, or mistresses whilst the aircraft roared down the runway, the accumulative effect of all those tiny wavelengths bouncing around the cabin might derail the odd take-off or two. But since we tell passengers to switch off their phones, the airwaves are free for me to text my new girlfriend.

And that brings me to my current status.

I'm a married man with a faithful wife and two fab children. I love them dearly, but my wife has recently shown the strains of a life apart. It's not a voluntary lifestyle, but one forced upon the both of us by the airline that pays me. If this unwilling estrangement is to continue I wonder if my marriage will. I am convinced that this is the chief contributing factor to my wife's emotional distance. I have plenty of love to give, but my wife is drawing only a fraction of that love; the rest has been withering away, lost forever. Until now.

Like many men, I need to be needed; I need someone to look to me for companionship, for support, for manly jobs. And someone had come along to fill that need. Regrettably it wasn't Tabitha; incredibly it was the most sexually thrilling woman I have ever known, usurping even Julie. And she wanted my knob. She hadn't properly had the aforementioned body part, but the text I'd received a short while ago signalled that the status could be changed very soon. The red rash had gone, and the green light was on. But first I had to survive a flight to Amsterdam with Rivers as my first officer.

I hadn't noticed the change to my roster. It had been Rivers, floating into the breakfast room with an air of excitement, who delivered the news. 'Dude, we're cloud surfing buddies tomorrow,' he'd said, raising his hand for a 'high-five.' It took only a few spaced out moments for me to decipher the message. I was getting to understand his mixed up American now, and I hoped he was impressed.

Whilst I was keen to see the fabled hippy in action, I saw it more as an opportunity to lose my job. Something told me a day out in the sky with Rivers would be strewn with challenges. Had I not been in a state of boyish delirium over Kelly and thus incapable of rational thought, I would have sought a roster change – the last thing I needed now was another trip to Manchester.

I hadn't told Kelly about Rivers. It was probably an attempt to keep my involvement with her as a separate, boxed-up section of my life. But this unconscious thinking didn't explain why I'd told Rivers about Kelly, and now I considered that I'd got it the wrong way round. So my text to Kelly was an effort – albeit a poor one – to introduce her to the new man in my life.

> Hello darling, might not see you later, flying
> with Keanu Reeves and could end up having
> a Bill and Ted style adventure! xxx

Bless her! She had absolutely no idea what I was talking about. She had heard of the Hollywood actor, but not of the surreal and juvenile time travelling movie that had propelled him to fame. I wasn't surprised; even if she were my age, it wouldn't have been her kind of movie.

Rivers and I made the short trip to Gatwick airport together. It had been a tiresome effort dragging him to the car early enough to allow for parking problems and the long bus ride to the crew room. 'Dude, just ride with it, man, we late, we late, chill,' he had said. I wasn't sure about this advice, so I pulled rank – and his sleeve – and coerced him into the car (against his 'human rights, man!').

Since Rivers and I arrived in the crew room together, and knew one another, we avoided the ten-minute search through the dozens of other pilots that usually characterises the start of our day. There was also no risk of duplicating the flight paperwork, thereby saving at least one rainforest.

'Double Amsterdam, dude, four flight plans, weather for the entire continent, and notices about Blackpool airport.' Rivers dropped the pile of paper on the briefing table and shoved it towards me. The company's filters, which were intended to extract only the relative information for each flight, were notoriously inaccurate. It was quite usual to get weather information for sections of Europe that we wouldn't fly through even if we were hijacked. And NOTAMS (notices to airmen) concerning navigation aids at airports in the opposite direction to our flight commonly appeared.

'Thanks, Rivers. Five tonnes?' I suggested a fuel figure without looking at the briefing pack. There are six runways in Amsterdam, most have the capability of landing in heavy fog, and there's always at least one that will be into wind should it be howling a gale. Five tonnes was more than enough. In fifteen years of flying to Amsterdam (five of which were before I joined the airline world) I have never been delayed on arrival: no holding and no lengthy radar vectoring to sequence me behind a string of Dutch planes. But why should there be any delays? Three times as many runways as Heathrow, six times as many as Gatwick, and half the traffic. And no eco-warriors protesting against the forced displacement of the lesser-spotted snail and its undergrowth buddies.

Heathrow is still clinging to its status as busiest international airport in the world, whilst Gatwick is the busiest single runway airport in the world. When controllers tell us there is 'no delay' it means there is no delay beyond the tacit twenty minutes we all expect. Seriously. And neither airport, straining at the seams of safe operation, can secure an additional runway. Within the next ten years I predict Heathrow will cease to be the preferred transit hub to other continents, overtaken by the modern multi-runway leviathans: Schipol, Charles de Gaulle, Madrid. The residents of Hounslow may cheer, but the airport is a city of business and humanity. Both will be lost as it becomes nothing more than a ghost town. At least the snails will be happy. After all, they were there before humans discovered concrete, and they don't jet off on holiday twice a year. Besides, by the time they make it to the airport, the flight would have left.

Rivers nodded. 'You got it, dude, I'll phone it through.' He made his way over to the phone that half a dozen first officers were already queuing to use. Meanwhile, I performed a sweep of the cabin crew trying to guess which one was Olga.

'Stand ten, buddy. No slot. Plane'll be here in ten whirls of your dial.' Rivers had pushed in ahead of three other guys, telling them we were late. He wasn't British; he didn't queue.

'Ten whirls? Of the big hand or the fast hand?' I asked, with a wry smile.

'You dumb-ass, ten–' and then Rivers spotted my grin, 'Hell, buddy, I think we're beginning to understand each other.'

'Come on, mate; let's find Olga.' I led him on a circuit of the crew room asking each crew with a female senior if they were going to Amsterdam. At one table Rivers decided he liked the look of a girl and begged me to phone Crewing to arrange some sort of crew swap.

'Over here, mate,' I called when I finally found Olga. Rivers prised himself away from true love and floated over to our new table.

'No offence, Olga,' I said, 'I'm sure Rivers really wants to fly with you as much as I do.'

'I don't care,' she said in heavily accented English. 'I have boyfriend, he very big and rich.' She pronounced her aitches with the guttural scraping of someone trying to clear their throat, and omitted all grammatical articles, both traits of the Russian language. Her lips were bright and red, as though she'd just dipped them in wet paint, and the bling on her fingers glinted sharply under the room lights.

'*Ah, ty Rusky?*' I asked.

'*Da,*' said Olga, confirming my deduction.

'*Ya magu govorit pa Rusky,*' I claimed.

'Yes, I know you speak Russian, you already speak to me in Russian.' Olga was unimpressed, and there was no attempt to continue in her language or to learn the origins of my language skills.

'Right, ahem,' I said, shuffling my feet. 'It's Forty-five minutes each way, the weather's fine, coffee white none. Thanks.'

Olga wrote this down with such firm strokes of the nib that I wondered if she was carving the information into the table beneath. She looked up and jabbed her pen at Rivers. 'You?'

'Er ...' River's face jerked as though the pen had made contact, and his eyes searched the table as though the answer to Olga's unspoken question was hidden somewhere on its surface.

Olga continued to stare at Rivers (though she had lowered the pen in some sort of Glasnost gesture) until he recovered his composure.

'Coffee, black, none – please.' He managed eventually. Olga wrote this down too, then looked straight at me.

'We go!' she said, already reaching for her bag.

'Er, yes, let's live the dream,' I said, and made for the door.

I hadn't met any other Russians in the company before; I always assumed there weren't any given that Russia wasn't in the EU, and so I wondered how Olga had blagged herself a work permit. '... *he very big and rich.*' Perhaps that had some part to play in the answer. Big and rich: mafia probably; embassy worker; oligarch; all three perhaps. I had worked for a guy who was two of these and I well understood their ability to secure whatever they wanted. And far from their girlfriends being happy to lounge around on yachts all day, they were fiercely independent and driven people. Although sometimes they were just fierce. I had also learned that it was unwise to question them too far. For now, I was happy to accept that Olga worked for us legally and that's all I needed to know.

'So, Olga, your boyfriend, is he some kind of mafia oligarch then?' As the last treacherous word tumbled from my slack mouth, I recalled my experiences that suggested it was wise not to question mafia girlfriends. But it was too late.

'*Niet!* No, he is businessman, he work with my father.' She spat out her words, emphasising each consonant as though she despised every one of them. It would be the same in her language. Russians usually sounded like they were rowing, even when making love.

'Of course, just kidding, I didn't really expect him to be mafia. Does he work in the UK?'

'No, he work in Moscow, but he come here sometimes.'

'So what brings you to the UK?' I asked, becoming intrigued.

'My father, he want me to learn about job.'

'Cabin crew?' I asked doubtfully, expecting a rebuke.

'Da, he want to start airline in Moscow, and fly to Gatwick, I will be cabin crew trainer.'

'Wow! And your boyfriend will be chief pilot,' I suggested playfully.

'No, he hate pilots, he say they get too much salary and screw too much cabin crew.'

He was probably right, I thought grimly. He'd make a good flight operations director.

Once the inbound crew had handed over, Rivers and I settled on to the flight deck and tried to make ourselves comfy. Olga and her team were busy performing their security check on the cabin, and a friendly dispatcher was gently nudging us with overt glances at his watch.

Prior to all flights a thorough check must be made of the cabin to ensure that passengers have remembered to take with them all their personal belongings. Any items – however innocuous – left on-board must be removed (except newspapers). But there is always something. And that day was no exception.

'Stupid man!' spat Olga. 'How he walk off without stick?'

Rivers and I looked over our shoulders into the cabin to see Olga waving a walking stick around like Ivan the Terrible slaying peasants. We decided not to ask for coffee before Olga chose to make it. I wasn't sure what kind of cabin trainer she would turn out to be, or indeed, what type of airline her father had planned. All I knew was that I wouldn't be flying his planes.

'We are like hospital,' said Olga. 'Passengers they get on sick, and they get off well. Now ambulift is here, but he no wait, he cured. But I have his walking stick. Maybe I hit him with it if he come back.'

What Olga lacked in compassion she balanced with a shrewdness that made her a dangerous foe; the type of woman who would spot deceit a mile away and punish it mercilessly. She was probably right about the forgetful man with the stick: some passengers request assistance knowing they will board the plane first, then bound off at their destination as though trying out for the Olympics. I really hoped he wouldn't pop back for his walking stick; I would hate to see bloodshed so early in my working day.

The smell of petrol fumes heralded the arrival of a fuel man seeking a signature. It was always a good idea to refrain from flicking any electrical switches or using a mobile phone whilst the guy stood in such a confined space. One loose spark and the flight deck could shoot into orbit. His exit was followed by a return of the dispatcher. He was an amiable young man, and a fully qualified pilot in search of a break. I knew him vaguely (there are so many dispatchers in Gatwick) and he seemed polite and enthusiastic. He glanced at his watch again, and whispered the time to himself in the hope we would be gently cajoled into respecting 'on-time-performance'. That was the latest big thing; nothing must get in the way of departing on time. But the problem that day was that Rivers was flying the first sector, and he won't be rushed.

'Two minutes, Tim. Nearly there,' I said to the young dispatcher. 'Any delay, put it down to ramp congestion – just say another plane was blocking our push-back.'

The dispatchers were responsible for bringing together all the elements of a turnaround to ensure an on time departure. If they failed, with no external contributing factors, then they were held responsible and financially penalised; they were barely taking home minimum wage as it was.

'Cheers, guys,' he said and we swapped paperwork. I got a copy of the loading sheet, and he got a little strip of paper from the technical log. This was the 'paperwork' pilots often talk about when they tell passengers, during the 'Welcome on board' announcement, that 'We're just finishing off the last of the paperwork ...' Although by that time, we've usually finished it off, but it gives us something to say.

Passengers were now boarding and I could hear Olga demanding boarding cards. 'Yes, boarding card, thank you, free seating, yes, boarding card, thank you, free seating, yes ...' Perhaps in her head she was actually saying 'Get on, sit down, shut up, get on sit down shut up.' She was perhaps mid twenties, but appeared oblivious to her country's evolution from communist times; for Olga, it seems that customers were simply people who got in the way of an easy life.

Eventually she marched on to the flight deck and, without any preamble, blurted out the number of passengers on board. According to my load sheet it was wrong by one, and for a moment I considered not querying it. I looked at Rivers and hesitated. He shrugged unhelpfully, but then Olga caught sight of the little piece of paper in my hand and saw the contradictory number.

'Blyad!' She seethed, then stormed from the flight deck to begin another head-count.

'Dude, you totally chickened out!' teased Rivers.

'Do you blame me?' I asked, embarrassed at my own diffidence.

'Fair comment, dude, fair comment.'

'We'll think of something to crack a smile in that masterpiece of facial plastering,' I promised. 'She must have a lighter side to her hidden somewhere beneath all that make-up.'

'Yeah, buddy, but I reckon it's gonna have to be a major sting.'

The passenger discrepancy had been resolved after Olga had counted twice more and reached the same number. A system error had checked-in a child who had been a baby when the ticket was booked. Babies, not having their own seat, are counted separately from adults and children, and no one had picked this up until Olga had got busy with her clicker. I was surprised she hadn't thrown the child off for turning two years of age after his ticket had been purchased.

Rivers turned out to be a skilled flyer. He hand-flew the Airbus A320 along the entire departure from Gatwick without the assistance of any of the automatic systems. His accuracy was exceptional, as was his situational aware-ness in one of the world's busiest chunks of sky. Finally, at fifteen thousand feet, he engaged the autopilot, undid his seat belt, and sat back with the satisfaction of someone who's just had sex with a movie star.

'Where's my coffee, man?' He drawled. 'Go and tell that bitch to stop beating up on passengers and get her pretty little butt in the galley.'

'Sure, Rivers, I'll pop out now and lay down the law.'

'Cool, dude, you better take the fire axe with you.'

We laughed loudly in the way that guys do when they're trying to cover up some shortfall in their masculinity. Suddenly the door buzzer sounded and we almost jumped from our seats. We twisted round to stare at the monitor behind us. It was Olga.

I considered denying her access by flicking the door lock control switch beside my chair, but Rivers spotted two cups of coffee in her bejewelled hands and suggested she may not have heard our cocky exchange. I unlocked the door and Olga entered, wearing a face that could freeze vodka.

'Why you make me wait? What you do in here that is secret?' She demanded.

There was something erotic about hearing a Russian woman using the word secret; it was like the old days, like being interrogated by Xenia Onatopp in the Bond movie *Goldeneye*.

'Sorry, Olga, we were just talking to air traffic control,'

'This is crap.' She dismissed my excuse with characteristic diplomacy. 'You want coffee, you don't make me wait. You boys cannot be trusted. Next time I bang together your heads.' The last word began with a fearsome clearing of her throat as she pronounced the h like *ch* in Scottish loch. I was sure I saw her swallow straight after – always better than spitting. And then she was gone.

'I reckon she's actually sending herself up,' I told Rivers. 'You know, just playing on the Russian stereotype.'

'Yeah, we can jape her ass for sure, man.'

Gatwick to Amsterdam is just a forty-five minute flight and we didn't expect Olga to contact us again before landing, so we cooked up a few practical jokes for the way back.

Air traffic controllers in Holland, like most other non-Mediterranean nationalities, are competent and slick, though sometimes a little too slick. They have a style all to themselves, combining the colloquial familiarity of Americans with the patience and clarity of Northern Europeans. But it takes a lot of getting used to. A typical exchange between pilot and controller is like chatting with a jovial shopkeeper, and being told which aisle the cheese is located. 'Turn right, go straight to the beacon and take your time, there's a queue already', could be a typical instruction when talking to an Approach Controller. Once I was given my four number code for the transponder as, '4378 for the little box.' No call sign, no standard phraseology, and no bloody clue what he was talking about. Later, the same controller, having noticed I hadn't switched on the transponder said, 'Put another fifty pence in the little box.' And whilst they're not always sympathetic to those who fail to latch on to their aviation patois, they offer nothing worse than a humorous riposte: 'Is this your last flight today, Sir?' came the question one night when I was being a bit slow to respond, to which my answer was yes. 'Thank goodness for that!' said the controller. I often wondered if their ATC manual was written over lunch in one of their 'special cafés' that Rivers so loved.

On the ground at Schipol, Olga disgorged the passengers with a flat 'Have a nice day' whilst I began programming the flight management computer for the return trip. After several minutes Olga shouted through that all the passengers were off, then she disappeared to begin the security sweep of the aircraft. Rivers ventured outside to kick the tyres and I wandered into the cabin, checking for messages on my phone as I walked.

I started to tap out a text message to Kelly. Nothing major, just a 'Hi, how are you?' kind of message. But my smile didn't go unnoticed.

'You have lover?' said Olga with her dead-pan face.

'What?' I almost dropped my phone. 'No, why, what? Why would you say that?'

'Men no smile like that when they send text to wife. She is cabin crew, yes?'

'No! Look, I'm texting a friend, that's all.' It was true, in a way, and for the first time, Olga smiled. Somehow, I didn't suppose it was quite the smile I'd hoped to elicit.

'Cabin is ready for boarding – Captain.' She emphasised my title, almost giving it a Marilyn Monroe intonation.

'Good, clear to board,' I said, putting the phone in my trouser pocket and disappearing back onto the flight deck.

Whilst I watched the passengers rush across the apron towards the plane in pursuit of some cherished seat (for the forty-five minute flight) I was reminded that the Dutch are one of the tallest nations on the planet. It's intelligent evolution of the most practical kind. If the planet keeps warming up like they say, then given the shallow contours of the Netherlands, the Dutch will have to be the tallest people around. Tallest man drowns last, and becomes King of his country for the last few moments of his life.

The Dutch dispatcher, and potential future Queen, gave us a cheery wave and gathered up her paperwork before toddling off to her next flight. Turnarounds in Amsterdam were usually conducted with the kind of Teutonic efficiency that still prevails in territories that contributed bloodlines to the Anglo-Saxons. Had William the Conqueror (otherwise known as Guillaume le Bastard) not invaded the land of Anglo-Saxons in 1066 and diluted the Teutonic blood with Frenchness, perhaps the British would also be efficient. Anyway, we were in and out of Amsterdam before you could say 'Doesn't she look fetching in those wooden clogs?'

Once in the cruise Rivers and I prepared to begin Operation Crack, an undercover attempt to stretch a smile onto Olga's attractive, though frequently dour face. But as we finalised the plan, Rivers suddenly appeared to suffer another attack of Tourette's.

'Shit!'

'Now?' I asked, deadpan.

'What?'

'Shit.'

'Fuck!' he blurted in confusion.

'First?' I asked as his face looked like it might gain some colour.

A silence followed during which he stared aghast at me, as though unsure how to proceed.

'Shit,' he repeated, then continued as though talking to a retard. 'There-is-a-wasp-crawling-out-of-the-air-vent. There. Look.' And he pointed with the same slow motion with which he had enunciated his words.

'Shit!' I agreed, jumping in my chair. I reached for a newspaper and began rolling it into a weapon.

Wasps have to be one of the most sinister creatures on the planet, second only to humans. Not only can they sting more than once, it seems to be their aim to do so. Whilst the venerable honey-making bee will use its venomous tail only as a last resort, the wasp is definitely jab-happy. I'd confronted pissed-off lions and AK-47 toting guerrilla leaders whilst working in Africa, but nothing stirred panic in me more than a bored wasp.

'Wait, dude, I got an idea,' said Rivers ominously. 'Why don't you run out of the flight deck yelling 'Terrorist attack!' then ask Olga to fetch the wasp repellent?'

'Oh, I don't know, Rivers, that's a bit much.' I could already feel Olga banging our heads together.

'Come on, dude, it'll be a hoot,' he insisted. 'Look! It's flying around now.'

'Bloody hell!' I shouted, and waved my arm around like a helicopter with a broken rotor blade.

'There!' screamed Rivers.

I jumped up and ruffled through my hair with frantic strokes of my fingers in case the wasp had somehow snuck in under some kind of rear guard assault. I was now seriously considering leaving the flight deck whilst Rivers ridded us of this malevolent stowaway.

'Do it, man, you're almost there anyway,' goaded my first officer.

I looked through the peephole and saw Olga in the front galley. Fuck it, I thought, it'll entertain the passengers and they'll love it. Going the extra mile, that's what made the airline so popular with passengers (that and the rock bottom ticket prices).

I wrenched the cockpit door open and fled into the cabin with only partially faked panic radiating from my face.

'We're under attack!' I spoke calmly but loudly, and perhaps for the first time in my career I had the attention of the entire plane. No one chattered away now, no rustling newspapers, no theatrical yawns, no childish hand gestures. The combined sea of faces turned towards me at the same time and reflected the cabin lights forward; it was like having a spotlight flashed on me.

The stage was not my natural environment and I suddenly lost all enthusiasm for the joke. Olga stared at me with that 'bang your heads together' look, and I knew instantly the joke had been a mistake.

I threw a hand over my shoulder at the cockpit door and said meekly, 'Er, wasp, th-there's a wasp on the flight deck. I don't like them.' I ducked quickly into the toilet.

Once sheltered from the blanched faces of my passengers I stared at my own in the mirror, then covered it with my sweating hands. How could I have been so stupid? I could see the papers already, lying there in full view on the Chief Pilot's desk, his face not at all white, but rage red. Not a good colour in any circumstance. After several minutes

I left the sanctuary of the toilet and returned to the flight deck without saying a further word. Olga followed behind. As she closed the door I heard Rivers telling ATC that the cockpit wasn't secure. I shook my head vigorously, but he went on to explain that the cockpit was under the control of an armed and dangerous wasp. When he put the mic down he grinned up at the two of us.

'Come on, Olga,' he said. 'It won't kill you!' He widened his face into a joker's grin as though that alone could force one from her.

'Rivers, we might have just joked our way out of a job, mate,' I said, feeling sick. My stomach lurched as though I'd been forced to suck on the corpse of the wasp that had triggered this act of utter stupidity, a corpse that now discoloured the windscreen with its innards. At least he'd managed to kill it; that was something, I supposed.

Olga did make good her violent threat to bang our heads together, and it was indicative of our futile remorse that we allowed her to do so. Probably not the wisest decision that day given that we had to fly a plane, but not the worst by a long way.

It is naïve to believe that what happens on board stays on board. Plenty of flying careers have ended abruptly following on-board antics that made the press. Airlines might want their pilots to think they're nothing grander than a train or bus driver so they can pay them less, but passengers still regard us with curious reverence. Even a mild quip about the weather gets passed on to the friends of some passengers: 'And the pilot said hope you've got your brolly with you – he didn't say umbrella, he said brolly! Brilliant!' So there was no way my passengers were going to disembark in Gatwick and find nothing at all to say about their flight from Amsterdam that day.

'Did you have a good flight, darling?'
'Yes, the usual, had a nap, listened to cabin crew trying to sell coffee, and that's about it.'
'Glad you're home safe then, darling.'

As if that was ever going to happen.

When Kelly switched on the news the next morning and my name bounced from the small speaker, it shocked me awake like a bucket of cold water. The story was being covered in a comical manner, more of a 'And finally' item than a headline, but they had my name, and it was written on the screen. Even the hard of hearing would know about it.

'You're such a clown sometimes, John,' said Kelly. 'And you don't even know you're being funny. That's why I love you.'

Wet the bed! What did she say? We hadn't even shagged yet; we'd had a few dates and shared a bed three times but, as early days go, this was still the section of the Bible that deals with Adam and Eve. How could she love me? I really didn't feel comfortable with this declaration, particularly in light of the story that had provoked it.

'Thanks, darling, I love you too.' *Bollocks! Think before*

you speak.

Kelly chucked the remote control onto the floor and raised her bare leg over mine. Her kisses were warm and soft. She trailed her lips over my face leaving behind a tingle with each little peck. Slowly the rest of her naked body slid over mine and she lay on top of me, tickling my neck and chest with her dark, dense locks of perfumed hair. Even after a boozy night and a curry she smelt like the sweetest flowers in the garden.

'I'm ready,' she whispered, and took hold of me with gentle hands.

The nerves that had stemmed from an over-active groin during our first few dates were now replaced with those created by the opposite problem. Thoughts of my stupidity and newfound infamy were throbbing in my head with more vigour than I could ever hope for else-where on my body.

'I'm so sorry, darling,' I moaned. 'You're so beautiful and I've fallen helplessly for you, but all this stupid busi-ness has shot an arrow right through my libido. Please don't be angry with me.'

'Ah, bless. This calls for DR ABC,' she purred, moving down the bed for a closer inspection. 'Let's see. Scanning for vital signs. Well, there's life, Jim, but not as we know it!'

It was depressingly indicative of my state of mind that, whilst she busied herself below, I wondered whether this Eighties girl, raised in Portugal, knew she'd quoted a line from Star Trek – a Sixties American sci-fi series. No wonder her exceptional skills were having little effect on me if this was my preferred line of thought.

'It's not good news, Captain,' she continued. 'There's a pulse, but he's weak; I'm not sure he's going to make it.' She crawled back up the bed to lie quietly by my side. 'It's all right, darling, just a little cuddle, then I'll put the kettle on.'

Perhaps I did love her; there were certainly plenty of reasons to do so.

Rivers and I travelled north together; at least they'd sent a taxi for us and, as bad luck generates bad luck, it was the same driver as last time. He didn't need to interrogate me; the papers had provided all the details he could possibly want to know. 'Pilot creates a buzz,' stated one tabloid headline. 'Sting in the tail for wayward pilot,' wrote another. Most stories I'd read treated the incident as a bit of a joke, but The Guardian focused on my mental state and questioned whether the airline itself was doing enough to screen unsuitable pilots. I imagined my boss would accuse me of bringing the airline into disrepute, and that was a capital offence.

Rivers had been unusually reticent to offer his thoughts on a likely outcome, his sardonic outbursts stifled by something I couldn't fathom. His only contribution to this ill-considered affair had been a less than clever call to ATC, but we've all said stupid things over the radio from time to time. He could claim the microphone was stuck in the transmit position and that he was just winding me up by pretending to call ATC. It happens regularly.

I decided to probe his mood. 'Rivers, mate, you're in the clear, I'm the one that acted stupidly. Your name didn't even make the news. Don't worry.' I gave him a friendly nudge with my elbow.

'Nah, buddy, why do you think I left the Amsterdam base for Gatwick? No one volunteers for Gatwick!'

'I thought the cafés wouldn't serve you anymore.' It was a light-hearted quip to echo the one he made when first we met.

'The Base Captain, man, he hounded me outta there – said I was disruptive, disrespectful and unprofessional. He hated me, buddy, told me he'd frame me for something if I didn't clear out of his base.'

'Yes, but he's not the Chief Pilot, he's just one vindictive guy in another country. If he had any influence they wouldn't just move you to another base, they would have fired you there and then.'

'You're wrong, man, I'm on a UK contract now; it's much easier to fire me. I'm a gonner, John.'

I gaped at him, wondering if I had heard correctly: he'd used my name. For the first time in the two weeks I'd known him, he'd actually used my name. I wasn't sure what it meant, but he looked like a man on death row whose eleventh hour appeal had just been rejected. The taxi ride was Rivers's slow walk.

We sat in silence for about an hour. Even the taxi driver was quiet. I'd asked him to switch the radio on but he said it was broken; seemed about right.

Rivers took out his mobile phone and tapped away on

the keys with the corner of his thumb. I looked across expecting to see him typing out a text, which would have been another first, but he was playing Sudoku. I'd never seen Rivers use his phone before, and I suddenly realised there was probably a lot about this guy I didn't know.

I'd grown to like Rivers. True he was a caricature, someone who seemed to have stumbled off the set of Wayne's World and onto The Beverly Hillbillies, but he had challenged my conservative beliefs and habits. I was enjoying myself: we'd been going out, drinking beer, and swapping aviation horror stories like rival adventurers comparing injuries. I never talked about my experiences in Africa; it was likely that all those who met me since those days knew nothing about it, except Tabitha.

Ah, yes, my wife.

I hadn't called, but she was sure to know about yesterday's fateful caper. Even if she hadn't seen the news or read a paper, her mother would have been on the phone first thing. Interestingly, Tabitha hadn't called *me*.

'Deep breath, dude,' said Rivers. 'We're going under.'

The taxi pulled up outside the door to our company's head office. We stretched out our limbs through the open doors and climbed apathetically from our rear seats onto the pavement.

'I'll *bee* waiting here for you,' said the driver winking and nudging thin air with his elbow like an unfunny vaudeville act.

'It was a wasp, actually, but no matter,' I replied, though I'm not sure why.

I had been right about the newspaper; it must have been a premonition. Why does a premonition always turn out to be bad news? Try as I may, I never have premonitions about winning the lottery, or bumping into some hot Hollywood actress in a hotel lift, then getting stuck for three hours with no air conditioning. Lord knows how much I've thought about it. No, I see newspapers sat on the Chief Pilot's desk – with a picture of me staring out! Where on earth did they get my picture from?

The meeting was brief. It started with the words 'I'll keep this brief,' and ended with Rivers shouting 'Fuck you!' I couldn't blame him; he had just been fired.

My only contribution was to nod and say 'Yes, sir' when asked if I understood the consequences of appearing before him again, ever. Unlike Rivers, I had survived, but only just. From this point onwards I was destined to see out my career, with this company at least, as a first officer. I thought about asking if I could expense the cost of having a set of stripes removed from my uniform jacket, but the Chief Pilot didn't do humour – that's why I'd been here three times in the last month.

My head buzzed (oh dear!) with ambivalent emotions. Part of me was relieved that I'd kept a job, but when the cost of commuting and living away were factored in, my new salary would be insufficient to justify being away from home. I might as well throw it all in with this lot and fly regional planes for someone else out of Exeter, or simply walk away from aviation and find some other employment. Still, another part of me ached that such a decision would end things with Kelly, though surely that would be a good thing. Living at home would solve all my problems with Tabitha and I could go back to being a full time husband and father. But Kelly? *Bollocks.*

As I slumped down in the taxi, I realised how selfish I was being. Rivers had nothing. No job, no wife, no family, not even a girlfriend. I had all of these things and I was agonising over the trouble they were causing. Nice position to be in?

'Sorry, mate, this really is the pits. What will you do now?' I asked in a low voice I hoped would convey the concern I felt.

'Get drunk until my money runs out, then join the Foreign Legion.'

I stifled a giggle. The thought of Rivers in the army, particularly one as tough as the French Foreign Legion, was risible in the extreme. But I was glad he still had the capacity for humour. There were two kinds of Swedish men: the humourless ones who nurse a beer all night then proclaim 'Ja, we had a good time tonight, but now we must go to bed', and those that drink and live on the edge of sanity. Rivers was the latter.

'We'll drop by the recruitment office together,' I suggested, and punched his arm playfully.

I had been suspended for the rest of the month, after which I was to return as a first officer on about half the salary. Under the circumstances, I couldn't get away with spending the next two weeks near Gatwick, so I called Tabitha to explain that I would be home the following day.

As expected she'd received a call from her mother, who'd read the Daily Mail's account to her. According to a sub-heading I had been drinking, though the story went on to state 'as though he were drunk', and even then it was an unnamed passenger the reporter claimed to be quoting. It took a number of increasingly frustrating attempts to convince her that the report's author might have shown keener skills as a novelist than a journalist.

I would see Kelly that night and explain to her that I must be at home during my suspension. She was bright enough to understand and mature enough to accept it. In the meantime, I really needed to work out where I wanted to be.

'All the best, mate,' I said to Rivers as the taxi arrived back in Gatwick.

'Jet easy, buddy.' He held his hand out and we shook before walking away in opposite directions.

Chapter 11

A blessing cruelly disguised

It was called gardening leave, but I've never considered mowing the lawn and pulling out weeds a satisfying way of spending my spare time.

I was alone during the days; the children were at school and my wife was with her mother most of the time, volunteering at the hospital. She had been livid about my antics on the Amsterdam flight, and appeared to be just as displeased with my suspension. I told her I was sorry if my prolonged presence unsettled her daily routine, and she had snapped back at my sarcasm. After she left the house I called Kelly and told her what a bitch my wife was being. It now seemed clear in my mind where I wanted to be, and I contrived to find an excuse to get back there.

That was the thing about gardening. I'd never understood it before, but with a head full of problems and an overgrown lawn in which one could lose small children, I got it: gardeners had plenty of time to think. Pushing a lawn mower around and pulling out weeds didn't require any concentration. I wondered how my life would have turned out had I discovered gardening earlier. Perhaps I would have mulled over my marriage until I'd thought it into an early grave, all without the aid of a wonderful and beautiful young accomplice.

I released the handle on the petrol mower and the engine died instantly. My ears stopped rattling and I stooped to detach the bulging grass box from its retaining hooks and empty the contents into a recycling bag. The garden was only average sized for a modern housing estate but all kinds of vegetation sprouted from its borders and quarters. This compartmentalised design made it look like a miniature National Trust garden.

My wife's prized flower bed was still unfinished, and there had been no sign of her Polish gardener since my deal with him. That had been a waste of effort anyway; it hadn't exactly earned me the favour with my wife that I'd intended, but at least I hadn't yet paid him. With the grass clippings now transferred, I turned back towards the mower in the middle of the lawn.

A blossoming apple tree stood firmly near the corner of the garden and its leafy stance obscured the side gate. It therefore took a comically false cough from the figure standing there to attract my attention.

'Sorry to bother you, sir, I'm looking for a Mr John Reilly,' said a dark clothed man, moving from behind the tree. As he stepped into view my pulse quickened and a small frisson poked at my stomach. The cough had come from a uniformed police officer. And then a policewoman pushed through the gate, fatally dislodging the remaining hinge, and we all watched the wooden barrier creak its way to the floor. No, I hadn't fixed it. The policewoman nodded a tacit greeting and went to stand by her colleague.

I wondered if adultery, however partial, had become illegal again, or maybe it was now against the law to cut the grass before 11.00 am on a Thursday morning; it seemed like everything was being criminalised these days.

'I'm John Reilly. I didn't want to cut the grass anyway, officer.' I smiled to let him know it was a joke.

'Can we go inside, sir?' He gestured towards the back door as though he didn't expect me to know the way.

'What's this about?' I asked, following his hand signal. Something told me it wasn't the time for more jokes.

The policeman pointed to the sofa and invited me to sit down. I wanted to check the deeds of the house to make sure I still owned it, but the grave faces of the two officers quickly emptied my head of frivolous thought.

The woman delivered the news. 'It's your daughter, sir; there's been an incident at the school. She's in hospital. Stable, but it is serious.'

'An incident?

'Yes, sir, she's stable–'

'Stable. What happened …'

'We're investigating–'

'Serious? Is she alright?'

The policewoman looked at her colleague whilst I tried to make sense of her words, though they were clear enough.

'Try to stay calm, sir,' spoke the man. 'We'll–'

'I am calm …

'We'll take you straight there. There's a teacher with her at the moment. We can find out more when we get to the hospital.'

'A teacher?'

'Yes, sir, someone has to stay with your daughter–'

'Where's my wife?'

'We were unable to get hold of Mrs Reilly.'

'But she's at the hospital, actually there at the hospital. She's helping out in the café.'

'Perhaps, sir, but she didn't answer her phone when the school called her. They left messages, but were unable to reach her. Come on, sir, we'll get you down there now.'

We raced through the town with blue lights flashing and sirens wailing. At any other time I would have been thrilled to tick-off a 'must do before you die' event from my list, but their use suggested that Lucy wouldn't even have time to make a list of her own, let alone start ticking things off. My eyes prickled with the thought.

It's a sight no parent should ever see, but too many do. Lucy lay on her back, tubes and wires violating her young body like a vile alien preparing her for some unearthly use. A steady beep accompanied the spike trace on a small machine beside the bed, another controlled the drip of pale liquid into the back of her hand. My step faltered as though a hole had opened beneath my feet, and the policeman grabbed my arm to steady me. 'Lucy', I called,

The Life of Captain Reilly

but she couldn't hear me.

I clasped her still fingers, squeezing gently, my eyes following the tube from the cannula in the back of her hand up to the silent machine. 'Lucy', I called again.

'She's unconscious,' said a pointless voice. 'But she's stable now.'

A woman in plain grey clothing moved into my peripheral vision and held a hand out to touch my arm.

'I'm Doctor Monroe. Lucy has suffered major trauma. We will need to operate within the next hour to relieve swelling on the brain.' Her voice was sympathetic but business-like. That was the information she had to convey, and there was no easy way.

'What happened? No one is telling me what happened.' I stared at the only other person in the room now that the police had retreated. 'Are you the teacher?'

'Yes, I'm Susan Clarke, Lucy's form teacher. Lucy was hit by a delivery truck that had taken a wrong turning within the school grounds. It was driving somewhere pupils wouldn't expect it to be, and she just ran out from behind a wall. It wasn't her fault.'

'Lucy, can you hear me?' I patted her hand and wriggled her fingers with my own. I felt my eyes stinging, and I blinked hard. When I opened them again, tears fell.

The doctor moved forward and gently ushered me away. She was talking, but I didn't hear her.

'No, I can't leave her. She can't be on her own. She's my little girl ...' I knew I was still speaking as my voice faded, though I didn't know what I was saying.

'I'm sorry, Mr Reilly, we need to prep her for surgery. We'll take care of her, I promise. This is Sally, she's the senior nurse; she'll show you to the relatives' room.'

I turned round to see a tall woman in a dark blue uniform. She smiled and reached out her hand. The last time I had been in the relatives' room my dad had just died. The first time was when my mother had died. The nurse assured me it was just a waiting room where I could spend some time until Lucy came out of surgery. I didn't feel any better. And then I remembered Tabitha.

'Where's my wife?' I asked. 'She's meant to be working in the café today – with her mother.'

'I'll go and find her,' offered Susan Clarke. 'She hasn't answered her calls, but I suppose she's not meant to use her phone in the hospital.'

The relatives' room was comfortable and private, and I began to think of it more as the waiting room described by Dr Monroe than a room associated only with the death of a loved one. The smiley nurse brought me a cup of coffee and I blew gently across the top of the insipid froth before taking a few quick sips.

Where the hell is Tabitha? I thought, digging my phone out and pressing re-dial. She answered before I'd heard it ring at my end.

'Yes, hi, I'm on my way. Oh my God! What happened?'

'Hit by a van inside the school; she's just going for surgery.'

'What did the doctor say? Have you spoken to a doctor, what did he say?'

I hesitated just a second, distracting myself puzzling over her whereabouts.

'John! Is she okay, what did the doctor say?'

'The doctor says she's stable, but there is swelling on the brain, they're going to operate now.'

'I'm fifteen minutes away, see you then.'

'Drive carefully.' It was a meaningless caution; she had already hung up.

I pushed the magazines around the table searching for something that would leap out and divert my mind from the morbid thoughts that prevailed. It was unlikely that a collection of celebrity filled glossies would achieve that outcome, particularly since I didn't recognise anyone pictured on the front covers. So I pushed myself into the back of the sofa and placed my hands behind my head. Staring at the ceiling I allowed those morbid thoughts free rein. What if I'd been in Gatwick when Lucy had her accident? Worse still, I could have been night-stopping down route somewhere with no chance of getting back. I'd never see my daughter again. *What if she dies?* I clamped my eyes shut to help visualise and understand just what I was thinking.

A metallic sound brought me from my reverie and I watched the door open slowly. A head appeared nervously around the edge.

'Oh, you're here,' said Tabitha, pushing the door open more quickly. She rushed into the room and straight to where I sat on the sofa. 'I can't believe it,' she cried, throwing her arms around my neck.

We sat in silence for what seemed like minutes but was probably only a matter of seconds. Tabitha sobbed on my shoulder. I could feel her blonde hair tickling my cheek and I smelled the soft perfume I'd bought her for Christmas.

'Everything's going to be fine,' I said. 'The doctor didn't seem worried.'

'They never do.' It was a fair reply, and one against which I had no argument.

Tabitha released her grip and searched her bag for tissues. She wiped both eyes then tried to compose herself.

'Swelling on the brain is serious. At worst she could die; if she's lucky she might survive with brain damage,' she said.

'Or she could recover with no lasting effects,' I countered, trying to raise her spirits.

'Unlike you to be so positive!' Her words caught me by surprise. I wasn't expecting a fight.

'What do you mean by that?'

'You know, you're always so miserable these days, you have such a downer on everything.'

What the bloody hell was she on about? Our daughter was in intensive care and Tabitha was having a go at me! I didn't reply; this was something to discuss another day.

The next few hours passed with few words. I was desperate to ask her where she'd been that morning but I knew I would be accused of prying, so silence seemed to be the way forward.

Occasionally the smiley nurse popped in and asked if

we needed anything. 'Only information', I replied, but it seemed that was the only thing she couldn't provide. Mrs Clarke also stopped by to say she couldn't find Tabitha and was surprised and relieved that my wife was already there. It was the obvious moment to ask her my burning question, but Tabitha's quick glance slapped me back into silence. She interrogated the teacher with an attitude I hadn't witnessed since my army days.

'You are responsible for my children's safety, Mrs Clarke. I want to know exactly what happened.'

'It seems that–'

'It seems?' said Tabitha, jutting her head forwards.

'If I may, Mrs Reilly. Lucy was being chased by other children when the accident occurred. I'm not sure why–'

'You're not sure why?' Tabitha interrupted again, her head snapping backwards this time.

'Tabitha, let her speak.'

My wife shot me a sideways glare without moving her head away from the beleaguered teacher. I didn't think I was quite in her peripheral vision so it must have been a real effort to see me. I thought her eyeballs were going to reappear at her ears judging by the speed at which they slid across her face.

The teacher continued. 'We're still investigating, but I wanted to bring this news to you as soon as I could. We'll get to the bottom of it, Mrs Reilly. Mr Reilly.' She nodded at me.

Tabitha found a new direction for her anger. 'Why was the van in the school grounds?' she demanded.

'He had a permit, but had taken the wrong turning. True, he shouldn't have been there, but by all accounts he was driving slowly. Lucy just came out of nowhere. I don't think we can blame him.'

'I'll blame whomever I please, Mrs Clarke! My daughter could have been killed.'

'Okay, Tabitha, calm down. Let's wait until we know more.' I took her in my arms and she sniffled softly. I wondered if she'd left snot trails on my shirt like Lucy would have done.

Another hour ticked by on the noisy clock above me. It was like water torture, relentless drips tapping on my head, beating me into madness. I stamped to my feet and began pacing the room, stopping at every notice, every advertisement pinned to the wall. I'd already read them from the sofa, but now I read them from a new angle. Tabitha was texting, and for the first time since the police had appeared in my garden, I thought of Kelly.

For some reason it just didn't seem appropriate to text her, even to think of her. My daughter was undergoing emergency surgery; she might not make it, and her mother – my wife – was sat there with me. Tabitha and I might not be talking much, but we were in this together, and that was the most important thing.

Suddenly, the keypad beeps accompanying Tabitha's texting ceased and she slammed her hand down on the sofa. 'For Chrissakes, stop pacing around like a caged animal! Why don't you go and get us both a coffee?'

I huffed and hesitated, mulling over my options, then realised I didn't have any. I left her in peace to tap away on her phone, and went to find the smiley nurse.

Miserable! That's what she'd said! Was she right? I didn't think so, but if I was miserable or 'had a downer on every-thing' then she had a part to play in that. I didn't enjoy working away from home every week. It wasn't something I had jumped up and volunteered for and, although there was now some extra-marital compensation, if I had the power to turn back the clock one year then I would do so in a heartbeat. Life had been cosy; it was everything I'd thought about when I was young: dream job, beauti-ful wife, gorgeous children, great social life, lovely part of the country. But thanks to greedy accountants and selfish bosses my job was being driven down inexorably into little more than bus driving. My family life had been devastated by the closure of a profitable base; a closure that appeared to be motivated by nothing more than the promise of greater profit elsewhere.

It was unthinkable, though, to walk away from the job I had worked so hard, and sacrificed so much, to achieve. A job I'd wanted to do since I woke in my cot as a baby and stared at the model planes hanging from above; model planes which my flying-mad father had made for me. Being a pilot is almost like being a priest: it's a way of life, something you simply don't renounce just because you're fed up with it. I couldn't do anything else, nothing worthwhile anyway, and certainly nothing that would bring in the same kind of salary. Flying is a profession, like medicine, or law: you train hard and then that's what you do until you retire or get struck-off.

Rivers, having been fired, would find it impossible to get commercial flying work in the UK. He was a good pilot, he just didn't fit the company profile and they'd found a way to be rid of him. Aviation is a cosy industry. Pilot recruiters would know Rivers Andersson's name long before his CV dropped onto their desk.

And then there was my family. I couldn't simply give up on them either. A wife is for life, not just for convenience. There must be a way to combine a cherished career with a happy family, without being 'miserable.'

Doctor Monroe shuffled around the corner still in her surgical gowns, though minus what I gruesomely imagined would be bloody gloves.

'Ah, Mr Reilly, shall we find your wife and have a chat?' Why did people keep asking me questions that were clearly instructions?

'Is everything okay?' I asked. That was a question, plain and simple.

'She's going to be fine, but let's go and chat in the relatives' room. Is your wife there?'

'Yes, I was just going for coffee but …'

'I'll ask the nurse if she could get you some, and I'll be along in a minute.'

I thanked her and went back to the room.

'The doctor's on her way,' I told Tabitha, who was just ending a phone call.

'My mother,' she said, nodding at the phone. 'Did you

get the coffee?'

Well obviously not! Do you see coffee in my hands? I was asking those non-questions now – albeit to myself. It must be contagious; perhaps they had something at the hospital for it.

'The doctor is coming.' I reminded her about the important news in order to take her mind off coffee.

She jumped to her feet as though hearing the news for the first time.

'What did she say? Have you spoken to her? Did she say anything? Is Lucy okay?'

I put my hands on her arms and reassured her that everything was fine.

'But did the doctor say that? They always say that, they never tell you the truth – they don't want to worry you. But that worries–'

'Look, just take a deep breath and sit with me for a minute. The doctor will be here soon. She said Lucy will be fine.'

Tabitha sat down but immediately rose again as Doctor Monroe entered.

'How is she? Is she going to be okay? Can I see her?'

'Yes, she's fine. We've reduced the swelling and she …' the doctor paused briefly as she appeared to search for the best phrasing. 'There's no reason she shouldn't make a full recovery, but it could be a long process. Head injuries take time to heal.'

'Can I see her?' Tabitha asked again.

'Soon. She's still under the anaesthetic at the moment,

but she should come around within the next hour. Give us a few moments to settle her into a room and then the nurse will fetch you. Now, I'm sorry, I really need to change for another operation, but I'll stop by a little later.' And with a short smile, the doctor turned and left.

'Oh, thank the Lord,' exclaimed Tabitha, sitting down. She buried her head in her hands and began to weep, her shoulders shrugging up and down. I sat beside her and for the first time in a long time she kissed me on my cheek.

'I'm so glad you were here today,' she said, wiping her eyes.

I used my thumb to help dry her cheek, then pulled her head towards my chest. What did it matter where she'd been all morning? I didn't have the right to know her whereabouts all the time. I accepted Tabitha and the children had to carry on with their lives despite my regular absences, and I suspected there were plenty of undisclosed activities they enjoyed whilst I was away. I put it from my mind; things were going to be all right.

Chapter 12

Duped by manager, initially. Wasted.

Lucy enjoyed the bedside service provided by the nurses, and loved the idea of watching television in bed. It cost me a fortune, though, since every time she switched the bloody thing on it debited my credit card.

Tabitha and I visited twice a day – sometimes together – and made sure there was someone with her most of the time. Lucy had said we didn't need to stay so long; she had made a friend in the next room, but with each visit Tabitha and I recovered a little more lost ground.

Everyone was thrilled the morning Lucy took her first steps out of bed, and I returned home from the hospital in the kind of mood reserved for fathers of happy families. Within minutes of settling down with my first crossword in weeks – *Duped by manager, initially. Wasted* – Mrs Clarke from the school called. She had news that slapped the smile from my face.

'Good morning, Mr Reilly, it's Susan Clarke from St.

Joseph's. I hear Lucy's doing well; we're looking forward to her coming back to school.'

'Hi, yes, I'm sure she is too!' I said, laughing. I'd laughed quite a lot in recent days, something that hadn't been happening at home for several weeks. I'd thought back over the last months and concluded that Tabitha had been right: I had been miserable, even if she hadn't helped, though I hadn't put it like that to her.

'I've been digging around, questioning the pupils about why Lucy was running away that day. It seems your moment of fame inspired some of the boys to a bit of mischief.'

I pulled a face as I listened through the telephone to Mrs Clarke's words. My fame? What was she talking about?

'They trapped a wasp in a bottle and threatened to release it down Lucy's blouse. Understandably she screamed and ran …'

I was no longer listening; I was frozen with shock. I dropped my hand and ended the call. My prank had nearly killed my daughter. An unfortunate van driver had been arrested; he could go prison, and all because I'd played a stupid joke – a joke no one found funny anyway. I didn't blame Rivers. Yes it had been his idea but I'd done it; I'd performed the act of stupidity.

I sat in the lounge, slumped on an armchair and staring into the garden. My dangling right hand was still clutching the phone, the other holding the newspaper – *Duped by manager, initially. Wasted.*

My hand buzzed and I dropped the phone on the floor as

though it were electrified. I looked over to the clock ticking away above the fireplace and sighed when I realised two hours had passed since Mrs Clarke's call.

My phone continued to vibrate and shriek the old fashioned single ring you always hear in American movies. I looked over the arm of the chair to check the caller's number, but recognised it only as a Manchester code. Work, for sure. Like I was going to answer that. I waited until the message service kicked in, then picked the phone up and dialled the access number. After a few moments the message played back and I shook my head in utter dismay. The bastards. I dropped the phone once more and continued to stare into the garden. There was only one course of action open to me.

Working away from home had brought my family to a precipice beyond which lay certain misery. It simply wasn't worth it anymore. One becomes an airline pilot to be a captain. Bounced down to co-pilot with no chance of promotion is not what I had in mind. Half the salary, and I'd still be pushing the same buttons and taking the same crap – and still living away from home. No, it wasn't worth it anymore.

No phone call would ever been so satisfying. I pounded the keypad of my phone and waited.

'Hello. It's Capt– it's John Reilly,' I corrected myself. 'John …?'

The Chief Pilot paused, and I filled the gap to help out his amnesia. 'Reilly.'

'How can I help, John?' he said with a welcoming tone

311

that threw me off-guard.

'Er, yes. I've just had a message from the crew planning department. I'm afraid the answer's no.'

'No? What seems to be the problem … John?' He paused again.

And then it hit me: he had no idea who I was. Three times in three weeks I'd been before him. Twice he'd read about me in the paper. And a couple of weeks ago he had demoted me for the rest of my career – that is, if I chose to stay at his contemptible organisation. But he couldn't remember who I was.

'The problem, mate,' I began with recklessness, 'is that all you care about is numbers. Numbers on the balance sheet and numbers on a computer screen. As long as you keep pilots quiet whilst meeting your financial targets, you'll be happy. How much was your bonus back in January for trimming pilot numbers at northern bases? It was your first act as Chief Pilot. Pay off your mortgage, did it?' I wanted to go on, but the Chief Pilot had other ideas.

'How dare you!' His voiced bellowed out of the handset and into my ear forcing me to move the phone away from my head. I almost looked around to see if he was in the room.

I told the man to shove his job between the widening cheeks of his fat arse, and that I'd rather work in a hardware store than fly his planes. The last bit wasn't actually true. My idea of a tool kit was one of those 'handy-home' assortments that cost less than the first aid kit that ought to come with them. But it sounded good at the time.

I didn't wait for a reply. He was probably still trying to work out who the hell I was. I would have to put it in writing, of course, minus the vulgarity. With immediate effect, I was on permanent gardening leave. *Duped by manager ...?*

I slumped in my chair, fretting over how to tell Kelly it was over. I'd hardly thought about her in recent days – out of sight, out of mind, and all that. Part of me felt dishonestly pleased that we hadn't had full sex, though no prizes for guessing which part of me rued the missed opportunity. She was a gorgeously hot, lovingly beautiful young person and she'd stirred the kind of passion that fades within a few years of many weddings. It was like travelling back in time to my youth. And that was the problem. How many men fall for these unwitting traps? They sacrifice the love of a loyal wife and the happiness of their children for a trip down memory lane. Within a few years (if that) those adoring eyes and firm breasts go the same way as their wife's, and they're back to square one. The only difference is that the girlfriend wants to go clubbing and the divorced man wants to amble around garden centres. If he's really unlucky he's be wiped out by two divorces, and spends the rest of his life paying for other blokes to look after his children. Still, he'd be able to think back to all those nights shagging some other woman – until age claimed his memory.

I whistled through my teeth as I considered how close I'd come to ruining all our lives. It was time to get on with the rest of it now, and Tabitha had first rights to life-changing news. She would still be at the hospital, helping her mother in the café. I grabbed my car keys and made my way back. The drive to the hospital from our house was brief and I had a smile all the way there. I didn't even remonstrate with an old man who held me up at a junction because he couldn't turn his head enough to check for oncoming traffic. I didn't care. Take it easy old-timer – jet easy, as Rivers would say.

Tabitha's mum greeted me and poured my usual coffee; I'd seen more of her in recent days too. She wasn't so bad; she hadn't charged me for coffee in her little café all week (though this was depriving the charity of revenue) and we'd even chatted convivially. Progress all round.

'Is Tabitha not with you?' I asked.

'Er, yes, she's just popped out. Er, actually I think she's gone up to see Lucy again.'

'I'll just have my coffee, then pop up myself.' I didn't want to talk to my wife in front of our daughter, so I gave her some time with Lucy whilst I drank my coffee and mulled over the crossword.

'Duped by manager, initially. Wasted,' I said, but my mother-in-law just shrugged.

'Initially?' I tapped the pen against my top teeth. 'Duped by manager – initially.'

When I went up to the ward Tabitha wasn't there; my mother-in-law was clearly not in the loop, probably losing her marbles. I stood outside for a few minutes wondering whether to wait, but a nurse told me that Lucy was on the move and I didn't want her to see me so I made my way back to the café.

I was a little nervous about how Tabitha would take the news of my resignation. Her concern would be income, and where it was going to come from. I hoped I could convince her that family was the priority, and this was the best way to save it. I wouldn't be mentioning the precise cause of Lucy's accident.

Tabitha came out of the lift beside the café and looked startled to see me.

'Tabitha, I need to speak to you alone.' I said. Her face reddened. 'Don't worry, it's all good.'

'Oh, sure.' Her fair complexion returning as she smiled.

'I've decided that our future is the most important thing in our lives. Our children, you, us, our life in Exeter, they're what matters.' I began with a preamble that I hoped would soften the impending announcement of my unemployment. Tabitha started to shake her head slowly, but I continued.

'We've become closer since Lucy's accident and I realised how damaging me being away from home has been – me clinging to a deteriorating career, that is.' Tabitha lowered her head, still shaking it.

'So,' I breathed deeply, 'I've quit. I'm staying home. Permanently.'

'What?' she snapped, looking up. 'Why did you do that? You love flying.'

'True, but I love my family more. Besides, I've had enough of airlines.'

'You can't just throw away a well paid job simply because

you have to work in Gatwick.'

Throw away – wasted? 'Aha, well that's the problem.'

Tabitha narrowed her eyes and slewed her head to the side. 'What's the problem?'

'Crew Planning called today. They don't have any spaces for first officers in Gatwick. They want to transfer me to Warsaw on an Eastern European contract.'

'I think you should take it,' she said, her head nodding in encouragement.

'You have to be kidding. I have nothing in Poland.'

'You have nothing in Gatwick, either.' Tabitha dropped her head and let out a lungful of air.

'Tabitha? What's wrong?'

'John, look, you need to know something.' She looked at me again, and then turned away.

There was no way I could earn enough money as a first officer in Poland; the salary would barely cover the mortgage. And then there was the commuting. Even if the airline released more seats for staff travel, I would still need to fly into Gatwick then drive three hours home every week. It was impossible; I'd be better off working in a supermarket. I'd been duped by *my* manager, that was for sure. *Duped by manager, intially – M?*

Tabitha looked up again and drew breath. 'I'm sorry, John,' she said, looking down once more. 'There's someone else.'

Dumped! At least I'd solved my crossword puzzle.

From Russia with Stuff

Just when you thought it was safe to get back on a plane ...

Absolved from the stresses of modern aviation, disgraced former airline captain John Reilly spends his days packing boxes in a warehouse and his nights in bed with a beautiful young student. But an unexpected encounter with a former airhostess alerts Reilly to the prospect of the imminent re-acquaintance with stress.

When the creepy Oleg Ivanovich calls at his home and offers him a flying job in Moscow, John Reilly knows that trouble has already booked its seat on board.

Packed with humour and loaded with farce, the latest chapter in the life of Captain Reilly is a tongue in cheek tale of suspense, mystery and danger – with a splash of sex.

If the aviation authorities don't revoke his pilot's licence, mortality will.

J.T. O'Neil is the pen name of a full time captain with a major European low cost airline. Foolishly encouraged by the inexplicable popularity of his revealing blog, he has somehow contrived to patch together snippets of his life as a glorified bus driver, and churned out a couple of novels.

Born in northern England, but educated in the rest of the world, J.T. O'Neil claims not to remember the Sixties, which means he must have been around for at least some of that decade.

As a futile attempt at literary credibility, J.T. O'Neil studied literature and creative writing with the Open University, and now thinks he knows what he's doing.

jtoneil.com

12544146R00188

Printed in Great Britain
by Amazon.co.uk, Ltd.,
Marston Gate.